Blackbeard's Gift

By

James Clifford

Fiction

This is a work of fiction. Any resemblance to persons living or dead is coincidental. Except for Edward Teach, and Lt. Maynard, none of the characters was a real person. The events described, except for parts of the final battle between Blackbeard and the British war ship, are fiction and never happened.

Cover art used by permission © SuperStock, inc.
Art by Jean Leon Gerome Ferris

Dan River Press
PO Box 298
Thomaston, Maine 04861

For Julie

§

Prologue
Bristol England
1716

Allen Lawrence had the sensation that someone was following him, and a wave of fear surged through his body. He had never been this frightened in his entire life.

Why he ever agreed to help the investigator was beyond him. He should have taken his chances and kept his mouth shut. Instead, he had allowed himself to be manipulated by the arrogant little bastard for his own political gain, and now it was too late. He had no choice but to finish what he had started.

It was a dark, moonless night as Lawrence aimlessly walked along the cobblestone streets of Bristol. He no longer felt safe at home because Arthur Barrett and his gang of henchmen knew where he lived.

He laughed out loud, breaking the night's silence. He knew his mind was just playing tricks on him because, despite his growing unease, he was fairly confident that Barrett was unaware of his infidelities. But still, he had to be careful; his life depended on it.

Later that night he was to hand over documents that would destroy one of the most powerful men in all of England. He knew he was about to break one of Barrett's cardinal rules, and because of his betrayal, a large bounty would be placed on his head. Barrett, after all, had routinely killed men for much less.

The investigator had sworn that he would protect him, but Lawrence wasn't naive enough to believe the empty promise. During the eight years that he had worked for Arthur Barrett, he had witnessed a host of crimes committed by Barrett and his cronies, including treason and murder. Even with that damning knowledge, he still wished that he had refused to help the investigator. But in the end, he simply knew too much and had found himself in an untenable situation.

Lawrence turned off the cobblestone street and into a dark alleyway that led behind one of the many taverns that populated the seaport city. He could hear the raucous laughter coming from the patrons inside. He shook his head in disgust. After all this time, he still couldn't figure out how his life had turned out so badly. He wondered if his current actions would in some way make up for his misdeeds.

He seriously doubted it. The truth was that he hadn't helped the investigator out of the goodness of his heart or because of some honorable notion of correcting past injustices. No, he had cooperated only because the investigator had threatened to throw him in jail as an accomplice. He was only helping to save his own skin; it was that simple.

The alley led to a dirt path that brought Lawrence to a series of filthy rundown docks that lined the harbor. A horrible fire had destroyed most of the area years ago, and it had never been rebuilt. Lawrence stared out at the rotting docks and couldn't shake the feeling that he was an evil man. He hadn't directly hurt anyone, but he had kept his mouth shut for eight long years. How many lives had been destroyed by his silence?

Only after many sleepless nights had Lawrence reluctantly agreed to cut a deal with the investigator in order to avoid being thrown in jail. In return for the investigator's promise of immunity, he agreed to collect and turn over enough evidence to send Barrett to the gallows.

Despite the anguish over his betrayal, in the end the decision really wasn't that difficult. He simply couldn't bear the horrible thought of spending years in jail. His fear of being confined like an animal in a tiny cage was stronger than both his loyalty to and his fear of Barrett.

However, Lawrence was smart enough to realize that even if they hung Barrett, his life would still be in jeopardy. Indeed, he would have to leave England when it was all over. He would start a new life somewhere far, far away, and perhaps this time he would live honorably.

Lawrence slowly walked along the abandoned docks, deep in his own thoughts. He approached a gutted warehouse when someone grabbed his shoulder from behind. Startled, he jerked around, only to recognize the person that had just scared him half to death.

He recovered and then shook his fist, yelling at his friend. "Damn! What the hell is wrong with you, sneaking up on a man like that? You almost made my heart stop!"

His drinking companion and good friend Samuel Johnstone grinned. "Sorry, old boy. Didn't mean to startle you. I just saw you walking alone and thought you might want a little company. What are you so jumpy about, anyway?"

Lawrence shrugged his shoulders and laughed nervously. He didn't answer the question and instead motioned for Johnstone to follow him. As the two men walked along the old harbor docks, it didn't occur to Lawrence to ask his friend why he also happened to be in the most deserted part of town at such a late hour.

"Hey, look," Johnstone said as he stopped walking. He bent down and picked up an old rusty horseshoe lying on the ground. He looked at it for a second before casually tossing it into the harbor. "My mother always told me it was good luck to find a horseshoe."

Lawrence watched the horseshoe make a small splash before quickly disappearing into the dark water. Maybe the horseshoe was a good sign, Lawrence thought, because shortly he was going to need all the luck in the world.

"What are you doing out here, anyway?" Johnstone asked with a hint of amusement in his voice. "Couldn't find any pretty young lasses to keep you company?"

Lawrence laughed dutifully. They were both bachelors and spent a great many nights carousing the many bars and taverns around town.

"No, no girls tonight," Lawrence replied with a distant look. "I'm just out getting a little fresh air, that's all."

Lawrence thought about the irony of his statement. If he really wanted some fresh air, he certainly wouldn't have been walking around this part of the city. Over the years it had become nothing but a large garbage dump for local merchants, and the smell of rotting trash and dead fish had created an awful stench.

Despite the unexpected intrusion, Lawrence was grateful for Johnstone's company. He felt better having someone he knew and trusted with him. A few times when he had been out drinking with Johnstone, he had desperately wanted to tell him about the precarious position he had fallen into. But in the end, he had kept his mouth shut because he didn't want to endanger his friend in any way. He glanced over at Johnstone, who smiled back, and Lawrence knew he had made the right decision not to get him involved.

"I hope you aren't going to try and get me to go out with you later," Lawrence said lightheartedly. "I have a lot of work to do tomorrow, and I need to be leaving soon, anyway."

"All right," Johnstone said with a smirk. "We'll just walk."

The two friends walked silently for a few minutes before approaching a large wooden pier that stretched far out into the harbor. Despite the vast number of barnacles covering the pilings, the pier, unlike the rest of the area, was in relatively good shape.

"Come with me," Johnstone said as he motioned for Lawrence to follow him down the long pier.

It was eerily quiet. There wasn't the slightest bit of breeze, and the air was hot and sticky. Lawrence noticed that even the typically rough harbor was still, perhaps due to the unseasonably warm temperatures. He looked out over the harbor, and a pang of sadness swept through him. He was going to miss Bristol. It had been the only home he had ever known.

Lawrence pulled out his pocket watch. It was almost ten o'clock. He had to get going; the investigator would be waiting for him. The two friends walked to the end of the pier, and Lawrence turned to bid Johnstone goodnight.

But before he could utter a word, an explosion of pain ripped through his body. The agony that filled his body was so sudden, so intense, that he couldn't scream, he couldn't breathe. It happened so fast, and the pain spread so rapidly, that it didn't even occur to him that he was going to be dead in a short period of time.

He slumped down onto the wooden pier and felt a warm thick liquid flow from his side. He was in shock. For a brief second, he wondered if he was having a nightmare, but then his mind quickly realized there was no waking from this horror.

Another wave of pain racked his body, and he cried out in fear and agony. Feebly, he raised his head, and then he understood what had happened.

His good friend stood over him with a large knife in his hand. There was blood on the blade. His blood! He stared at Johnstone in disbelief, realizing that he no longer had to worry about Barrett, the investigator, or starting a new life.

The pain slowly started to diminish, and despite the hot temperatures, Lawrence started to feel cold. He had often wondered what it would feel like to die, and now he knew. Lawrence watched as Johnstone knelt down beside him. He should have felt hatred or anger toward him, but, surprisingly, he didn't.

Johnstone shook his head and ran a hand through Lawrence's sweat-soaked hair. "Damn you, Alan! Don't you remember making a promise – a promise of loyalty? Why did you make me do this to you? You left us with no choice. This did not have to happen this way!"

Lawrence tried to respond, but all that came out of his mouth was a gasping noise and a stream of warm blood. He watched as Johnstone stood up and threw the bloody knife into the harbor. Lawrence's friend and executioner then bent down and reached into his jacket. He pulled out the documents that Lawrence had intended to give to the investigator.

Johnstone stood back up and gazed down at Lawrence. "I'm sorry, old friend," he said. He then turned and left without saying another word.

As he watched his friend walk back down the pier, Lawrence grew colder. His vision began to fade, and his friend seemed to disappear, merging into the black night. When Johnstone completely disappeared, only then did Lawrence no longer feel any pain.

I
Fall, 1716

John Rutherford was born in Bristol, England in the year 1690. He lived in a simple and predictable fashion and would have been more than content to pass the rest of his days in the same manner. But an unexpected visitor changed everything one night.

"Who could that be at this hour?" his wife snapped.

Rutherford knew Anne didn't like to be interrupted, especially at dinnertime. Although the couple lived in a modest but respectable part of the city, that didn't preclude the occasional unsolicited visit from the less fortunate – and Bristol had its share of downtrodden souls.

"If it's another one of those beggars," she replied coldly, "slam the door on them. I am sick and tired of being harassed by those animals."

Rutherford rose from the tiny table, trying his best to ignore his wife's harsh comments. He walked out of the kitchen and through the small parlor room, where they entertained what few guests called upon them. The small one-story gray-stoned house was located in the merchant district of Bristol. It wasn't a mansion, but it was clean and comfortable, and Rutherford was proud to have been able to afford it, especially considering his meager background.

He opened the front door, expecting to see some poor sod begging for scraps of food, but instead was surprised to find a handsomely dressed gentleman standing in the doorway. The dapper man was tall and appeared to be in his late fifties. He was wearing an expensive tweed overcoat with a long red velvet scarf draped around his neck. The man obviously hadn't begged for anything in his entire life.

"Are you Mr. John Rutherford?" he inquired in an official, monotone voice.

"Yes."

"I have a letter requesting your presence at a meeting with Mr. Arthur Barrett of Barrett Trading Company tomorrow morning at eight o'clock. This is the office location."

He handed Rutherford a piece of stationary that had Barrett Trading Company's logo and address on it.

"This matter pertains to a possible job opportunity that I think you would have some interest in. You have been referred to Mr. Barrett by a mutual acquaintance. The position pays substantially more than your current wages. Mr. Barrett will be expecting you at eight o'clock sharp. Good evening." He tipped his hat, and Rutherford watched him turn and leave.

Rutherford closed the door and walked back to the kitchen, his mind racing with excitement.

"Who was that?" Ann asked between bites of stewed rabbit.

Rutherford sat back down.

Before he could answer, she spoke again, "You didn't give money to anybody, did you?"

He loved his wife, but sometimes . . .

She stopped eating and stared at him.

He had learned it was best not to keep her waiting for long. He replied in exasperation, "No, I didn't give money to anyone."

"Well, then, who was at the door?"

"You're not going to believe it," he answered excitedly. "You've heard of Barrett Trading?"

Anne frowned. "Of course I have," she said in a condescending tone. "They're the richest company in Bristol."

"Well, I've also heard that they're pretty ruthless as well."

"Oh, people say that about any successful company," Anne exclaimed with indignation. "So what in the world does Barrett Trading want with you? You don't owe them money, do you?"

"No, I don't owe them any money. As a matter of fact, somebody has referred me to Mr. Barrett. I have a job interview with him tomorrow morning."

"What? Are you playing a joke on me? Who was really at the door?"

"I'm serious. I have an interview with Barrett, and from what the man said, the job pays a lot more than my current position."

"Any job would pay more than what you are making now," Anne said.

Despite her sarcasm, John could see the excitement in Anne's eyes as she considered the possibility of his working for Barrett Trading. Of course, the thought that he would be making more money had a lot to do with her excitement.

Lately, Anne had been complaining mightily about their financial situation, and he had to admit it was starting to bother him some. He was the junior bookkeeper at Fredricks & Smith Barrister Firm, and at just twenty-seven years of age, he felt that he was making a reasonable enough living, especially considering his youth and lack of experience.

He didn't make a ton of money, and although he never expected to be rich, they lived well in his view, especially compared to most people in England. Poverty was rampant, and as a child he had known what it was like to be poor and to go to bed hungry.

The vast majority of families in England barely scratched out meager livings by farming in the countryside. Even worse, more and more families were being forced to move into the big cities like London to find work in grim factories for slave wages. Rutherford had heard that the conditions that those factory workers lived in were absolutely atrocious.

No, Anne didn't realize how lucky they were. They had a small but nicely kept house in a respectable part of the city. There was plenty of food to eat, and from time to time, he even had a little money left over to buy her a new dress or a piece of jewelry.

They had been married now for almost three years, and despite the fact that she sometimes drove him crazy, Rutherford loved his wife very much. She was two years younger than he was, and although most people wouldn't necessarily consider her a beautiful woman, he was very attracted to her.

Rutherford loved her long dark hair that fell down the entire length of her back. She had pale, almost milky skin that became flushed whenever she got mad or excited or when they made love, a rare occurrence anymore.

Recently, it seemed, he only got to see her cheeks flushed when she was mad at something he had done or had failed to do. However, despite the occasional fight, he truly felt lucky to have won her hand in marriage. After all, with his family's meager background, it wasn't like he was a prized catch.

Anne came from a well-respected family of tea merchants, and although they were not immensely wealthy, they made a comfortable living. It had taken a lot of convincing to finally get her father to agree to their marriage.

Rutherford believed that her old man had finally given in to his repeated requests only because she had three older sisters who had all been recently married. He suspected that her father had grown sick of paying for weddings and dowries and he knew he could get off cheaply by allowing Anne to marry him.

The rest of the night, Rutherford and Anne sat at the kitchen table, keeping warm in front of the fireplace. They drank coffee and speculated about the position and how much it would pay. Anne excitedly made plans on how she would spend the extra money, which struck Rutherford as rather funny, since he hadn't secured the job yet.

After a dessert of currant-filled pastries, they retired to the bedroom, and Rutherford received his last surprise of the evening. Anne's cheeks became flushed with excitement. And this time, it wasn't because she was mad at him.

After Anne had fallen asleep, he quietly lay next to her and ran his hand through her long thick hair. He watched as her back rose and fell with each breath. Rutherford couldn't sleep. He was nervous about his meeting with Barrett. He wondered what the man was like and what type of job he was offering.

A recurring question kept nagging at him: why would Barrett even want to hire him? After all, he didn't have any knowledge of the trading or mining industries. Surely there must be hundreds of more qualified and experienced people available.

Late into the night, he kept wondering, why him?

II

After tossing and turning for most of the night, Rutherford finally drifted off to sleep in the early morning hours. He dreamt that he and his father were fishing in Bristol's harbor. It was a beautiful day, and the sea was bright and calm. Every time they brought the nets up, they were full of fish, and his father would let out a huge holler of delight.

It was the happiest Rutherford had ever seen his father, and he wished they could stay out in the harbor and fish forever. Abruptly, his dream was disturbed when he felt a tug at his arm.

"Get up, John," a voice called out.

Rutherford realized the voice belonged to his wife, and the tranquil vision of the harbor and his father faded away. He lay in bed for a few minutes with the dream still vivid in his mind. The memory of his father left an empty feeling.

Then he remembered the interview with Barrett. He groggily rolled out of bed, cursing the night's fitful sleep. He quickly washed his hands and face with cold water from a bowl on the nightstand and then threw off his nightshirt and cap.

He grabbed his best suit and in rapid succession pulled on linen underwear followed by his gray breeches. He hastily stretched a pair of white stockings over the bottom of his breeches until they reached all the way up to his knees. Then he sat back down on the bed and buckled up his freshly shined black leather shoes.

He slipped on a white shirt that had large ruffles at the sleeves and neck and carefully tucked it into his breeches. Lastly, Rutherford put on his new black waist-coat that Anne had bought him for his last birthday.

Rutherford stared at his reflection in the mirror with casual indifference. He was resigned to his looks. He was neither tall nor muscular. He wasn't handsome, but he wasn't ugly, either.

His nose and mouth were undistinguished; however, his wife did comment that he had pretty baby-blue eyes.

He licked his fingers and patted down a few stray hairs that were standing up on his short-cropped brownish-blond hair. Only his lightning-quick reflexes distinguished him in any way. He had never lost a foot race. And, while playing any type of game, he seemed to have the unusual knack of anticipating other people's moves.

As a boy, he earned the nickname Lancelot from his playmates because no one could beat him in fencing matches. Rutherford was secretly embarrassed by the nickname because he had a suspicion that if he was ever forced to defend himself with real swords, he would tremble like a leaf and wouldn't be able to fight.

He shook his head. Too bad his speed and quick reflexes were of no use to him now. He was nothing but a file clerk.

He walked into the kitchen and kissed Anne, who was busy making a pot of tea.

"You look very handsome," she commented.

"Thank you, my dear." He grabbed a slice of buttered bread and wolfed it down before announcing hastily, "I've got to go."

He didn't want to take any chances and show up late for his interview. Barrett was not the type of man one kept waiting.

Anne accompanied him to the front door and handed him his wool overcoat and cocked hat.

"Wish me luck," Rutherford said as he opened the front door.

A cold gust of wind greeted them.

Anne smiled, "Good luck, and here is a kiss to ensure it."

It was a frigid day for October. But the heavy winds had died down and the sky was clear, blue, and sunny, which was highly unusual for this time of the year. Maybe the sunny weather was a good sign, he thought as he waved goodbye to his wife.

Rutherford walked up the steep road that led to the heart of the city's business district. Bristol was the second largest city in England in 1716; nearly fifty thousand people lived in the harbor city that was situated between the Avon River and the Atlantic Ocean. He marveled at how busy and congested the streets had become over the last few years. They teemed with sailors, merchants, milkmen, lawyers, laborers, beggars, children, pickpockets, and servants all hurrying to their respective destinations.

He wasn't paying attention to where he was walking and stepped right in the middle of a large pile of mule dung.

"Damn it!" he cursed angrily. "Not today!"

The streets of Bristol were usually in awful condition. When it hadn't rained, one could choke to death from all the dust. When it had, the streets turned into a muddy quagmire that made traveling a messy proposition. Whether it rained or not; the filth that was haphazardly thrown into the streets stopped many in their tracks. Animal guts from butchers, raw sewage, dead animals, rotting food, and every form of refuse imaginable could be found piled ankle deep.

Rutherford took out a handkerchief and carefully wiped the foul smelling excrement from his previously freshly polished shoe. He then threw the soiled handkerchief on the ground before continuing on his way.

Along the way, he passed a multitude of street vendors hawking every type of goods and services imaginable. Food, prostitutes, beer, knives, animals, clothing, cheap fiddles, and jewelry were just a few of the many items one could buy. Behind him, the harbor was packed with ships of all sizes from Europe, Africa, the Far East, and the American colonies.

The walk to Barrett Trading had only taken twenty minutes, and he nervously approached the entrance of the building, where dozens of people were filing in and out of the front doors. Rutherford stopped, straightened the collar of his overcoat, and took a deep breath. Well, this is it, he thought anxiously. Let's see what Barrett has to say.

Once inside, he was taken aback by the extravagantly decorated interior.

Every piece of furniture appeared brand new, as if it had come straight from the showroom. It was obvious that Barrett Trading was doing extremely well.

The first floor was enormous. Beautiful mahogany-timbered walls separated one office from another, and in the center of the huge room sat rows and rows of desks, each occupied by someone busily working away.

He spotted someone who looked like a manager and walked over. "Excuse me," he said. "I have an eight o'clock appointment with Mr. Barrett."

"Is he expecting you?" He asked rather curtly.

"Yes, he is. My name is John Rutherford."

He continued staring at him with a distasteful look on his face before finally glancing down at his appointment book. "Yes, Mr. Rutherford," he said with a newfound respect. "He is expecting you. If you could have a seat over there," he said, pointing to a waiting area, "someone will come by to escort you to his office shortly."

Rutherford left the receptionist's desk and sat down in a plush leather chair. After about ten minutes had passed, he realized he was not a high priority.

He wondered what his father would say if he could see him now. Would he be proud? His father had been a fisherman. And growing up, Rutherford had lived in what was basically a two-room shanty located in the poorest, most rundown section of the city. Another family had lived in the apartment next to them, and only a razor-thin wall had separated the two families. Rutherford had grown up an only child, and his father's biggest dream in life had been to save every shilling he could spare so that his son could get the education that he had never received. His father had hoped an education would be enough to break the generational cycle of poverty and tragedy that so many fishing families had come to know.

When he was a young lad, Rutherford's father had told stories of how his father and his father before him had made their living fishing. He told wonderful tales about the sea and how it was a beautiful and mysterious place. But without fail, after every amazing adventure story, he would warn Rutherford that the ocean was a dangerous and fickle place and that no one in their family had ever been able to escape its impoverished confines.

Eventually, his father's dream did come true. Rutherford only wished he had lived long enough to see it realized. His father's ship had been lost at sea when he was fifteen, and no trace of it had ever been found. Like so many others before, the ship and her crew had simply vanished into the sea.

Two years after his father's ship disappeared, his mother passed away. The doctor said it was a heart ailment, but Rutherford knew his prognosis was wrong. After her husband died, his mother lost her spark, and Rutherford believed she had simply given up the desire to live.

So at the age of seventeen, with no parents and no money, Rutherford seemed destined to follow in his father's footsteps. But his destiny changed one day when the owner of his father's doomed fishing boat paid him an unexpected visit.

Rutherford had met William Livingston only once before, when he was a small child, so Mr. Livingston's proposal came as a complete shock. Livingston explained that Rutherford's father had agreed to captain his fishing boat for him under one condition: if something were to happen to him and his wife, Livingston would take care of Rutherford and make sure he received an education.

So Livingston had made young Rutherford a deal he couldn't turn down. He offered Rutherford the chance to come live with him. He would provide shelter, food, and an education if Rutherford promised to work hard, attend classes, go to church, and stay out of trouble. The kindly old man kept his promise, and Rutherford knew that he would always be indebted to him.

The memories of his family and childhood were interrupted when, finally, after forty-five minutes, a rather nervous and sickly man came to escort him to Barrett's office.

He followed the man up the stairs and the atmosphere on Barrett's floor was entirely different than the one he had just come from. There were just a few offices, and Rutherford didn't see a single person. It was awfully quiet compared to the sea of activity down on the first floor. He wondered what went on behind all the closed doors.

The nervous assistant didn't utter so much as a sound. And when they approached Barrett's office, he just pointed at the door, nodded his head, and quickly disappeared back down the hall. Rutherford wondered if all of the employees were this scared of Barrett.

The door was shut, so he knocked lightly.

"Come in!" bellowed a rough voice.

Rutherford opened the door and hesitated as he entered.

Barrett stood with a cigar in his hand behind a huge brown cedar desk. He was a large, stout man in his mid-fifties. He had a bushy salt-and-pepper mustache that was matched by thick gray hair.

"Mr. Rutherford, I have been expecting you. Have a seat." He pointed to a chair in front of his desk.

Barrett's office was enormous. Rutherford sat down and stared at a large stuffed boar's head that hung from the wall. It had belonged to a nasty-looking beast with two giant tusks protruding from its massive jaw.

Barrett pointed at the boar. "I shot that fat bastard, but not before it gored two of my best dogs." He laughed. "You'd think I would have been mad, but in a way, I kind of respected that crazy boar. We chased it for two hours straight, and it fought until the very end. But you know what I admired most about the animal?"

Rutherford wasn't sure what one could admire about a half-crazed boar that had just killed two dogs. "What?" he mumbled.

"Even when the animal knew it was cornered and was about to die, it never stopped fighting. Even though it had been fatally wounded, the damn thing still tried to kill another one of my dogs. I respected that."

He turned and pointed back at the boar. "That animal had more guts than most men you'll ever meet."

Rutherford wasn't exactly sure what the meaning of the story was, and he looked down from the boar. His impression of Barrett was that if he took off his expensive suit, he could have easily passed for one of his mining or shipping employees. Behind the façade of his impeccable clothing, he was a rough-looking fellow who obviously had been around a bit. Rutherford nervously played with the brim of his hat while his potential boss inspected him.

Barrett sat down behind his desk. After a couple of seconds, he spoke nonchalantly. "First of all, don't worry about being late for your job at the law firm. I talked to your boss Fredericks, and he knows you're here."

"Damn it!" Rutherford cursed silently.

Fredrick's owned the law firm where he worked, and there was no doubt in Rutherford's mind that he had just gotten himself fired for trying to get another job behind his back. Rutherford had prepared a little white lie to explain why he was late for work, but obviously he couldn't use it now.

He could already see the look on Anne's face when he explained to her that not only did he not get the job with Barrett but he also got fired from the law firm. She would have a fit. For a brief moment, Rutherford wondered if she would leave him.

Barrett quickly interrupted his fears of impending unemployment and divorce. "As a matter of fact, it was Fredrick's who told me about you and suggested that I consider hiring you for a position that we have available."

Rutherford let out a sigh of relief, but the realization that the job recommendation had come from Fredrick's was somewhat of a shock. In his last job review, Fredrick's had told him that he was the worst bookkeeper that he had ever hired and that Rutherford should consider himself lucky that he even had a job.

Fredrick's tended to be a little harsh at times, and Rutherford knew that he didn't completely mean what he had said. Still, it certainly wasn't a ringing endorsement of his skills. He wondered if his current boss was just trying to take the easy way out by getting Barrett to hire him rather than having to go through the discomfort of firing him.

The more he thought about it, the more Rutherford realized that didn't make any sense. Fredrick's certainly wouldn't pawn him off to a man of Barrett's stature just to avoid a little discomfort.

Barrett took a puff from his cigar and blew a huge ring of whitish-gray smoke towards the tall ceiling. "I'm going to give you a little history of Barrett Trading," he began, peering coldly at Rutherford. "In 1585, the company was started by my great-great-grandfather, but it wasn't until my father had the foresight to recognize the massive changes that were occurring throughout Europe that Barrett Trading saw its fortunes improve dramatically. He correctly predicted the rapid increase in economic industrialization and the need for coal to fuel that demand. That's why he got into the coal business. And because of Barrett Trading, England has subsequently become the world's leading supplier of coal. Like my father, I believe I have a knack for predicting social and economic changes. But predicting those changes is the easy part; making money from them is the challenge."

Barrett reached over his large desk and snuffed out the cigar in a metal jar that was already too full. "I'm sure you know a little about the economic situation in the American colonies."

Rutherford didn't, but replied, "Of course." He prayed that Barrett wasn't about to ask him something in detail.

Luckily Barrett didn't test him and continued, "Well, I believe the new trading routes of the West Indies, Caribbean, and the American colonies are going to create wealth beyond anyone's wildest imagination, and I am betting everything on it. As a matter of fact, if it wasn't for my steadfast belief in the area, the city of Charleston would now be a ghost town."

"You helped found Charleston?" Rutherford asked in admiration.

"I was one of a group of the first financiers. But after a devastating hurricane, two consecutive years of bad harvests, and a malaria outbreak, my partners had given up hope. The city was in financial ruin, but I didn't waver one bit in my belief that Charleston would become a major trading hub. So I bought out my partners. And seventeen years later the city has flourished and I am making a fortune from the rice plantations and trading operations."

Rutherford was impressed. The man was obviously a smart businessman.

"The company will still remain in the coal business," Barrett continued, "but all future energy and resources will be allocated to building the largest, most profitable trading company the world has ever seen.

"Now because of this diversification and growth, we need to hire a few good men. We only hire outside the company based on recommendations from people we have known and trusted for many years. It just so happens at this time we are in need of a qualified individual to work in our administrative department, primarily handling bookkeeping and other clerical duties. Fredrick's tells me that you have experience in these matters but, more importantly, that you are a loyal employee who can be trusted."

Barrett slowly leaned over his desk and looked directly at him. "Well, Mr. Rutherford, is that true? Can you be trusted?"

Rutherford had always been nervous in job interviews, and today was no different. He hoped Barrett didn't notice. "Sir, I appreciate what Mr. Fredrick's has told you about my employment history at his company," he answered with a growing sense of confidence. "I think I have done a good job for him, and I think I could do an equally good job for you if you were to give me an opportunity here. You can definitely count on me."

It appeared Barrett was satisfied with his answer, and he continued on as if Rutherford already had the job. "The hours are long, and you are expected to work as long as it takes to get the job done." He paused and looked at him with a serious expression. "Even if it means not going home at night."

Barrett leaned back in his chair. His demeanor made Rutherford extremely uncomfortable. "But the second and most important requirement that I demand is complete secrecy and loyalty regarding our business dealings. Business is tough enough as it is, and we don't need competitors or the damn government interfering with our every move. If you can fulfill these two requirements, then you will have a very successful career here."

He paused and handed Rutherford a folded piece of paper. "This is your starting salary, should you choose to accept our offer."

Rutherford took the piece of paper and unfolded it. At first, he thought the figure was a mistake; it was nearly double what he was making at the law firm.

Barrett interrupted his state of disbelief and utter joy with one last warning. "However, Mr. Rutherford, I must warn you, if you cannot fulfill either one of these demands, then you will quickly find yourself no longer employed here."

Barrett looked Rutherford directly in the eyes with a cold stare. "Well, Mr. Rutherford, can I trust you?"

He wasn't sure what he saw in Barrett's eyes, but he knew the burly man meant every word. Regardless, all Rutherford could think about was the money. With the amount Barrett was offering, he would have no problem earning his undivided trust and loyalty.

"Yes, sir," he answered quickly. "I promise you will not be disappointed." Rutherford tried not to sound too eager, although it was hard for him to hold in his mounting excitement.

"Good," Barrett replied. "Welcome aboard. When you get back to work, give Fredrick's the news."

Barrett started to shuffle some documents on his desk, and Rutherford took that as his cue to exit. He got up to leave. "Thank you again for giving me the opportunity to work for you, Mr. Barrett. I won't let you down."

Barrett didn't look up from his papers. "I certainly hope not."

Rutherford left Barrett Trading and headed back to the law firm to give Fredrick's his notice. He tried to control his emotions, but it was hard to contain his excitement. He couldn't wait to see the look on Anne's face when he told her that his salary had almost doubled and that he was going to be an employee of Barrett Trading.

Still, something nagged at him. Despite his excitement about the job offer, he couldn't help feeling a little bit apprehensive. Something didn't feel right about Barrett's offer. It all seemed too easy. His father had always told him that nothing came free in this world.

But when Rutherford imagined the look on Anne's face after he gave her the good news, he managed to dismiss his misgivings pretty quickly.

The human mind was a wonderful device. It had the unique ability to completely ignore its own warning signs if there was money involved, and that was exactly what Rutherford's mind was in the process of doing.

III

A lanky but solidly-built man kept a watchful eye on the entrance of Barrett Trading from across the street. He was waiting for John Rutherford to leave because he had some important matters to discuss with Barrett.

He hoped that Rutherford turned out to be more dependable than Lawrence. What a disaster that could have been. Barrett was still fuming over the whole episode – and for good reason.

It had been pure luck that the constable had warned them about the meeting between Lawrence and the investigator. There was no question in Johnstone's mind that if Parliament had gotten hold of the documents that Lawrence was about to turn over to the investigator, they would have strung both him and Barrett up from the gallows.

Samuel Johnstone took a bite out of a sour green apple he had bought from a fruit vendor and watched Rutherford leave. He tossed the half-eaten apple onto the ground, crossed the street, and went directly to Barrett's office. He had worked for Barrett for over twenty years, and his loyalty was unquestionable. He had never forgotten where he had come from or the circumstances that had led to his employment at Barrett Trading.

Growing up had been a constant struggle just to survive. His parents had been a couple of drunkards who spent most of their time carousing in pubs rather than taking care of their family. So at an early age Johnstone learned how to steal and cheat in order to survive.

Over the years he became good at it – almost too good. As Johnstone got older, he discovered there were much more valuable items to pilfer than food, and that was how his path eventually crossed Barrett's. By his early twenties he, along with a few friends, had discovered that robbing certain warehouses and then selling those goods on the black market could be quite profitable.

Johnstone, like most criminals, never imagined that he would be caught. And of course, like most criminals, he was wrong. One night, his little group of thieves was ambushed while breaking into a warehouse down on the waterfront.

He could still remember the fear he felt sitting alone in his tiny cell awaiting punishment. Men were routinely hung for the crimes he had committed, and he had no doubt that would become his fate as well.

Early the next morning a stocky well-dressed man opened his cell door and walked in. He announced that his name was Arthur Barrett and that he thought Johnstone might like to meet the man that he had been stealing from for all these months.

It seemed like so long ago, but Johnstone still remembered Barrett's unusual manner of calm and confidence that had both scared and impressed him. Surprisingly, Barrett explained in the filthy cell that he admired the ingenuity and guts that Johnstone had displayed while stealing from him.

Then Barrett offered him two choices: Johnstone could come work for him, or stay in jail and take his chances with the law. Needless to say, he didn't really have much of a choice. He remembered foolishly asking Barrett how he would be able to get him out of jail. Barrett had just laughed at his question and told him not to worry about it. Later that morning the two left the jailhouse together, and Johnstone had been with Barrett ever since.

His friends that were arrested with him were hung in the town center without so much as a trial. Johnstone never asked Barrett about it, but he knew the hangings were meant to send a message to everyone in Bristol. And the message to those who dared trifle with Arthur Barrett was simple: be prepared to suffer the consequences.

Johnstone walked into Barrett's office without knocking because he knew how much it irritated the old man.

"Well, what do you think of young Mr. Rutherford?" Johnstone asked cheerfully as he proceeded to go straight over to Barrett's liquor cabinet and pour himself a large glass of brandy.

Barrett shook his head. "Dear God, Samuel, it's only nine-thirty in the morning!"

Johnstone raised his glass in a mock toast and took a large sip of the brandy. "Yes, it is, but it's not that often that I get to drink such a high class of brandy, and it's free."

"Somehow I doubt that very much," Barrett replied.

Johnstone sat down in the same chair that Rutherford had occupied just minutes before. "So, what do you think?" he repeated.

"He can't be any worse than Lawrence, now can he?" Barrett replied sarcastically.

Johnstone wished Barrett would just forget the whole Lawrence matter. "Look," he answered defensively, "how could any of us have known that Lawrence would turn out to be a traitor, especially after working here for so long. I mean, nobody could have guessed."

"Goddamn it!" Barrett growled as he slammed his fist down so hard that Johnstone could feel the vibrations in the glass he was holding. "That's what I pay you for. You better make sure it doesn't happen again."

"Don't worry about Rutherford," Johnstone said, trying to calm his boss. "He has no family money; his wife spends more money than he makes; and from what Fredrick's says, he is good with numbers. More importantly, we know how to use him if we need to. Anyway, he is too weak and naïve to ever be a problem if it comes down to it."

"Well, for your sake," Barrett snapped, "I hope you are right about him."

Johnstone wasn't concerned about Rutherford; he had come to discuss more important matters. "What about the beams? Do you want me to go ahead and ship them to the mine in Bath?"

"Yes, go ahead." Barrett looked proud of himself. "I have secured the disaster insurance from a group at Lloyds in London."

Johnstone nodded with approval at Barrett's brilliant scheme. Lloyds was nothing but a coffee house located in the shipping district of London, but it served a much larger purpose than serving just coffee. Ship owners, captains, merchants, and wealthy individuals used the coffeehouse to meet and carry on the business of insuring ships and their cargoes. Occasionally, if the premiums were high enough and one could convince enough of the patrons, they would underwrite other business ventures. And Barrett had done just that.

Barrett had somehow convinced a group of greedy merchants at Lloyds that a huge deposit of coal had been discovered in the Bath mine and that the prospects for future output were enormous. Lloyd's subsequently underwrote a large policy that would pay Barrett a small fortune if the mine suffered a catastrophic cave-in.

The Bath mine had been one of Barrett's largest producers, but now it was close to being completely depleted. In a short period of time, the mine would be nothing more than a worthless hole in the ground. No one knew this except for Barrett, Johnstone, and the pit boss, who just happened to be Barrett's nephew.

The beams that were going to be sent to Bath were structurally defective, and under the guise of safety, Barrett's nephew was going to have the miners replace all the support beams with the new defective ones. It would only be a matter of time before the beams collapsed.

"What about the miners?" Johnstone asked, not really out of concern for their safety but more to hear what Barrett's answer would be.

"Mining is a dangerous business," the old man shrugged. "Accidents happen."

Barrett's answer was exactly what Johnstone would have expected him to say. He got up and poured himself another brandy.

Barrett twisted the ends of his mustache. "We need more ships if we are going to beat East India for control of the Caribbean shipping routes, and the insurance money from Lloyd's is going to help pay for them."

Johnstone knew that Barrett was right about the potential for the new trading routes, although they faced an enormous obstacle with East India Trading. The rival company was founded in 1600 and for the last century had been by far the most profitable trading company in England. The wealthy nobles that ran East India Trading had close ties to the royal Parliament, since most were members or had close relatives who were. In effect, a small number of wealthy men had controlled England's economy for generations, and they certainly didn't want to lose their power to anyone, especially someone like Barrett.

East India had the resources and political clout that Barrett didn't have, and they had started to expand their business into the West Indies. One of Johnstone's carefully placed spies at East India had alerted him that they also wanted to expand their trading routes to include the Caribbean and the American colonies.

It was now a race to see who would be the dominant trader in the region. Johnstone knew that Barrett hated to admit it, but despite his wealth and influence in Bristol, he simply wasn't part of the elite circle of power that had dominated England's politics and economy for hundreds of years.

To counter that imbalance, Barrett sometimes had to resort to less-than-legal activities in order to even the odds and accomplish his goals. Johnstone truly believed that Barrett didn't consider his actions wrong or immoral; rather, they were logical choices to counteract the restrictions and prejudices that existed simply because of who one's ancestors were, or were not.

As Barrett had grown his operations over the years, the aristocrates had become more nervous and more desperate to bring him down any way they could. Johnstone ws convinced that was why Parliament had sent the investigator to Bristol. They wanted him to dig up criminal activites committed by Barrett so they could shut him and his company down once and for all.

Johnstone finished off his second brandy of the morning and stood up. "I'll get the shipment ready for delivery."

Barrett nodded his approval.

Johnstone left Barrett's office and smiled as he walked out of the building. He knew that was why Barrett employed men such as himself; he was willing to follow any order to ensure the success of Barrett trading.

IV

Sally Weston restlessly stoked the fire as she watched her husband gather his gear for work. They had been married for almost two years and had been through this ritual a hundred times before, but that still didn't make it any easier on her.

She loved Ben dearly, and that's why she hated his job so much. Her husband was a coal miner, and he made his backbreaking living by digging out the cursed rock from far beneath the earth's surface.

Bath was located on one of the largest coal deposits in Southwest England, and coal was the tiny town's only real source of employment. If a man didn't work in the mines, he was either too young or too crippled.

Coal. She hated even the mention of the word. Her worst fear was that because of England's incessant demand for it, Ben wouldn't make it out alive one day, and then she would be alone.

Accidents and deaths were a regular occurrence at the mine but, despite her misgivings, Ben swore that nothing would ever happen to him. Sally didn't know if what he said was for her sake or if he truly believed it. But one thing was certain: there was no denying the danger of his job.

"Damn it, Sally," Ben said, breaking the uncomfortable silence. "I don't know how many times I have to tell you this, but this is my job. This is what keeps a roof over our heads and food on the table. Why do you have to act like this every time I leave for work?"

Sally knew that what he said was true, and she tried to act brave and happy for him. But she couldn't hide her concern. "I'm sorry," she replied wearily. "I don't mean to make you upset. I just worry about you, that's all."

Ben walked over to her and lifted her chin. "Don't worry about me," he said as he smiled tenderly. "I'll be fine. As a matter of fact, a month ago Barrett sent down new safety beams, and we–"

"Barrett?" she tearfully cried. "You know good well and that he is just a lying weasel who doesn't give a damn about you or your safety."

Sally couldn't believe that Ben would actually consider trusting Barrett about anything. In fact, it was because of him that they were in this situation to begin with. Ben's father had died two years ago owing Barrett money, and to pay off that debt, Ben had been forced to work in the mine.

Ben walked over to her and wrapped his massive arms around her. He was well over six feet tall and close to two-hundred-and-twenty pounds of solid muscle.

Sally was petite, barely standing five-foot-two, and she felt like a small girl when she was in his arms. The closeness to him made her temporarily forget her fears. She had thick golden-blond hair and dark, almost mahogany-colored eyes, and her favorite thing to do in the entire world, besides being held by her husband, was reading books

Ben released his arms from her and grinned sheepishly. "Don't worry. Besides the new support beams, we always have Fat Boy and his friends watching out for us."

Sally laughed at the mention of Fat Boy. "Here. I almost forgot." She retrieved a large biscuit from the table and handed it to Ben. "For Fat Boy."

Ben had told her about the group of rats the miners worked with. At first she had been horrified to hear that he worked with dozens of rats crawling around, but after he explained why, she understood and was glad they were there.

Ben told her that rats were important to have around because they possessed an uncanny sixth sense when it came to survival. They could smell dangerous gases a half-mile away and could detect even the slightest movements in the earth.

The miners knew that if the rats had disappeared, they had done so for a reason and that they had better follow. So Ben and the other men regularly fed the rats to keep them around, and Fat Boy was the leader. Ben swore to her that the rotund rodent was the size of a beagle.

Ben put the biscuit into his satchel and picked up his gear. "I'll be late. I've got to go."

She forced a smile. "Be careful. I love you."

Ben hugged her one more time and left.

Sally stood at the doorway and watched him until he disappeared over the hill that led down to the town. It was a bitterly cold day, and even though it was morning, the sky was dark gray from burning coal and intermittent rain showers. Sally shivered and shut the door behind her.

Their small cottage did not provide much relief from the cold. The floor was nothing but flat stones placed right upon the earth. When the wind blew, drafts came from at least a dozen places, and to make matters worse, rain seeped through the wooden ceiling.

The day passed with the usual set of chores, and late in the afternoon Sally started to prepare dinner. Ben would be home soon, and he was always starving after working so hard all day. She fixed chestnut soup in a large cooking pot and started roasting the pigeons over the fire spit. The smell of the roasting birds made her smile. Ben was going to be happy about her little surprise; it was his favorite meal.

After the table was set, Sally glanced outside and saw a man approaching far off in the distance. She took the pigeons off the spit and set them on the table.

She glanced outside again, and her heart stopped. It wasn't Ben she thought she had seen; it was Joe Stanton instead. He and Ben were friends. She clenched her fists and squeezed shut her eyelids until tears ran out of the corners of her eyes.

Her mind raced in desperation. "No! Please, God!" she called out. Maybe Joe's here for another reason, she prayed, not willing to accept the awful truth of the situation.

A hesitant knock came from the front door. Sally froze; she couldn't make herself walk to the door. Joe knocked again, and she heard him call out her name. She forced herself to walk over to the door and then slowly opened it. The look on his face told her everything she needed to know.

"Sally, I'm so sorry." He seemed to be fumbling for words. "There was an accident."

She felt odd, as if she was not in her body but rather was observing everything that was happening from a distance. It was as if time and reality had ceased to exist. This wasn't really happening, was it?

"The mine collapsed." Joe shook his head, and his expression turned to anger. "Goddamn Barrett! Those beams were supposed to have prevented this from happening. I told them that the mine was a disaster waiting to happen. I don't understand why it collapsed. The beams should have at least given them some time to get out."

Sally hadn't said a word, and it didn't matter to her how or why it had happened. None of that would bring Ben back.

"Thank you for coming Joe," she said in a calm voice.

Joe reached out for her hand and squeezed it. "I'm so sorry, Sally." He turned and left.

Sally stood at the doorway and watched him walk back towards town. She shut the door and stared at the dinner setting, and finally the enormity of the situation hit her. Ben's chair would always be empty. She collapsed onto the cold stone floor and wept uncontrollably for a long, long time.

V
Spring, 1717

Six months had passed since Rutherford had taken the job with Barrett Trading, and he couldn't have been more pleased. Anne was happy, and he had settled into his new position with few difficulties. His responsibilities were similar to those at the law firm, which meant he basically kept track of purchase orders, accounts receivables, and accounts payable. He also recorded all the figures on ledger sheets and crosschecked the information to make sure no discrepancies existed.

He worked in the mining equipment division. Not only did Barrett own coalmines throughout Western England, but the company also manufactured equipment that was sold to mines throughout all of England.

It wasn't glamorous work, but he was being paid nicely for it. And contrary to what Mr. Barrett had led him to believe, the demands were not enormous, at least not yet.

The only thing Rutherford could complain about was the weather. It had been a brutal winter, with temperatures dropping as low as they had in years. A vicious wind constantly blew off the ocean, chilling Bristol and her citizens to the bone.

It had also been a bad year to get sick. A nasty flu epidemic had taken hold of the city, and more than eight hundred people had died. Even though the worst of winter was behind them, people were still dying from the wretched curse at a terrible rate.

Rutherford arrived home late. He called out to Anne, but she didn't respond. He walked into the bedroom and found her asleep in bed. He sat down on the edge of their bed and felt her forehead. She barely responded to his touch, and it felt like she had a slight fever.

"Are you all right?" he asked nervously.

Anne had suffered from bad colds from time to time, and it was probably nothing. But with the flu affecting so many people, it was hard for him to take her condition lightly.

"I just have a cold, John," she replied weakly. "It will pass."

Rutherford rubbed her back. "I know it will, but I want you to stay in bed the rest of tonight and tomorrow." He tried hard not to show his concern, but he was worried.

Anne was in no condition to argue. She shook her head, mumbled something, and rolled back over. She slept soundly throughout the night.

The next morning she appeared to be feeling better, so Rutherford left for work, but only after Anne promised to stay in bed and rest. Even though it was March, it was still freezing cold. The wind howled off the ocean, and a stinging rain pelted Rutherford's face as he walked to work. He made the short journey to his office in record time and, for once, he was happy that he worked indoors.

He settled in at his desk and started reviewing the usual equipment receipts and sale orders. Suddenly, something caught his eye. He thought it had to be a mistake. He had come across a sales receipt for a batch of iron support beams that was sold to a mining company in Exeter. He rechecked the invoice for a second time and felt his heart race.

The beams had been returned because they were found to be defective. Evidently, there had been some type of deficiency in the ore that had made the beams completely worthless. The company in Exeter had originally purchased the beams to help support the walls of a new tunnel that was being dug out. The very first week that the beams had been used, most of them had splintered, causing the tunnel to collapse. Luckily, no one had been in the mine at the time of the collapse. But needless to say, the company was quite upset about the beams, and the owners had threatened Barrett with all kinds of legal and possibly criminal lawsuits.

From what Rutherford understood, Mr. Barrett himself had traveled to Exeter to straighten the mess out. He didn't know what Barrett had told the mine owners, but it must have worked. No action was ever taken, and the entire matter seemed to have been forgotten.

The receipt for the sale of the beams to Exeter was not what bothered him so much; it was the fact that another shipment of identical support beams had been sent to one of Barrett's mines in Bath two months after the Exeter collapse. Whoever had authorized the sale to Bath must have known that the beams were also defective because they had come from the same batch. It was apparent, for reasons he couldn't comprehend, that someone had intentionally put those miners' lives in jeopardy.

Rutherford reread the sales receipt for a third time, and his confusion quickly gave way to shock and then horror. The receipt for the defective beams listed Bath as the mine, and the date the beams had been shipped was October 28.

"Oh my God," Rutherford muttered under his breath. He couldn't believe it when he remembered that the Bath mine had collapsed on December 16th. Twenty-eight miners had been killed, and the entire mine had been shut down after the cave-in.

His hands were shaking as he reread the receipts and pieced together what had happened. Whoever authorized the delivery of the beams to the mine in Bath had to have known that they were defective, but they had shipped them anyway. Why?

Rutherford couldn't believe what he had discovered, and he already wished that he had never come across the receipts. Questions raced through his mind. What should he do next? Should he inform the authorities? Should he talk to Mr. Barrett? Perhaps he could just pretend that he had never seen the invoices and just forget about it. No one would ever know anyway, right?

For what seemed like hours, he sat at his desk and studied the invoices, trying to figure out what he should do. He felt a light touch on his shoulder and instinctively grabbed the unknown hand before it could be pulled back.

"Whoa, Rutherford!" Jenkins cheerfully exclaimed. "I just came by to see what you are up to."

He had known Jenkins since school, and the man was just as annoying now as he had been as a child. Rutherford quickly shuffled the invoices and receipts so Jenkins wouldn't be able to see what he was working on.

"You haven't lost one bit of those famously quick reflexes, have you?" Jenkins asked in a nasal voice while peering down at his desk.

"I suppose not," Rutherford grunted.

"What are you working on?"

"Oh, nothing much," Rutherford managed to stammer. "Just the usual paperwork. You know how it is."

Jenkins had a concerned look on his face. "Are you all right? You look like you have seen a ghost. You're white as a sheet. You aren't getting sick, are you?" he asked, obviously more concerned for his own health than Rutherford's.

"No, I am fine, thank you," Rutherford lied. He was not physically sick. But someone in the company was responsible for those men's deaths, and he knew it. He had to get rid of Jenkins so he could think about what he was going to do.

"If you are getting sick, stay away from me. I can't afford to get sick right now, especially with Barrett on our butts the way he has been. I don't want to get Lawrenced."

"Lawrenced?" Rutherford repeated.

"Oh, I forgot. You started here afterwards," Jenkins said with an air of seniority. "Lawrence worked here until he was found stabbed to death last summer."

"That's terrible."

"Yes, it is. They say it was robbery, but the joke is that Barrett had him killed because he wasn't doing his job."

"What in the hell are you talking about?" Rutherford asked in disgust.

"Oh, I'm just kidding with you. It's kind of a saying – that you better do your job correctly, or you'll end up like Lawrence."

Rutherford didn't find it the least bit funny to joke about a man's murder.

"Hey, by the way, did I tell you Elizabeth and I are expecting another baby?"

"Congratulations," Rutherford said, barely listening to a word that the pesky clerk was saying. "That is great news."

"Well, when are you and Anne going to have one? I am starting to get worried about you two. It's been what – almost three years since you were married?"

Rutherford couldn't take it any longer; he sniffled loudly and coughed heavily. "I'm sorry," he said, trying to make his voice sound ragged. "I guess you're right. I don't feel so good."

Jenkins hastily retreated to his desk after he realized Rutherford might have the flu.

Rutherford, meanwhile, sat at his desk and continued to ponder his options. The more he thought about the situation, the more he concluded that he should bring the matter to Barrett. He should be the one to deal with whoever authorized the sale and to contact the authorities if necessary.

In the seven months that he had been at the company, Rutherford had rarely been in contact with Barrett. In fact, the longest conversation he had had with him was the day he was hired. Even then, Rutherford had hardly said two words.

The only time he saw Barrett was when they passed from time to time in the halls. Barrett would give him a courtesy grunt, but that was about it. Rutherford wasn't sure how he would break the news to him or exactly what he should say, but he decided telling him was the right course of action.

He slowly walked up to the third floor, contemplating what he was going to say.

He knocked at Barrett's door. "Mr. Barrett, it's John Rutherford," he called out. "Would you happen to have a second? I've come across something I think you should know about."

"Is it important, Rutherford? I'm very busy."

Barrett was obviously annoyed at having been bothered, but Rutherford wasn't going to back down. He opened the office door, and Barrett looked up from a stack of ship designs. He didn't look too happy for the intrusion.

"Well, what's so important, Mr. Rutherford?" Barrett asked impatiently.

"I think you need to know about something I have come across. It is regarding the mining accident that occurred in Bath a few months back. I found some receipts regarding the support beams that were delivered to your mine over in Bath – the one that had the cave-in."

When Barrett heard the word cave-in, Rutherford noticed a distinct change. His hands fumbled with the ship designs, and for a split second Rutherford detected a slight change in his facial expression. It was as if Barrett already knew what he was about to tell him.

"Yes, what about it?"

For the next ten minutes Rutherford explained in careful detail what he had found and what he believed had happened. Barrett's face never changed expressions, and he interrupted Rutherford only a couple of times to repeat certain facts.

After he finished, Rutherford immediately felt better. A huge burden had been lifted from his shoulders, and it was Barrett's problem now.

Barrett remained expressionless. He turned around in his chair and bent over. Rutherford heard the dials turning on a huge black safe Barrett kept behind his desk. The safe door clicked open and then slammed shut again. Barrett swiveled his chair back around and faced Rutherford. He had two large cigars in his hand.

"I just revealed a secret to you, Rutherford," he said, handing him one of the cigars.

Secret? What the hell was Barrett talking about?

Barrett clipped off the end of his cigar and threw it in a trashcan by his desk. He struck a match and slowly lit the cigar. "That safe," he said as he pointed behind him, "all it holds is cigars." He blew out a giant stream of white smoke. "You haven't met Samuel Johnstone yet, have you?"

"No."

"Well, he has been away for most of the time since you were hired. He runs my trading operations. Poor Johnstone – for years he has been trying to find out what I keep in there. Every year without fail he tries to get me to reveal the secret. I wouldn't be surprised if he's tried to break into it a few times."

A cold smile came over Barrett's face. "Who knows what he thinks I have stashed in it? Gold, perhaps, or secret documents." He laughed. "Knowing Johnstone's ego, I wouldn't be the least bit surprised if he thought I had some incriminating evidence against him, just in case."

He winked. "Do me a favor, Rutherford," he said with a conspirator's tone.

"Let's keep what's hidden in the safe a secret between you and me. It will be our little joke on Johnstone."

Rutherford heard him really laugh for the first time, and the sound was exactly what he had always imagined a jackal sounded like moments before closing in for a kill.

Rutherford nodded his head in confused agreement, and Barrett handed him the matches. He didn't really smoke cigars, but Rutherford didn't want to turn down the offer.

"Come over here and look at this, Rutherford."

Rutherford lit the fat cigar and walked over to the huge desk, where Barrett unrolled a design of a ship.

"This is the new ship I am having built. Her name is going to be *Barrett's Gold.*"

Rutherford looked at the design; he had to admit it was impressive. It was as large as any ship he had ever seen in Bristol's port.

"Isn't it supposed to be unlucky to name a ship after your family?" Rutherford asked, quickly realizing the stupidity of his question.

Barrett looked at him rather contemptuously, and then a smile appeared on his face. "It is . . . if you believe in letting the fates determine your luck. I make my own luck. You know, Rutherford, I have been following your work here, and you have turned out to be an excellent employee – better than I even expected. Don't get me wrong; I would not have hired you in the first place if I didn't think you would do a good job. It's just that, well, you can understand it is hard to always hire good people. Even if you think you are hiring a quality individual, sometimes things just don't work out for one reason or another. But that certainly has not been the case with you."

"Thank you, sir," Rutherford managed to blurt out, trying not to choke on the cigar smoke. He wasn't really sure why Barrett was giving him the unexpected praise, but he certainly didn't mind it one bit.

"I am glad that you came to see me, Rutherford. As a matter of fact, I have been meaning to have a talk with you about a promotion within the company. You have performed extremely well in our mining division, and a position is opening in our trading department in the next couple of months."

Barrett took a couple more puffs from his cigar. "I think you might be just the man for the job. I'm not sure how much you know about our shipping business, but like I probably told you when I first met you, it is my belief that vast fortunes will be made trading goods between the West Indies, the Caribbean, and the colonies."

"This ship," Barrett pointed to the designs, "will be the tenth one built to trade goods in the West Indies and the colonies. I want to build at least ten more over the next five years. You have no idea how profitable these markets are going to be Rutherford. We can all get rich beyond our wildest imaginations."

For the first time since Rutherford had known Barrett, he truly looked happy while discussing his grand plans for his company.

"Now what does this all mean for you?" Barrett rolled up the ship designs. "The new position would entail overseeing and bookkeeping all goods and supplies that are shipped over the trading routes."

"And of course," he added, "with the additional responsibilities, you will be compensated with a nice salary increase."

Rutherford was shocked by the offer. He had come to Barrett's office with disturbing news that he knew was going to upset him, but instead of getting angry like he had expected, Barrett was offering him a promotion instead. Even with the scandal about the beams and dead miners, Rutherford wasn't about to let the unexpected opportunity slip away.

"Mr. Barrett, it would be an honor to be considered for the position when it opens. I can guarantee that I won't let you down. Thank you for the consideration."

He had become so excited about the possibility of the new job with the overseas trading routes that he almost forgot why he had come to see Barrett in the first place. Despite the offer, he couldn't leave without asking Barrett about what he had discovered. "Sir," he said with some reservation, "what should we do about the invoices concerning the beams?"

Barrett's face became solemn, and he displayed a concerned look. "This matter of the support beams," he said in a serious and deep tone, "is a very serious matter indeed."

Rutherford nodded in agreement.

"Obviously, someone made a mistake somewhere, but according to the reports – and I have been in the mining business my whole life – those beams played no part in that accident.

"Mining is a dangerous job," Barrett went on, "and accidents happen, and people die. It is a risk that all miners take freely and accept. What has happened cannot be changed, but I promise you I will personally look into the matter. Can I have the papers regarding this matter, please?"

"Of course." Rutherford handed over all the documents and receipts.

"Are these all of them?"

"Yes. I went back though the other ledger books, and that's it."

"Good work. Thank you for bringing the matter to my attention. I will handle it from here."

Rutherford got up to leave.

"Before you go, there is one other thing, John."

"Yes, sir?" he replied. It was the first time Barrett had ever used his first name.

"Because you have lived up to my two requirements, I think you have a long and bright future here." He paused and gave Rutherford what appeared to be a forced smile before continuing. "You work hard, and it is evident that you would never do anything to jeopardize the company. So keep up the good work."

Rutherford nodded at the compliment and left Barrett's office a little dazed but excited. He couldn't wait to tell Anne about the possible promotion. Perhaps that would make her feel better.

VI

Rutherford tossed and turned late into the night. He kept thinking about Barrett, the defective beams, and the collapsed mine. He couldn't imagine how terrifying it must have been to be trapped. He hoped that nobody had suffered for long because in the right circumstances men could become trapped in air pockets and end up dying a slow, agonizing death from suffocation.

Rutherford tried to relieve the burden on his conscience by telling himself that it was Barrett's responsibility now. He had done all that he could by informing him. And anyway, like Barrett said, the cave-in probably had nothing to do with the support beams.

It all sounded good, yet it didn't completely relieve the burden on his mind that something wasn't right and that someone in Barrett's company was responsible for those deaths. He had a nagging suspicion that Barrett would get rid of the paper trail and that would be the end of it.

Another thought crossed his mind: was Barrett dangling the job opportunity in front of him so he would keep quiet? The more he thought about it, the more it seemed an unlikely coincidence that Barrett had offered him a new position and a pay raise the very same day that he came forward with evidence of possible criminal activity.

Anne stirred in her sleep. For a few days her cold had gotten better, but now it was back again, and it was getting worse. She coughed heavily, and Rutherford rolled over and felt her head with the back of his hand. His dilemma about the mining accident and Barrett was quickly forgotten. Anne was burning up.

He sat up in bed, unsure of what to do. A coughing spasm woke Anne from her sleep.

"Are you all right, honey?" he asked, rubbing her neck.

She opened her eyes, and Rutherford couldn't believe how fast her appearance had deteriorated. Her face was a pasty gray color, her hair was soaked from sweat, and her eyes were swollen and blood red.

"I don't feel so good, John," she replied in a raspy voice.

She closed her eyes once again, and Rutherford stroked her damp hair with a trembling hand. "Don't worry. You'll be all right. I'll get the doctor tomorrow."

He carefully tucked the sheets in around her because, despite the fever, her body shivered uncontrollably from chills.

Rutherford hadn't wanted to admit it before, but now he had to: Anne had developed a bad case of the same flu that was devastating the city. He quietly slipped out of bed and walked into the kitchen.

He grabbed a bottle of brandy, poured himself a drink, and sat down at the kitchen table. He downed the entire glass and poured another. The brandy warmed his belly but not his heart.

He had never imagined what his life would be without Anne, and now that he had to face that possibility, it frightened him in a way that he had never felt before. He downed a second glass and grabbed a wet cloth and the bottle of brandy. He walked back into the bedroom and sat down next to Anne. He raised her chin and said, "Anne, here. Drink this. It will help you feel better."

He helped her sit up, and she drank the brandy. Rutherford wiped the wet cloth across her forehead to try and cool her down some. She only had enough energy to take a few sips, and then she slumped back down onto the bed.

It was the worst night of Rutherford's life. Anne's condition seemed to get worse with every passing minute. She suffered from coughing fits that continuously shook her out of her tortured sleep, and her breathing became shallow and ragged.

Throughout the night, she mumbled incoherently as the fever tortured her mind. Her body shook uncontrollably, and she complained of being cold. He had never felt this helpless in his entire life. He didn't know how to help her, and even worse, he didn't know if she could be helped.

As soon as the sun rose, Rutherford ran down to the doctor's office. He restlessly paced in front of the office until the doctor finally showed up.

Dr. Smithton was a tall wispy fellow who favored fanciful, bright-colored clothes. The physician had an excellent reputation, unlike a lot of the doctors in Bristol. Rutherford explained the situation, and the doctor followed him home.

Once inside the bedroom the doctor took a look at Anne and shook his head. He pulled the sheets back and began examining her. He felt her head, took her pulse, listened intently to her lungs and chest, and tried to get Anne to respond to a few questions.

She opened her eyes only once, and appeared to be totally disoriented. She didn't respond to any of the doctor's questions, and finally he pulled the sheets back up to her shoulders.

He looked concerned. "John, let's go out to the kitchen."

Rutherford led him into the kitchen. He didn't want to hear the doctor's prognosis.

"Would you like something to drink?" he offered, stalling for time.

The doctor waved his hand. "John, I'm sorry to tell you this, but Anne is very sick."

"Are you sure?" Rutherford interrupted. "Perhaps she just has a bad cold," he said with growing desperation in his voice. He started to feel lightheaded, almost dizzy.

"I wish that was the case, but it isn't."

"Is she going to die?" He could barely speak.

The doctor put his coat on and grabbed his medicine bag. "John, I don't want to give you false hope. There is always a chance she could pull through, but it is a very small chance. She has a very bad case. Her lungs are terribly congested, and her fever is very high. I haven't seen anyone this sick make it."

Even though deep down Rutherford knew Anne was dying, the doctor's words stunned him. He supposed hearing it from him not only made it real, but it took away any hope he might have had for some type of a miracle.

"What should I do?" he asked somewhat pitifully.

"Just make her as comfortable as possible. If you need anything, you know where to find me. I'm sorry." The doctor patted his shoulder and left.

Rutherford stayed by her side constantly for the next two days. Early on the third day, Anne completely lost consciousness. It was actually a blessing because Rutherford couldn't stand to see her suffer anymore.

He sat in a small chair by their bed and watched her for hours. The gloomy day turned into an even more depressing night as Anne's breathing became more and more labored. Rutherford didn't think she would make it through the night. He was so tired and distraught that his mind was completely numb.

Late in the night, Rutherford started to doze off in the chair by the bed. He didn't want to fall asleep, but he knew it was inevitable. He crawled into bed and wrapped his arms around Anne. Immediately, he fell asleep, and for the moment, the awful reality of the situation was replaced by a wonderful dream.

He and Anne were canoeing up the Avon River. They were all alone on the entire river. The water was calm and tranquil, and they could see their reflections in the sparkling blue water as they lazily paddled. The sun was bright, warm, and inviting.

They pulled over to the riverbank and jumped out. Anne laughed as Rutherford almost fell back into the river trying to get out of the canoe. He grabbed a huge wicker picnic basket, and they walked hand in hand down a tree-lined trail that opened into a large field.

Knee-high wild flowers surrounded them. There must have been millions of flowers of every shape and color: purple, red, yellow, blue, and pink. The flowers swayed gently in the warm breeze.

Anne unfolded a blanket, and they sat down in the middle of the field. Their only company was a single majestic eagle that was soaring high above them in the brilliant blue sky.

Hours and hours seemed to pass, and they just lay on the blanket, holding hands, watching giant puffs of white clouds pass by. A tremendous sense of peace and security washed over Rutherford.

The sun started to sink into the sky. Anne rolled over and told him it was time for her to leave. He didn't want her to leave. He felt safe in this place, but Anne had a look in her eyes that told him she was ready. She stood up and took his hands in hers. She pulled him up from the blanket, and they hugged tightly.

Anne let go, smiled, and started walking back down the tree-lined path. He stood and watched her leave; he knew he couldn't follow her to the place where she was going.

He woke suddenly and was holding Anne tightly. He gazed at her. She no longer looked sick, and the pain and suffering that had distorted her face had disappeared. She looked so peaceful.

Rutherford held her hand and kissed her cheek softly. "Goodbye, darling," he whispered.

VII

Samuel Johnstone passed by one of his favorite watering holes and briefly thought about stopping in for a quick glass of ale before meeting with Barrett.

He had returned to Bristol a week earlier after a five-month stint in the Caribbean. He was now in charge of the Atlantic Triangle trading routes, and even though that meant he would spend little time in Bristol, he couldn't have been happier about the change.

Barrett's ships delivered manufactured goods such as textiles, tin, and pottery to Africa. From the Dark Continent, slaves were picked up and sold in the West Indies and American colonies.

On the return trip the ships were loaded with rice, sugar, tobacco, tea, and furs to be sold at profitable prices. He still found it hard to believe how much Barrett Trading had changed over the last twenty years. What had once been a moderately successful coal company was now one of the most dominant trading companies in all of England, and Johnstone knew he was a big reason for that success.

Business was booming, and Barrett had rewarded him handsomely for his successes. Over the last few years he had patiently built up a nice little nest egg, and his plan was to retire to Jamaica within four years. Perhaps sooner, if he could score a big hit somewhere along the way.

He envisioned buying a little plantation overlooking the ocean. He would spend his days on the beach drinking rum out of coconut shells and being waited on by pretty young local girls.

Johnstone looked at his pocket watch and decided that he didn't have enough time for that drink. He passed a beggar lying in a heap of garbage on the side of the street. The foul-smelling man pleaded with Johnstone for some spare change.

Normally, depending on his mood, Johnstone would have totally ignored or, more often than not, kicked the dirty rascal. But not today. In fact, he did something that was totally out of character. He reached into his pocket and threw the beggar a pound note.

The haggard man squealed with delight. He quickly snatched the note from the street and ran off, no doubt to drink himself into oblivion with his newfound fortune.

Johnstone's unusual display of generosity momentarily confused him, but he shook off the feeling and continued on in good spirits while marveling at his generosity to the less fortunate. He approached the Ox and Musket Tavern and saw Barrett standing outside.

The Tavern was one of those places that attracted a diverse mix of people. Not only did sailors, pickpockets, prostitutes, and all forms of riffraff frequent the place, but so did doctors, ship captains, lawyers, and merchants. Despite its seedy appearance, quite a few merchants met in the back rooms to conduct business transactions or to gamble at cards or dice.

Johnstone waved to Barrett.

"Samuel, good to see you!" Barrett called out. They shook hands in a manner that was more affectionate than businesslike.

"Come, let's see what this Teach bloke has to say."

They walked into the tavern, and Johnstone pushed through the rowdy crowd, clearing a way for Barrett. The bar's owner, a fat, cherubic man who drank the profits as fast as they came in, motioned to them that their host was in the last room in the back.

The suffocating crowd smelled of smoke and sweat, producing an awful stench. Johnstone squeezed his way toward the back of the large room past a long bar, where a group of drunken Portuguese sailors were arm wrestling and screaming at one another in some incomprehensible babble.

Once off the main floor, they walked down a hall and into a private room. An imposing-looking man stood up to greet them. He was at least six-foot-three and had a long black mustache that drooped downward towards his chin.

His long hair was pitch black and unruly. Despite his unkempt hair, he was dressed in excellent clothes and displayed all the manners of a gentleman.

"Mr. Barrett." He nodded and then looked cautiously at Johnstone.

"Teach, I'd like to introduce you to Samuel Johnstone. He's in charge of our trading routes. Anything you say to me, you can say to him."

Teach nodded, and the men exchanged pleasantries. They took a seat at the table, and Teach ordered a round of drinks.

Barrett had previously explained to Johnstone that Teach came from a respectable and moderately wealthy family that owned a furniture and ironwork company. Barrett couldn't figure out why Teach wanted to meet with him, but his note had spurred an interest.

A skinny waitress who couldn't have been more than fifteen years old set the drinks down and quickly left.

Teach stroked his long mustache and raised his mug. "Cheers!"

The men toasted.

Barrett, as was his nature, got straight to the point. "So why are we here, Mr. Teach?"

"I have a business proposal for you. A proposal I think will be very lucrative for both of us."

"Let me ask you a question first," Barrett interrupted. "If you have such a lucrative business proposition, then why are you not in it with your family?"

Johnstone could tell by Teach's reaction that he had anticipated the question. He had an uneasy feeling about the man. Johnstone couldn't explain it, but he knew instantly that he didn't like or trust him. His gut told him that Teach was dangerous, and long ago he had learned to always follow his instincts.

Teach drained a mouthful from his beer and wiped the foam from his mustache. "First, let me tell you what I propose," he answered in a husky voice. "And then you will see why I have come specifically to you.

"King George has commissioned seven warships that have the legal authority to attack and confiscate all goods of enemy vessels in the West Indies and Caribbean. The goods taken from these ships are then brought back to England and added to the royal coffers. I have worked the last two years as a privateer on such a ship."

It surprised Johnstone to hear him say that he was a privateer, especially with his family's financial position. Most privateers were just common sailors who took the added risk of getting killed while attacking other ships in order to rob them of their goods. The crew generally received a percentage of the stolen goods, but a privateer's take was usually low. In fact, most privateers were just petty criminals who had been given the choice of jail or serving the King.

"I know of your family," Barrett replied. "Why in the hell would you get involved with that line of work? You could have taken over your family's business and not had a care in the world."

Teach frowned. "I have no desire to sell wooden furniture for the rest of my life," he replied with contempt. "You couldn't pay me enough to take over my father's rotten business. Anyway, I can make my own wealth and on my own terms."

Johnstone thought the man was an arrogant little bastard. There was something about him that reminded him of someone, but he just couldn't figure out who it was.

Teach looked around to make sure no one was listening and drew closer to Barrett. "I cannot tell you the amount of goods we were able to take with very little resistance. Gold from Spanish ships, slaves from Africa that we later sold in the colonies, silver and indigo from the French, jewelry of all types from Portugal. You name it; we stole it. Then we either kept it or later sold it for gold or liquor."

Johnstone was confused. Why was Teach telling them this? "Great! So you are nothing more than a bloody pirate. That still doesn't answer the question. Why are we here?"

Teach turned and gave him a contemptuous look.

Johnstone didn't see an ounce of fear in his eyes, and that gave him another reason to be apprehensive of the man.

"What I propose is a business partnership," Teach answered sharply, turning to Barrett. "One that has some risks, but one that will make us both rich."

"I'm already rich," Barrett cut in.

Johnstone laughed, and Teach returned the smile. It was evident they were all testing one another.

"I'm aware of that," Teach replied. "I plan to go out on my own. I want to raid merchant ships and steal their goods. Only I don't want to give England or the King any of the profits. I need someone to give me enough money to buy one decent ship, hire some good men, and get the necessary equipment. For your investment you will receive half of the profits."

A brawl had broken out between the Portuguese sailors, but Barrett ignored the tables being broken and the bottles being smashed around him.

"So you want me to give you enough money to buy a ship so you can go out and become a pirate? You know pirates are hung. Why would I take such a risk?"

"I have heard certain things about you, Mr. Barrett–"

Barrett cut him off sharply. "Don't always believe what you hear, Mr. Teach. That could get you into trouble."

"Listen, Barrett," Teach said, smiling as his voice took on an almost venomous tone, "you can fool most of the people in this town, but you can't fool me. Take off that expensive suit, and you're no better than a common criminal. And that thug of yours," Teach said as he pointed at Johnstone, "is nothing but a pirate anyway."

"This man's a fool!" Johnstone yelled angrily, standing up from the table. "He's wasting our time. Let's get the hell out of here."

"There is something else in it for you, Mr. Barrett," Teach interjected, ignoring Johnstone's outburst.

Barrett looked at Johnstone and motioned for him to sit back down. "And what is that?" he said, turning to Teach.

"Through this partnership, I can provide protection for your ships, so you don't have to worry about people stealing from you. More importantly, I know of your problems with East India Trading Company and the Parliament. I can make it very disruptive for them to conduct their business. That I can guarantee."

"What if I decline your offer?" Barrett asked.

"Then I will find someone else to finance my operation. Perhaps East India would like to back me. Of course, that would mean all of your trading ships will be open game."

"Is that a threat?" Johnstone asked incredulously.

Teach laughed loudly. "Of course not, Mr. Johnstone. Men of your stature cannot be threatened. I am not just talking about money here, but the chance to dictate shipping in the entire region. Do you know what is happening in the colonies? I made a lot of contacts in the area while I was in the service. Those people depend on us for supplies in order to survive, and they don't care where it comes from. I am talking about the potential for enormous wealth and power. You're a smart man, Barrett. You know that the real power is going to come from whoever can control those shipping lanes. I could be a very valuable tool in helping you destroy your enemies and achieve control of the whole area."

Johnstone glanced over at Barrett and immediately knew by the expression on his face that Teach had convinced him. After twenty years he had come to understand Barrett's true character. Men like Barrett were driven by only one force of nature – a force stronger than the lure of money or the possession of a beautiful woman. It was the force of power. And for those rare men who so desired it, their souls were never content. Some were good. Many were evil. Regardless, the power worshippers could not know satisfaction.

Teach must have sensed that he had persuaded Barrett as well. He stuck out his hand. "What do you say, Barrett? Partners?"

Barrett hesitated for a brief moment before he extended his hand to seal their partnership.

The rest of the night was spent hashing out the details of their new partnership. Barrett was going to arrange to have enough funds deposited in Teach's account to buy a ship and get the operation up and running.

Johnstone felt that Barrett was making a huge mistake, but there was nothing he could do about it. Once Barrett had made up his mind on something, that was that.

As they were getting ready to leave, Barrett had one last warning for Teach. "Remember, Mr. Teach, don't double-cross me. If you do, you'll be very sorry."

Barrett stood up to leave, and Johnstone followed. He looked back at Teach, who had remained seated. Teach pointed his finger at him in jest and smirked coldly. Johnstone knew he would have to watch his back with this man.

Once back outside the tavern, Barrett turned to Johnstone before leaving. "Samuel, there is one more matter."

"Yes?"

"I want you to pay a visit to John Rutherford tomorrow. Give him that job in shipping that I promised him a while back. If something goes wrong with this Teach business, we'll need someone to take the fall."

Johnstone smiled. It amazed him how Barrett was always planning ahead.

On the way home it finally came to Johnstone who Teach reminded him of. He laughed in amusement at his keen observation. The person Teach reminded him of was Barrett. He wondered how long the two sharks would be able to work together before one tried to eat the other.

VIII

Summer, 1717

It was probably around midnight, but Rutherford couldn't be certain of the time. He sat in an old rickety chair in the parlor room and listened to his own slow, rhythmic breathing. The house was quiet. So very quiet.

It had been months since Anne had passed away, but he still couldn't bring himself to sleep in their bed. It was too painful. Since her death he had fallen into a depressing cycle: he went to work and came home. Nothing in life seemed to matter all that much anymore.

He remembered the old priest telling him that time healed all wounds. The words were comforting at the moment, but now he wasn't so sure the priest knew what he was talking about. He was convinced that the only thing time brought was nothing but more pain. How could God be so cruel? he wondered.

He took a long pull from the half-empty bottle of brandy and curled up on the cushioned seat. He was exhausted, but only with the aid of brandy could he manage to sleep. He felt his eyelids growing heavy, and he welcomed the dreamless dark sleep that began to overtake his body.

He thought he had just fallen asleep when he felt the warm sunlight on his face. He slowly opened his swollen eyelids. Was it morning already? He rolled off the chair with a loud moan. His body creaked in half a dozen places. He had a splitting headache, and his back was aching.

Tonight, he swore, no more booze. But he had made that pledge every morning for the last couple of months and had yet to keep it. He threw some cold water on his face and left for work. It was going to be a long day.

Once at his desk, he sipped on a cold cup of tea and pretended to work. He was so consumed with the throbbing in his temples that he didn't notice the man approaching his desk.

"Mr. Rutherford, good morning. Allow me to introduce myself. I'm Samuel Johnstone, and I am in charge of trading."

Rutherford quickly snapped to attention. He wondered if he looked as bad as he felt. He had heard a lot about Johnstone, but he had never met the man in his almost eight months of employment at Barrett Trading. The wild gossip from his fellow employees ran the gamut, although Rutherford believed most of it was just nothing but crazy rumors.

Johnstone extended his hand, and Rutherford shook it. Rutherford quickly forgot about the pain in his head because, for a second, he thought the son of a bitch was going to break his hand. Johnstone's grip was like a vise. Mercifully, just when Rutherford was about to cry out, Johnstone released his grip and sat down in front of his desk.

Rutherford's hand was throbbing. What the hell was that about? he wondered. He couldn't believe how strong the man's grip was for someone his size. Johnstone was an inch or two taller than Rutherford and was solidly built. But that still didn't explain where his strength came from.

Rutherford studied Johnstone. He had long black hair, which was completely out of style, and a handsome, almost boyish face. His most distinguishing feature was the color of his eyes: a menacing, almost translucent gray.

"John, I have heard some very good things about you from Mr. Barrett, and he seems to think that you are just the man we could use in our trading department."

Rutherford had almost forgotten about his discussions with Barrett earlier in the spring. It looked like Barrett was keeping his word about the job after all.

"I'm sorry about your wife, John," Johnstone said as he shook his head. "I know it must be hard on you."

When it came to discussing his wife's death, Rutherford had developed a standard reaction to everyone's well-meaning but uncomfortable condolences.

"Thank you," he responded in a low but unemotional tone. "It's been a difficult time, but she's in a better place now."

Of course, Rutherford didn't believe the words, but he found that it seemed to make other people feel more comfortable to be around him.

After all these months, it still pained him to talk about Anne. He wanted to change the subject. "Are you married?"

Johnstone gave a wry smile. "No, I'm not, and for that matter, I probably never will be. With all the new ships Barrett has built, I travel too much. Besides, there are too many fine women in this world to be tied down to just one."

Rutherford had heard rumors that Johnstone had fathered a vast number of illegitimate children in both Bristol and various ports around the world.

Johnstone shifted in his seat. "I know you are busy, John," he said in a businesslike manner. "So I will get to the point. Mr. Barrett wants you to finish up any loose ends here and report immediately to the trading department. As he has probably told you, the future of this company lies in overseas trading, and that's where we need our best people."

Best people? Rutherford knew why he was being given the job; it was a reward for keeping his mouth shut.

"You will report directly to me, and I do have to stress one point. I need your word as a gentleman that all aspects of our business remain within the company. If you have any concerns, you see me and me only. Is that acceptable to you?"

"Of course," Rutherford replied without hesitation.

"Terrific. I look forward to working with you."

Johnstone detailed exactly what kind of work he would be doing. Rutherford was pleased to hear that Johnstone would be spending most of the year traveling to the Caribbean and the colonies; his boss was going to be gone for most of the year. Rutherford started to like the job more and more.

Another meeting was taking place on the other side of town. The discussions were being held in a plain faded-brick building that served as Bristol's chief law enforcement and court building.

David Hitchcock had been sent by some highly influential members of Parliament to investigate Barrett. Rather, he had been sent under the guise of an investigation. His employers just wanted to do away with Barrett any way possible.

At thirty-one, he was the youngest commissioned investigator ever – a fact that was attributed to his family's connection to the Duke of Lincolnshire. But his appointment wasn't entirely due to family connections. He was a decorated war hero and considered one of the best young officers in the whole British Army. Hitchcock loved the Army, but he had higher goals in mind – goals that could only be achieved through political office.

Hitchcock knew that the politicians had the real power and influence. He wanted to be the one telling the Army generals where and whom to fight, not the one carrying out someone else's orders.

Hitchcock couldn't believe how unlucky he had been. Last year he had spent weeks convincing one of Barrett's employees to help him, and he had succeeded. Allen Lawrence was going to give him enough evidence to send Barrett to the gallows. Everything was going according to plan until Lawrence failed to show up with the documents and was later found murdered.

With Lawrence dead, his case against Barrett was finished, and he had to return to London empty-handed. But powerful men wanted Barrett done away with, and they convinced Hitchcock to return and finish the job. This time they promised him a position in Parliament if he could find a way to bring him down.

Hitchcock sat across from the constable, and Bristol's chief law enforcement officer didn't seem all that happy to see him.

"Damn!" Hitchcock swore. "If Lawrence hadn't been killed that night, we would have had Barrett nailed. I know he had enough concrete information on the scoundrel to bring him and his whole rotten, corrupt company to its knees. It sure was awfully convenient that he wound up stabbed to death on the very same night he was supposed to meet me."

"Wait a second," the constable cut in. "You're not implying that Barrett had Lawrence murdered because he found out that he might – and I stress might – have given you some type of information that backs up your claims. You don't have any proof of that. This is the second time in a year you have been here, and you've got absolutely nothing. Doesn't Parliament have better things for you to be doing?"

"Look," Hitchcock replied in exasperation, "don't you find it pretty damn ironic that the one person who was willing to deliver evidence against Barrett just happened to turn up dead before he was to hand that evidence over to me?"

"Bad luck is what I would call it. Crime is not as rampant here as it is in your city. But these things happen from time to time."

"I'm still going to need your help," replied Hitchcock, ignoring the insult about his hometown.

"I will do whatever I can to help you. But unless you have real proof, there is no real reason to pursue this matter any further."

Hitchcock smiled. "I don't have any hard evidence yet, but I still have one more trick up my sleeve. I have a new contact within the company that's willing to help."

Hitchcock was lying. He did have one more person he wanted to talk to, but he didn't know if the man knew anything or if he would even cooperate. He lied to the constable because he didn't want him to think that the case had come to a dead end.

"Well, you best do that in a hurry," the constable replied irritably. "Because I have better things to do around here than to waste my time with another dead-end investigation."

The investigator forced a smile, stood up, and left.

IX

As part of his promotion, Rutherford had moved up to the second floor, and he couldn't have been more pleased. He now had his own little office, and the work was much more interesting than filing papers all day long. Barrett's new ship was due to be completed by Christmas, and Johnstone was going to sail with it to Jamaica, leaving him in charge.

Rutherford wasn't sure if it was the new job, a change of scenery, or something else, but he was spending less and less time brooding about Anne. He felt a twinge of guilt about it, but perhaps the old priest had been right after all: time did heal all wounds.

He still missed her dearly, but the anguish over her death had dulled somewhat. He had reached a point where he felt that life was worth living again. And in order to live again, he had to accept that she was gone forever. Nothing he could do was ever going to change that.

He finished completing the inventory checklist for a cargo ship that was set to sail to the Congo. He loved reviewing ships' manifests and their travel logs. It amazed him how many different goods Barrett's company traded and the different locations the ships sailed to.

His stomach rumbled loudly, and he looked at his pocket watch. His appetite had slowly come back over the last couple of weeks, and he had stopped drinking so much. He set aside the ship's manifest and headed out for an early lunch.

He leisurely strolled down to the harbor. It was an exceptionally nice day, and he decided to take advantage of the weather. He sat outside at an outdoor café and ordered a plate of dumplings and a glass of cider.

Normally, he read the newspaper while eating lunch. But not today. He was content to enjoy the beautiful blue sky and watch the ships in the harbor.

As spring had progressed into summer, the flu epidemic that had plagued the city in the late winter and early spring had finally dissipated. Rutherford noticed a sense of relief in the faces of the people who passed by.

The deadly flu had taken its toll on the city. Over a thousand people, including Anne, had died from it. But mercifully, the suffering and dying had finally ended, for now.

The waiter brought his dumplings and cider, but before he had a chance to take a sip of his drink, a gentleman approached the table.

"Mr. Rutherford, good afternoon," the man said as he tipped his hat. "My name is David Hitchcock. I am an investigator for the Royal Parliament. Do you mind if I sit down and have a few words with you?"

Hitchcock appeared to be in his early thirties and was impeccably dressed. He acted and looked like he came from the highest reaches of society.

Rutherford had no idea what he could possibly want with him but saw no harm in letting him take a seat. "Not at all," he answered nonchalantly. "Would you care to order anything?"

"I would love a glass of beer."

Rutherford motioned to the waiter, who brought over a beer.

Hitchcock raised his glass in a salute and took a sip, clearly enjoying the taste. "The reason I have come to see you, Mr. Rutherford, is that I would like to ask you a few questions about the company you work for."

Warning bells started going off in Rutherford's head, and he stopped eating the dumplings. "My company?" he asked rather hesitantly.

"Mr. Rutherford, let me get straight to the point. We have been investigating your company, in particular Arthur Barrett, for some time now."

"Investigating!" Rutherford interrupted loudly. "What possibly for?"

Hitchcock gave him a sarcastic grin that seemed to imply that he should know exactly what he was about to tell him. "To start with: tax evasion, conspiracy, bribery, piracy, and, of course, murder."

Rutherford couldn't believe what he was hearing and wasn't sure how to respond. "I'm sure you must be mistaken," he said, wondering what the hell he had gotten himself involved in. "Barrett Trading Company has been in business a long time, and I'm sure no one in the company would do those sorts of things."

"Mr. Rutherford, everything I've told you is true. What I don't know is if you have had any involvement in these crimes or not."

Rutherford squirmed in his chair. He hadn't forgotten about the miners in Bath. Is this about the cave-in? he wondered.

"I'm not sure I can help you, Mr. Hitchcock," he said hesitantly. "I have no knowledge of the things you say. I have only been with the company for a short period of time." Rutherford's heart was pounding against his chest; surely the investigator didn't suspect him of any misdeeds. "I don't know why you have told me all this or what you want from me. If you know all these things are true, why don't you go and arrest Barrett?"

Hitchcock leaned back in his chair and took another sip of beer before setting it back down on the table. His silence was making Rutherford uncomfortable.

"Believe me," he finally answered, "I will. But I still need some more hard evidence before I send anyone to the executioner, and that is where you can help me."

"Help you?" Rutherford protested. "I really have no idea what you are talking about. How can I possibly help you?"

Hitchcock smiled and took the last swig from his glass. "Listen, I don't expect you to give me anything this second. Just think about it and keep your eyes open. I know it could be difficult for you, but you have to remember, in some cases we are talking about people who have lost their lives because of that bloody bastard!"

Rutherford was surprised by the sudden outburst; Hitchcock didn't appear to be a man who was easily flustered.

"The reason I am talking to you," Hitchcock continued in a more gentle tone, "is because from what I have heard, you are a good and decent man. Everything I told you about Barrett is the truth, and I don't think you would be able live with yourself if you had a chance to save innocent lives but instead looked the other way."

Hitchcock stood up and threw a couple shillings on the table. "Rutherford," he warned, "before I leave, I want to make myself perfectly clear. If you choose not to help me, when I arrest Barrett, if I have even the slightest evidence implicating you, I will make sure that you go to jail for a long, long time."

After delivering his threat, Hitchcock turned and left. Rutherford was in shock. He pushed away his plate of dumplings; he no longer had an appetite.

On the other side of Bristol, Johnstone, Barrett, and the constable sat around a splintered wooden table in one of Barrett's warehouses. They met there because their privacy was assured.

The constable had been on Barrett's payroll for years, and Johnstone knew that Barrett had considered him one of his best investments. There had been more than a few times that the constable had helped out in situations that could have ended in disaster.

But the constable's cooperation came at a steep price. Johnstone had known greedy men before but none quite like this one. In fact, the man didn't just love money; he worshipped it. Johnstone was convinced the moneygrubber would have pushed his own mother in front of a charging horse in exchange for a few pounds.

The funny thing about the constable was that his love for money was so great he refused to spend even a single shilling. The man was tighter than a cooper's barrel. Johnstone had discovered that he hid all of his money in a special safe dug underneath the floor of his house – a fact that Johnstone kept secret, even from Barrett, because he planned to steal the money before he left Bristol for good.

The three men met to discuss what to do about the investigator. He had become a thorn in Barrett's side, and Johnstone knew the bosses patience was starting to wear thin.

"I don't think Hitchcock has anything on us," Barrett said to the constable. "He will probably give up in a couple of weeks like he did last time."

The constable shook his head. "I don't know. He is a persistent little bugger. The only reason he left the first time was because his star witness . . . " The constable paused slightly and coughed. "Uh, had an unfortunate accident."

Johnstone laughed. "Yes, it was unfortunate, wasn't it?"

The constable didn't appear to care for Johnstone's humor. He turned to Barrett. "Hitchcock has political aspirations back home, and bringing down someone like you would certainly win him some favors."

"What about paying him off?" Barrett asked.

The constable thought for a moment. "No, with most men that would work, but not with Hitchcock. His family's already wealthy. Besides, he is out to make a name for himself. I think it would be too great a risk to try and bribe him."

The constable glanced over at Johnstone, who sneered his displeasure. There was no love lost between the two men, although Johnstone didn't mind dealing with him because he was so easy to control.

The constable ignored Johnstone and turned again to Barrett. "The reason I wanted to meet with you," he continued, "is the investigator told me there is another person in your company who is cooperating with him."

Barrett slammed his fist on the table. "Damn it! Did he say who it was?"

"No, but I have the situation under control. I don't want to get Hitchcock too suspicious. He's already a little leery of me, especially after Lawrence was found murdered the very night they were supposed to meet. I'll find out who it is, but you just have to give me a little time."

Johnstone knew the fat bastard was stalling. Obviously, he was trying to get more money out of Barrett.

"Get me that name within a week," Barrett replied, "and I will double your pay for the next three months."

Johnstone could almost see the money dials spinning in the constable's cherubic head.

"I'll find out who it is. Then what?"

"Just get the damn name," Johnstone shot back in a venomous voice, "and I will take care it."

Johnstone looked at Barrett, who nodded his approval. He turned back towards the constable. "And if you don't have his name in a week's time," he said, peering straight into the constable's swollen red eyes, "then I will be forced to take care of Hitchcock. And I don't think that would look too good for you. Now would it?"

"I told you," the constable protested, "I'll get the damn name. I'll have one of my men follow Hitchcock around. Now if you'll excuse me, I have to get back to work."

As he watched the fat man hurriedly storm off, Johnstone growled to Barrett, "Look! That pig is so fat he waddles like a duck when he walks."

Barrett laughed. "Don't worry, Samuel. He will get us that name by the end of the week."

"What makes you so sure?"

"Didn't you see the twinkle in his eyes when I promised to double his payment? I wouldn't be surprised if he was on his way to see Hitchcock right this minute."

X

Rutherford sipped on a cup of tea while silently rehearsing what he was going to say to Hitchcock. The damn investigator had demanded another meeting to discuss the Barrett matter, and Rutherford was at his wits' end.

He almost wished he had never been offered the job at Barrett Trading. He hadn't counted on things getting so complicated. He silently brooded and wondered if it was possible that he was in serious trouble over the Bath incident. He had had his suspicions about the defective beams, but he didn't know who had sent them or why.

Could it be possible that Barrett was involved? If so, Rutherford couldn't figure out why he would have jeopardized one of his own mines. It didn't make sense.

It especially disturbed him that Barrett had been implicated in so many serious crimes. He was confused and wasn't sure whom to believe.

Rutherford watched as the investigator approached his table and sat down.

"Mr. Rutherford, good afternoon." He tipped his hat with what appeared to be a casual indifference to the whole situation.

Despite his misgivings about Barrett, Rutherford had decided to get the matter regarding the investigator over once and for all. "Mr. Hitchcock," he immediately blurted out, "I don't mean to disappoint you, but I have thought about what you said, and I really can't help you. I have no direct knowledge of any criminal activities regarding Barrett. I'm sorry."

Hitchcock's posture and confidence seemed to slump a little. He stared off towards the street and didn't say anything for a few seconds. Rutherford matched his silence.

Finally, Hitchcock sighed heavily. "All right, Rutherford, we'll leave it at that for now. But let me give you some friendly advice: watch your back. Over the years, a lot of people associated with Barrett have mysteriously ended up . . . " He paused, as if to stress his point. "Let's just say they met with unfortunate accidents."

With that last warning, Hitchcock got up and left abruptly.

Well, that was that. Rutherford felt somewhat relieved. Hopefully, he wouldn't be seeing him again. He finished his tea and vowed to forget the entire episode.

On the way out of the café, Rutherford accidentally bumped into a small man. "Excuse me," Rutherford said.

"That's quite all right," responded the man, who had a large birthmark on the side of his face.

Johnstone walked into a small dirty restaurant in the old part of Bristol – the part that had long been forgotten by gentlemen. The only person in the rundown building was a frail old lady, who was busy cleaning off a table. The place smelled of wild goats.

She stopped working and looked up. "You here to see the constable?" she spat out.

"Yes."

"He's waiting for you in the back." She pointed to a room in the back of the restaurant and returned to her work.

Johnstone walked back and saw the constable sitting with another man: a nasty-looking bugger who had a port-wine birthmark that covered his neck and a good part of his left cheek. No doubt one of the constable's snitches.

"What have you got?" Johnstone asked impatiently.

"This is Ralph Bellows."

The man stuck out his hand. Johnstone ignored it, and Bellows pulled his hand back, obviously offended.

"I haven't got a lot of time," Johnstone said. "What did you want to see me about?"

"I think we have found out who your little informer is."

Johnstone perked up. "Who is it?"

The constable looked pleased with himself. "I took the liberty of having Bellows follow Hitchcock around to see if he met with any of your employees."

"Just tell me who it is," Johnstone said impatiently.

"I'll let Bellows tell you."

Johnstone looked over at the man, who coughed nervously.

"I followed the investigator yesterday to a café, where he sat down at a table with another gentlemen. I found out his name from the waiter."

Johnstone had lost his patience. "By God! Just tell me the damn name!" he swore loudly.

"John Rutherford," the constable answered.

Johnstone nodded his head and left.

XI

"It arrived yesterday," the constable said as he handed the letter to Hitch-cock.

The official Parliament seal gave the contents of the letter away; Hitchcock's time was up. He quickly read the letter, already knowing what it was going to say.

In three terse sentences, Parliament's sergeant-at-arms ordered him to close the Barrett case and return to London immediately. Hitchcock shook his head in disappointment; they should have given him more time.

"Something the matter?" the constable asked.

Hitchcock sighed. He hated to admit that he had to shut the case down again. "I'm needed back in London," he replied dejectedly.

"Did Parliament finally figure out you were just wasting time down here?" the constable asked with a smugness that irritated Hitchcock even more.

Hitchcock ignored him but knew the fat bastard was going to have more to say about the matter.

As expected, the constable droned on, "I know how you feel – I really do. You forget I was your age once, trying to make a name for myself."

It took all of Hitchcock's concentration not to burst out laughing at the ri-diculous statement. He couldn't believe the overweight, drunken joke of a man was actually trying to compare the two of them. Somehow, he managed to hold in his laughter.

The constable put a beefy arm around his shoulder. "You are a fine investiga-tor," he continued on with his asinine comments, "and I know you will do well in the future. You were just barking up the wrong tree. And to show you I am not such a bad guy, why don't we go out for some going away drinks? I'll buy."

Hitchcock was fast on his way to becoming a true politician. Despite his ha-tred of the man, he knew it was important never to burn any bridges. He decided a few drinks wouldn't hurt. After all, one never knew when one might need a favor.

As promised, the constable and Hitchcock spent one last night together. Hitchcock could not believe how much alcohol the man could consume. Hitch-cock prided himself on the fact that he could keep up with just about anyone when it came to drinking – any man except this one. He was drinking two drinks to every one of Hitchcock's. So far, they had been to three different taverns, and Hitchcock was already drunk. He knew it was going to be a painful journey back to London, and if he didn't quit drinking soon, he might not even be able to get out of bed the next morning.

Hitchcock finished his beer. "All right," he said, trying not to sound too ine-briated. "I have to go. I have a long trip ahead of me tomorrow."

The constable belched loudly and yelled to the bartender to bring two more drinks. "You can't leave now. We've just begun. The night is young."

"Thanks. It has been fun and all, but I have to go." Hitchcock couldn't stop thinking about the headache he was going to have tomorrow.

The constable gave Hitchcock a look of contempt. "Why is it that every Londoner I know drinks like a woman?" he asked loud enough so that the whole tavern could hear him.

Shouts of agreement rang out, but Hitchcock wasn't going to let him goad him into staying longer. "I have to go," he said flatly.

"Fine," the constable relented, "go back to London. But at least drink this last beer I just paid for." He handed Hitchcock a new glass.

Hitchcock grabbed the last beer, figuring at this point one more wasn't going to matter; the damage had already been done. Hitchcock, though, was getting sick of listening to the lazy drunk talk about all the important cases he had worked on. He swore he had never seen someone so full of himself.

He was barely listening as the constable rambled on about the Lawrence murder. Then the constable said something that caused Hitchcock to sober up in a hurry.

"What did you say about Lawrence?" Hitchcock mumbled, trying not to sound all that interested.

"Oh, I was just poking a little fun at you. I couldn't believe you thought that Lawrence fellow was going to give you documents that would somehow tie Barrett to the deliberate sinking of that East India merchant ship."

The constable broke into such a fit of drunken laughter that he could no longer talk. He went on drinking, not even realizing his slip. Hitchcock had had enough. He set down his unfinished beer and left without saying goodbye. The constable didn't even try to stop him this time.

Hitchcock had to get out of the tavern and get some fresh air. At the front door, he turned back and saw the constable ordering a new drink. The son of a bitch had been on Barrett's payroll from the start!

Hitchcock had told him about the documents that Lawrence was going to hand over, but he never told him that they had anything to do with Barrett's connection with the sinking of the East Indian ship. There was no way the constable could have known about the contents of those documents, unless he had seen them or someone had told him about them.

How could he have been so stupid? It all made sense now: the lack of support, the stonewalling. Then it hit Hitchcock: in a way, he was responsible for Lawrence's death. He had told the constable about his meeting with Lawrence. The constable must have then warned Barrett, who then had him killed. Hitchcock couldn't believe his stupidity.

But what could he do now? The constable's blunder didn't change one thing. He still had no evidence and couldn't prove a thing. Hitchcock was a realist. He had a great future ahead of him, and despite not delivering on the Barrett matter, he could still become a member of Parliament. It just might take a little longer.

Besides, he now knew that the corruption in Bristol went to the highest levels, with Barrett in total control of it all. It dawned on Hitchcock that he was probably lucky to get out of the city alive at this point. It wouldn't have taken much for Barrett to arrange for an accident to happen to him as well.

He knew this was a battle he could not win at the present time, and sometimes, one had to cut one's losses. There was nothing he could do but finish packing and head back to London. Eventually, he would get both Barrett and the constable.

As Hitchcock stumbled back to his hotel, he couldn't believe he had almost forgotten about Rutherford. Even though he had never mentioned Rutherford's name directly to the constable, he had foolishly bragged to the constable that he had someone else in Barrett's company who was willing to cooperate. He was positive that he had been followed when he had met with Rutherford.

Hitchcock knew that after he left town, Rutherford wouldn't last two days. With Lawrence's death weighing heavily on his conscience, Hitchcock made a decision. He changed directions and headed to Rutherford's place.

It was late when Hitchcock banged on Rutherford's door. He had to at least warn him before he left town.

Rutherford was sound asleep when he heard someone pounding on his front door. He reluctantly got out of bed, cursing whoever was at his door this late at night.

His annoyance was soon replaced by surprise – and then anger – when he saw Hitchcock standing outside the door.

"Jesus, Hitchcock," he snapped as he opened the door. "What in the hell are you doing here in the middle of the night? I told you I don't know anything!"

"Shut up, Rutherford, and just listen to me for a minute. I have something important to tell you."

There was a look of concern on Hitchcock's face that he didn't like. It could only mean trouble. "Well, what is it then?" he stammered.

"You have to get out of town immediately."

"What? Are you crazy?" Hitchcock smelled like he had consumed an entire brewery. "You're half-plowed. Go back to your Inn and sleep it off. You don't know what you're talking about."

Rutherford turned to go back inside.

But Hitchcock grabbed him by the shoulders and spun him back around. He had a deadly serious look on his face. "Rutherford, I am leaving town tomorrow, and when I do, it will only be a matter of time before Barrett has you killed. I am telling you this because I don't want your blood on my hands. Trust me. I have no reason to lie to you."

Rutherford was confused and a bit scared. "But why would Barrett want me killed?"

"Barrett had a previous employee named Allen Lawrence. He was murdered because he was going to give me documents that would have been enough to have both Barrett and Johnstone executed."

"I've heard of Lawrence. I thought he was killed during a robbery."

Hitchcock shrugged. "He was killed the very night he was supposed to meet me. Come on, Rutherford," he said with irritation. "I know you are a smart man. Use your brain. You are a dead man if you stay in this town. Barrett thinks that you were going to cooperate with me because of those times we met. I was followed, and Barrett knows it was you I was meeting with."

"But I didn't even tell you anything!" Rutherford protested.

"It doesn't matter. Barrett doesn't know that. All he knows is that you were meeting with me. I told the constable that someone in Barrett's company was cooperating. They'll think it was you."

Rutherford couldn't believe this was happening. "If what you say is true, then I could go to the constable."

Hitchcock shook his head. "Rutherford, don't be a fool. He's the one who told Barrett about Lawrence. He's been on Barrett's payroll for years. I am leaving now. If you stay in this town, you will end up dead. Consider yourself forewarned. Move far away and start a new life. Goodbye. And good luck."

Hitchcock left, and Rutherford stood at the door with his mouth wide open. It was a few minutes before he finally shut the door.

Rutherford went into the dark kitchen, lit a candle, and drank a large glass of spiced rum. Since Anne's death, he had found that he could think more clearly after a few drinks.

He had long suspected that Barrett had covered up the mining accident, but the rest of it – could it be true? Was he really in danger?

What if he went and talked to Barrett? Even if he knew he had met with Hitchcock, surely Barrett would listen to him if he told his side of the story. Obviously, Barrett would see that he hadn't told Hitchcock anything, especially since Hitchcock was returning to London.

After another glass of rum, Rutherford decided the best thing he could do was to march straight into Barrett's office the next morning and explain everything. Before he drifted off to sleep, he wondered if he would feel so bold the next morning.

XII

Rutherford stood nervously outside Barrett's door and knocked softly. "Mr. Barrett, it's John Rutherford. Do you have a moment?"

"Come in, John," Barrett replied immediately without his usual annoyance.

Barrett sat behind his desk smoking a cigar that was practically the size of a loaf of bread. "Take a seat," he said, pointing to the chair in front of his desk.

Rutherford sat down.

"What can I do for you, John?" He didn't seem mad or upset in any way. If anything, he was unusually cordial.

Without hesitation Rutherford proceeded to tell him about the investigator, the meetings, and the accusations. Barrett listened intently, and not once did he display a single sign of emotion.

After Rutherford had finished the entire story, Barrett smiled and shook his head. "John, I appreciate you coming in and telling me about your little run-in with the investigator. You don't really believe what he told you, do you?"

Rutherford wasn't sure whom to believe at this point. The only thing he knew for sure was that the investigator, who was already on his way back to London, was absolutely no help to him now. Barrett, on the other hand, seemed completely reasonable about the entire matter. A glimmer of hope surged through Rutherford. Perhaps he could clear this mess up after all.

"Well," he mumbled, "that's why I came to you."

Barrett smiled broadly. "Listen, John. Hitchcock works for Parliament, which has a financial interest in the success of East India Trading Company. They are our biggest competitors, and they have been trying to put us out of business for years. Hitchcock was on a witch hunt; he was just trying to stir things up. I may be somewhat ruthless in my business dealings, but you don't honestly believe I would kill anyone in cold blood, do you?"

He returned Barrett's smile. "Of course not."

"You did the right thing, John. I appreciate you telling me about the investigator. And don't worry: I won't hold anything against you. As far as I am concerned, the case regarding the investigator is closed."

"Thanks, Mr. Barrett," he replied with a tremendous amount of relief. "I appreciate your understanding."

"Now there is one other matter I would like to discuss with you," Mr. Barrett said. "Johnstone is inventorying a large supply of rice that just arrived from the Carolinas. After work tonight, I would like you to meet him down at the warehouse on Bleeker Street and help him close the books on the shipment."

"Certainly," Rutherford replied, happy to have apparently cleared his name. "I'll be there."

Rutherford went back to his desk with no doubt in his mind that everything had been straightened out. Barrett's explanation seemed logical, straightforward, and honest.

Later that day, Johnstone met Barrett at his club for a late lunch. They were seated at Barrett's private table. Barrett ordered salmon and a bottle of white wine for both of them. The waiter brought the wine and filled their glasses.

Johnstone shook his head. "That damn investigator has been a royal pain in the ass. I'm glad he's heading back to London."

Barrett held a glass of wine under his nose while Johnstone drank half of his in one swallow. Barrett still hadn't said anything about Rutherford, which surprised Johnstone because he was expecting to get an earful at any moment.

"Samuel, you have no appreciation for fine wine," Barrett said in a soft and relaxed tone. "You drink it as if it were a glass of cheap beer at some rundown tavern."

Johnstone grinned. The old man was in an unusually good mood. "Do you think Rutherford was going to help him?" Johnstone asked while finishing off the rest of his glass.

Barrett took a small sip and swilled the wine in his mouth for a few seconds before swallowing it. "No, I don't think so, but I can't take any chances. Rutherford knows too much as it is. He became a liability when he discovered those receipts for the support beams that were used in Bath. It's only a matter of time before Parliament sends someone else. I can't afford to keep him around."

The waiter brought the salmon to the table and set the plates down in front of the two men.

Johnstone took a bite of his fish. "This is delicious. It's too bad about Rutherford; we could have used him in the future."

Barrett grunted in agreement. Somewhere between the salmon lunch, another bottle of wine, and the lemon tart dessert, it was decided that Johnstone would dispose of Rutherford immediately.

XIII

Rutherford finished up the last of the day's work and left to meet Johnstone. The Bleeker Street warehouse was located down in the port area and was a ten-minute walk from the office. He arrived to find Johnstone alone in the warehouse pouring over a huge stack of invoices.

Johnstone saw him walk in and stopped working. "John, how have you been doing?"

Rutherford smiled and nodded. "I'm fine, thank you."

"That's good. Barrett hasn't been working you too hard, has he?"

"Not any more than usual."

"Come, help me sort these invoices."

They had worked for about two hours when Johnstone got up and began to stretch his legs. "I need some fresh air," he said while yawning heavily. "Let's take a walk. I can tell you some stories about my adventures in the Caribbean."

Rutherford was grateful for the break, and he followed Johnstone as they walked towards the harbor.

"So tell me the truth," Johnstone said, looking slyly at Rutherford. "Barrett is a pain in the ass, isn't he?"

Rutherford smiled. "No, not at all."

Johnstone grinned back. "Don't worry. I won't tell him. I know he can be a royal jerk sometimes."

"Well, perhaps just a little."

They both laughed.

"What is Jamaica like?" Rutherford asked. He had heard many wild stories about the island.

"You have no idea. Those Jamaican women can make your head spin, if you know what I mean. And the rum down there!" Johnstone let out a loud whoop. "They call it dark and stormy."

"I thought dark and stormy referred to the women."

Johnstone burst out laughing. "Oh, Rutherford, that's a good one. I will have to remember that."

It was a nice night out, and Rutherford felt relaxed. The investigator was long gone, he had straightened things out with Barrett, and Johnstone was in great spirits. He followed his boss down to the old pier.

Johnstone motioned to him, saying, "You've got to see this ship. It's unbelievable."

They walked down to the end of the old pier, and Johnstone pointed out into the harbor. "See it? It's over there."

Rutherford leaned up against the rail, trying to spot the ship. The full moon was shining brightly in the night sky and a gentle breeze had picked up.

"Which ship?" he asked.

Johnstone stood behind him. "That one over to the left, about three hundred yards out. See it?"

Rutherford strained his eyes. He suddenly sensed movement behind him and then he caught a reflection of something in his peripheral vision. Somehow, he knew something was horribly wrong.

Reflexes and instincts that he thought were long gone took over, and he dodged to the left just as Johnstone tried to stab him in the back. The long knife missed him by not more than half an inch, and Johnstone's momentum brought them to within inches of each other.

Rutherford didn't know how – possibly it was by pure luck – but somehow he was able to hook his arm around Johnstone, and with a rush of pure adrenaline and his own momentum he heaved him over the pier railing into the harbor. It all happened so fast that it took his brain a few seconds to register what had actually taken place: Johnstone had just tried to kill him.

It was a fifteen-foot drop to the water, and he looked over and saw Johnstone swimming away. He didn't know what else to do, so he ran towards his home as fast as he could. As he ran, Rutherford realized the only reason he was still alive was because the moon's light had reflected off of the knife's blade.

With adrenaline surging through his body, Rutherford ran straight back to his house at a dead sprint. He opened the front door and collapsed on the floor. It took a couple of minutes for him to catch his breath.

When he did, he realized Hitchcock had been right all along. How could he have been so naive? He knew he was in big trouble, and to make matters worse, he couldn't even go to the constable for protection.

He had to get out of the house fast. Johnstone would come here first, and he better not be around when he arrived. He grabbed some money and clothes and threw them into a bag.

He then sneaked out the back door and quickly made his way down the alley. He had to somehow hide long enough to get a plan together. But one thing was evident: he would have to leave Bristol for good.

Rutherford found a small inconspicuous inn and paid for a room for the night. He set his bag down and collapsed onto the tiny bed. What in the hell was he going to do now? He couldn't believe everything that had happened.

He felt physically and mentally exhausted. Even though he didn't want to sleep, his body needed the respite, and he immediately fell into a deep sleep.

XIV

Rutherford awoke with a startle. At first he couldn't figure out where he was, then events of the previous night came flooding back. He felt sick to his stomach at the thought that he should, by all rights, be dead.

For the next few hours he sat in a small chair in the corner of the room, trying to figure a way out the mess he now found himself in. He didn't have a lot of options, but an idea kept popping into his mind: the American colonies. That would be the last place Barrett and Johnstone would expect him to go.

Rutherford knew people went to the colonies for many different reasons, but mostly they went to start over, whether to escape from husbands, wives, debts, or the law. In Rutherford's case, he was trying to escape with his life.

He knew there were a few ships in port that were due to sail in the coming week. He had to find a way to get on one of them without being caught. He had a lot to do in a short period of time, but he had to be careful: Johnstone and Barrett would be looking for him. He waited until nightfall and left the inn.

Rutherford didn't care about any of his belongings at his house. It was too dangerous to go back there anyway. But he did need some more money, and he had a good idea how to get some. He was going to see William Livingston, the only man in Bristol he could now trust. He cautiously made his way to his house and knocked on the door.

An older man dressed in a brown tweed business suit opened the door. A smile came to his face. "John, to what do I owe the pleasure? Do come in."

Rutherford walked into the house and followed William into the study. He felt ashamed that he hadn't visited William since before Anne's death. And now he was doing so because William was the only one who could help him.

"Would you like a drink?" William asked as he poured himself a whiskey.

"I'll have the same."

William handed him the drink. "What's wrong, John? You look awfully tired."

He took a sip of the whiskey and wondered if William noticed the trembling in his hands. There was no point in beating around the bush, so in rapid succession he explained the whole story to him and why he had to leave Bristol. After he finished, he was surprised by William's reaction.

"John, I never told you this, but I was worried when you went to work for Barrett. Everyone in this town knows that man is as crooked as they come. You got involved with powerful men and ended up in the middle of one of their power struggles. There is not much you can do about it except to get the hell out of their way."

"I know." Rutherford nodded in agreement. "That's why I came to see you. I have a big favor to ask you."

"What is it?"

"I want you to give me an advance on my house. I will sign an agreement allowing you to sell my house and all the goods that I have in it after I leave. I need you to find me passage to America on the first available ship. I have decided to go to the colonies and start over."

"Of course," William responded as he got up to pour two more drinks. "It shouldn't be too much of a problem."

"I don't know how I can ever repay you for everything you have done for me."

William smiled warmly. "I'll miss you, John. You were like the son I never had."

Rutherford felt a lump in his throat, and it was all he could do not to break down in tears.

It was decided that Rutherford would come back in two nights. Hopefully by then William would have found him a way out of Bristol.

The next two days were pure torture for Rutherford, who was confined to his little room. The anxiety ate away at him, and he grew increasingly restless and bored. He spent most of the day peering out of the room window, praying that Johnstone wouldn't find him.

He had nothing to do except think about his life and what had become of it, and he did a lot of that. He wished that Anne was still alive and that she was going to the colonies with him. He felt as if he had become isolated from the rest of the world, and it was a lonely feeling.

Anne was dead. He had no family or friends, except for Livingston, and he was leaving his only home forever. He remembered his father's advice, that nothing came free in this world. Looking back, he could see that Barrett had intended to use him from the very beginning. But his greed had clouded his judgment. God, how he wished he was still a junior bookkeeper at the law firm and that Anne was alive.

He glanced out the window and swore he saw Johnstone walking past the inn. He almost wished it were him. It was a passing feeling, but one that took him by total surprise. For a fleeting moment, he felt the urge to confront Johnstone face to face. He didn't feel afraid of him any longer, and he wanted to exact revenge on him, even if it meant he might die in the process. Rutherford couldn't be positive if the man out front had been Johnstone, but luckily, whomever it was he never stopped.

Finally, the second night came, and once again Rutherford reluctantly left the inn and sneaked over to William's house. He prayed that William had come through for him.

William opened the door before he could knock a second time. They went into his study, and William pulled a large envelope out of his desk drawer.

William had a funny expression on his face, as if he was trying not to laugh. Rutherford wondered what could be so funny to him in light of the circumstances.

"Here are your traveling documents and money," William said, as he handed him the envelope.

Rutherford felt a huge amount of relief; William had not failed him.

"You're sailing to Charleston, Carolina tomorrow morning."

Rutherford nodded. Charleston. He supposed there were worse places he could go.

"I hope that is enough money. It was the best I could do on such short notice."

Rutherford glanced at the stack of pound notes. "It's more than enough. Thank you so much. For everything."

"You're welcome." William laughed mischievously.

"Damn you! You have had that silly smirk on your face ever since I arrived. What on heaven's earth is so amusing to you?"

"Look at the name of the ship."

Rutherford took the ship document out and read the name. He couldn't believe it. "The *Sea Biscuit*!" he shouted. "You mean to tell me I am sailing three thousand miles across the Atlantic Ocean on a ship called *Sea Biscuit*?"

William was laughing so hard he had a hard time talking. "Yes," he finally managed to say.

Rutherford joined in on the laughter. "Who in the hell would name a ship *Sea Biscuit*?"

William regained his composure. "It used to be owned by a company that shipped flour. It was sold a few years ago to a trading company. You know it's bad luck to change the name of a ship, so *Sea Biscuit* it remained."

"I expected to be sailing on a ship called *Fury* or *Hell's Revenge*, not *Sea Biscuit*. That has got to be the worst name I have ever heard in my life."

"It's the best I could do. Come, let's have one last drink together, shall we?"

Rutherford heard a touch of sadness in William's voice.

"Listen, John, you're going to have to be careful. Barrett and Johnstone are looking for you. They have informed the authorities that you stole money and are on the run. They have the constable and his gang of thugs out looking for you."

"Damn!" Rutherford cursed. How far would Barrett go to find him? "You don't believe their lies, do you?" Rutherford asked defensively.

"Don't be ridiculous, John. I know you didn't steal any money from Barrett."

"I'm sorry," Rutherford quickly apologized, ashamed at his outburst, especially after all that William had done for him. "I'm just a little nervous about tomorrow."

"Listen," William said, "I know you are going to find this hard to believe, but if you can get out of here safely, it might be the best thing for you. You will have a chance at a new life. Ever since Anne died, you have been going in the wrong direction. Charleston may be a little primitive, but there should be some good opportunities for you to get back on your feet."

Rutherford nodded in resignation.

William went over to his liquor cabinet and poured himself another drink. He had a funny smirk on his face. "I have also been thinking about your situation and have come up with a little plan to increase your odds of getting out of Bristol alive tomorrow."

"You have done enough," Rutherford protested. "You don't need to take any more risks on my behalf."

"It's too late," he replied. "I left an anonymous letter with the constable saying you are going to sneak back into your house tomorrow to get a few things and then leave for London on horseback. I figured the constable would place most of his men at your house and near the roads leading to London, which, of course, happen to be directly opposite the harbor."

Rutherford shrugged his shoulders. William's ploy made sense. "I can never repay you for everything you have done for me."

The two men hugged goodbye. Both of them knew they would never see one another again.

XV

The last day Rutherford would ever spend in Bristol had arrived. Rutherford was weighed down by an immense feeling of desperation and despair, and he wondered where his resolve to confront and fight Johnstone had gone. Even though he was dreading the walk to the harbor docks, at least he wouldn't have to spend another night alone in this hellhole.

It occurred to Rutherford that he was like a flower petal aimlessly spinning in the wind, its destiny controlled by forces other than its own.

It was time to leave. He forced himself to get out of bed, and he packed his few belongings. With a weary acceptance, he left the Inn and made his way down to the harbor as quickly as possible, taking as many alleyways as possible.

He did have one piece of luck: a thick fog had rolled in during the night, making visibility difficult. The white blanket that had descended on the city made him feel invisible, like a ghost. Hopefully, it would help in his escape. Despite the fog, he still couldn't shake the dread in the pit of his stomach. He knew to be caught now would in all likelihood result in his death.

Rutherford approached the harbor with trepidation. His heart was pounding, and all his senses were on high alert. Because of the fog, it was hard to make out the ships in the harbor. He could only catch glimpses of tall masts that hung in the air like solitary church steeples rising from the harbor.

He approached the docks, and he thought his heart was going to stop. He could make out plenty of ships, but he couldn't see the *Sea Biscuit* anywhere. What if something had happened to it? That ship was his best chance to get out of Bristol alive. He didn't think he could survive another day without being caught.

He walked over to a dirty longshoreman, who was busy lighting his pipe. "Excuse me, sir. Can you tell me where the *Sea Biscuit* is?"

The longshoreman looked at him with what seemed to be amusement, although it was hard to tell because his eyes were so bloodshot.

"Aye, I can tell you where she is," he said with a smirk. "She's right over there." He pointed to a ship that was anchored off the far side of the dock.

Rutherford was filled with relief. He walked over to the dock to get a closer look. Other than cargo, he didn't know much about ocean vessels. But he knew one thing: the ship he was looking at didn't look like it could even sail out of the harbor. He wondered if it was possible for such a dilapidated-looking thing to sail across the entire ocean.

The events of the last three days had been so sudden and so unexpected that he had actually given little thought to the dangers of a voyage across the Atlantic Ocean. The three-thousand-mile journey would take three months to complete, depending on the winds. Sailing was a dangerous business, and he had heard plenty of horror stories. The ocean bottom was littered with thousands of ships. And even if the ship reached its destination, that didn't mean he would. The death rates for ocean voyages were tremendously high. Illness, diseases, accidents, mutinies, malnutrition, dehydration, fires, and storms all took a heavy toll. Despite the odds, his fate had been set. Rutherford had decided it was better to die out in the Atlantic than to stay here and surely be killed. He hesitantly walked over to the ship to get a closer look.

The *Sea Biscuit* had three masts with large square sails. A tangled mass of rigging and ropes hung off the large sails, and it was hard to figure out what everything was connected to. The ship was about a hundred feet long, and both the bow and stern were a deck higher than the midsection.

Rutherford stopped a sailor who appeared to be part of the crew. "Excuse me. Do you know when the ship will be sailing?"

The sailor was a dirty little fellow who didn't look like he was a day over the age of sixteen. He stopped what he was doing and answered the question with one of his own. "Are you on this ship?"

"Yes, I am. Here are my documents."

He grabbed the papers out of Rutherford's hand and pretended to read them, but Rutherford could tell the dirty bugger couldn't read a single word.

The sailor did his best to appear like he was approving the documents. He handed them back roughly. "We sail in one hour. Be back here in half an hour to board." He spat a big brown wad of tobacco juice that landed a hairsbreadth from Rutherford's shoe and then smiled at Rutherford. His front teeth were stained a yellowish-brown. "And if I were you, I would be on time so we don't sail without you."

One more hour and he would be gone. Even though it was probably dangerous, Rutherford decided to walk around the docks. It would be the last time his feet would be on solid ground for a long time. He walked to the end of the dock and took a look back towards Bristol. The city slowly rose up a gentle hill, and he could see dark outlines of the buildings through the white mist. He wondered how in the hell he had found himself in this position.

He turned to head back to the ship when he felt a tug on the back of his trousers. Rutherford turned, expecting to be arrested or worse. To his immense relief, it was just a young lad who was probably no older than ten.

"Mister, are you sailing today?" he asked.

"Why, yes, I am," Rutherford answered. "I am going to Charleston."

"Wow. That's on the other side of the world. Are you an explorer or something?"

"No," Rutherford said, laughing. "I'm not an explorer."

"Since you are going on such a long and dangerous journey, you need to buy a good luck charm!" the boy exclaimed, adopting a salesmen's pitch. He pulled out a thin leather necklace with a Saint Christopher's medallion attached to it and showed it to Rutherford. "Saint Christopher is the patron saint of travelers. He will protect you from sea monsters and storms."

Rutherford didn't really believe in sea monsters, but the way things had been going the last year, he figured he could use all the protection he could get.

Rutherford vaguely remembered the story of Saint Christopher. The power-fully-built saint had traveled the world in search of novelty and adventure. One day he came to a dangerous stream, and a young child asked his help in crossing.

Saint Christopher carried the child on his shoulder, and when they were half way across the stream, the child began to feel as heavy as the world. When Chris-topher realized that he was carrying Jesus and thus the weight of the world was on his shoulders, the child disappeared. It was ironic, thought Rutherford. Like Saint Christopher, he felt like an enormous weight had been placed upon him.

Anyway, he felt sorry for the little lad. His clothes were ragged, and his face was dirty. The poor kid probably never got enough to eat by the looks of his frail body.

"How much are you selling the charm for?"

"Only two shillings, sir. And I promise you: when you hit your first big storm, you will be glad to have Saint Christopher on your side. He will guarantee your safety during the voyage."

Rutherford laughed nervously at the sales pitch, even though he knew the young boy was right about one thing: a dangerous journey did indeed lie ahead of him. "You guarantee it, huh? In that case, here." He handed the boy four times his asking price.

The boy happily grabbed the coins out of his hand. "Thanks, mister!" he ex-citedly cried out as he handed over the charm.

Rutherford put the necklace on and tucked it inside his shirt.

"When will you be coming back, sir?"

Rutherford paused, and for the first time it dawned on him that he would probably never set foot on English soil again. He couldn't bring himself to say it, however.

"One of these days," he replied softly. "One of these days."

It was time for him to get back to the ship. When Rutherford arrived, most of the goods and passengers were already on board. The young sailor who had tried to read his documents earlier impatiently motioned for him to board. He walked to the gangplank that connected the ship to the dock and paused. Gingerly, he walked across, holding his breath the entire time.

He reached the end of the plank and finally took a deep breath as he stepped onto the deck of the ship. There was no going back now.

Rutherford stood with the rest of the crew and passengers as the ship slowly made her way out of Bristol's harbor. His heart was torn. It was painful to leave the only home he had known, but at the same time he was enormously grateful to have escaped it with his life and a chance at a new start.

The sun had burned off the last of the fog, and there was just the slightest hint of a breeze that carried with it the sweet salty fragrance of the ocean. It turned out to be a spectacular morning after the fog burned off. The sky was clear and blue, and a bright yellow sun hung low in the sky.

The ship slowly sailed out of the harbor and into the Atlantic Ocean. England became smaller and smaller until it disappeared below the horizon. It was hard to imagine that he wouldn't see land again for nearly three months.

Johnstone had run all the way from Livingston's house, and he was sweating profusely. He hoped that because of the morning fog, the ship had been delayed. He ran down the docks, knocking over more than a few people in the process.

He looked out at a mass of docked ships and grabbed a dockhand by the lapels of his coat. "Where's the *Sea Biscuit?*" he yelled.

The dockhand had forearms the size of a small barrel, and Johnstone instantly regretted grabbing him.

The man threw Johnstone's arms off violently. "What the bloody hell's wrong with you, mate?" he cursed at Johnstone in a heavy Scottish accent.

Johnstone remembered getting into a brawl with a Scottish sailor a few years ago. It was one of the few times he ever lost a fight.

He cautiously stepped back from the burly man. "Sorry," he replied in a contrite voice. "It's just that I'm trying to get an urgent message to someone. Has the *Sea Biscuit* left yet?

The Scot appeared to relax a bit. "Aye, there she is." He pointed out into the harbor.

Johnstone turned, but not before he had put plenty of distance between him and the burly man. He walked over to the end of the dock. He had missed Rutherford.

What a waste, he thought. If only he had paid a visit to Livingston earlier.

The old man had surprised Johnstone. Not a lot of men could have stood up to the amount of pain that he had suffered while trying to help a friend. Johnstone first had threatened him with torture. Usually that alone would have opened the mouths of most people, especially after he described in detail what he was going to do. But not Livingston. He vehemently denied any knowledge of Rutherford's whereabouts.

So in order to find out if he was telling the truth, Johnstone cut off one of his thumbs. And much to his surprise, the old man still didn't confess. So he severed his left Achilles tendon, and yet the man still refused to answer. At that point, Johnstone thought Livingston had to have been telling the truth, because no one could endure that much pain.

But just to be sure, he broke his nose with a rusty iron hook. And as a last measure, he started to cut off one of his ears with a pear knife. Johnstone never thought it would be so hard to cut someone's ear off, but it did the trick. The old man finally cracked and revealed that Rutherford was on the *Sea Biscuit.*

After the confession, Johnstone put the man out of his misery. He cut Livingston's throat, but not before telling him how much he admired the amount of pain he had been able endure. Johnstone had to admit it was truly amazing.

Unfortunately, because of Livingston's bravery or stupidity – he guessed it depended on how you looked at it – he had arrived too late. The ship had already left, and Rutherford had escaped for now. Johnstone took one last look as the ship sailed out of the harbor and into the Atlantic Ocean.

"Don't worry, Mr. Rutherford," he said as he shook his fist, "we'll meet again."

He turned and left. He had to go give Barrett the news.

XVI

Rutherford watched the waves lap up against the bow of the ship, and he realized that he had made many mistakes in his life. But this was a new beginning, a chance at redemption.

There were sixty-three passengers and twelve crewmembers on board. Of the sixty-three passengers, ten were men of property, and with their wives and children they totaled eighteen. Another twenty were artisans or skilled craftsman, and the rest of the passengers were indentured servants who were required to work anywhere from two to seven years in exchange for their passage.

Rutherford studied the ship more closely. The hull was about as deep as the ship was long, and it had two decks. The lowest level stored most of the cargo, food, water, and supplies.

The upper part of the hull was divided into three sections. The captain's quarters and a few private cabins for the more wealthy passengers were located at the bow of the ship. At the stern more supplies were stowed, and the crew slept there in tight quarters. The middle of the hull contained the living quarters for the passengers.

Rutherford was transfixed by his new surroundings, and subsequently he was the last passenger to go down into the hull and claim his spot. When he climbed down below the deck, no stories could have prepared him for what he encountered.

The hull was dark, hot, and humid, and an overpowering stench permeated everything. God only knows what it will smell like after sailing for a few days. He couldn't believe these would be his living quarters for the next three or four months.

All the passengers slept together in one large area. Luckily, he had brought a blanket to sleep on. Rutherford noticed an empty space towards the back and slowly moved towards it, trying not to step on anyone in the process. He reached the empty spot and set down his few belongings, and that is when he saw her.

He hadn't even so much as looked at another woman since Anne had died, and he was momentarily taken aback by the strong feelings that the woman evoked in him. She took his breath away. The most beautiful woman he had ever seen was sitting alone on a little pile of blankets right next to his bench.

She was petite, with long, thick blonde hair, and her face looked like that of an angel. Surely she wasn't traveling alone.

"Excuse me, miss. There is no other space available. Do you mind if I put my things here?"

"Not at all," she answered softly without looking up.

He put down his few bags and arranged his little space. Rutherford couldn't believe his luck. If he had to be crammed in a small ship for months, he could not have been paired with a better neighbor.

She sat cross-legged with her shoulders hunched over and her chin resting on her hands.

"Hi, I'm John Rutherford," he announced casually.

She turned slightly in his direction and smiled weakly. "Sally Weston."

"Are you excited to be heading to Charleston?" Rutherford asked, knowing instantly that it was a dumb question to ask, since any fool could tell just by looking at her that she would have rather been anyplace else.

She raised her head and looked at him. There was sadness in her sparkling green eyes. "I'm scared."

Rutherford had never been good with words of comfort, and he struggled to say something that would cheer her up some. "Don't worry. I hear this is one of the safest ships in the entire British fleet."

Of course, he was lying, since he had no idea whether the tub of old wood named after a breakfast food would even make it out of the harbor, let alone across the entire Atlantic Ocean.

"And besides," Rutherford said, pulling out the necklace the boy had sold him, "Saint Christopher will protect us."

She smiled more confidently, and Rutherford felt a twinge of warmth in his stomach.

"Why are you going to Charleston?" he asked, still wondering why she was traveling all alone.

"I'm going to work for a rice plantation."

Rutherford knew there had to be more to it, but he didn't want to press her. They had a long journey in which to get to know each other.

"And you?" she inquired.

"I'm going for adventure and the opportunity to start over. I was a bookkeeper for a small business, but," he paused, "it went bankrupt. I have no family alive so . . . " He couldn't help but think of Anne. Would she disapprove of his feelings towards this woman?

"Are you going to be a bookkeeper in Charleston?"

He thought about her question for a second before responding. "I really would like to run my own business one day."

She took a sip of water from a bottle. "I'm sure you won't have any trouble starting a business. You seem very smart."

Rutherford beamed at the compliment and stretched out on his blanket. All of a sudden he felt exhausted. He closed his eyes and slept soundly.

The first couple of days passed uneventfully with calm seas and nice weather. Everyone settled into a daily routine that consisted of agonizing boredom and continuous anxiety.

Most of the passengers kept to themselves, and there was little trouble with the crew. Rutherford kept track of the passing days by carving marks into a wooden plank near his bench. He passed the time watching the ocean and playing chess with a merchant's teenage son, who, much to his chagrin, beat him every time. And, of course, he tried to spend as much time as possible with Sally.

Because the hull was so crowded, he spent most of each day up on the deck. The crew didn't mind as long as he stayed out of their way.

Rutherford was on the deck with Sally when he saw a magnificent sight. He pointed towards the bow of the ship. "Look, Sally!" he shouted.

A huge school of dolphins had swum beside the ship, and the dolphins were jumping through the wake of the ship.

Rutherford looked at Sally as she excitedly watched the dolphins play. Her hair sparkled as sunlight danced off her golden strands. She had never seen the playful animals before and was laughing in delight at their antics. The simplicity and beauty of the moment stirred feelings that Rutherford didn't know existed within him. Without a thought, he took her hand and held it.

Sally didn't resist his sudden advance and continued watching the dolphins with a large smile on her face. Finally, the dolphins disappeared as suddenly as they had appeared. She turned and smiled, and it was then that Rutherford knew he had fallen in love with her.

"Do you mind if I ask you a personal question?" he asked.

A guarded look came across her face, and she slipped her hand from his. "I guess not."

"How is it," he began, trying to measure his words carefully, "that you are on this ship and are indentured to work on a plantation?"

She sighed and looked out towards the ocean. "My husband was killed in a mining accident," she replied with a painful look. "He had debts, and I was forced to go to work for the man he owed them to."

"A mining accident?" Rutherford asked cautiously.

"Yes. We lived outside of Bath, and the mine he was working in collapsed."

Rutherford couldn't believe it. The shadow of Barrett Trading Company was still following him. He didn't know if fate was rewarding or cursing him, but he was sailing to Charleston with a woman whose husband had been killed during the cave-in at the Bath mine.

His mind raced. Should he tell her about his connection to Barrett? After a few seconds, he decided not to for the time being. He didn't think there was anything to be gained by the revelation. More importantly, he didn't want her to hate or blame him because of his connection to Barrett.

"I'm sorry," he replied in earnest.

She turned towards him. "What about you, Mr. John Rutherford? Any loves in your life?"

"I also was married. My wife died during the flu epidemic."

"Oh, John," she said with empathy.

They stood close to one another. He smiled at her, and she leaned closer and slowly hugged him. They held each other, and Rutherford wished the moment could last forever.

XVII

The weeks crept by, and a general malaise seemed to have struck everyone. The dwindling supply of drinkable water, plus the horrible food and abominable conditions, were all starting to take their toll. Most of the passengers, and even some of the crew, had grown lethargic and weak due to the deteriorating conditions aboard the ship.

On the thirty-second day of the voyage, the first passenger died. An old man near the front of the hull failed to wake up one morning. He had been sick almost from the beginning of the voyage, and Rutherford thought it was actually more of a blessing that his misery had ended. He wasn't sure what ailment the man had suffered from, but he had just lain on his bench all day and night, curled up in a ball, moaning in agony. His wife tried to comfort him, but there was nothing anyone could do.

Misery and sickness had become a daily struggle among the passengers. Rutherford told anyone that would listen to spend as much time as possible above deck. The hot and stagnant air in the hull was suffocating.

As the days passed, the list of ailments grew, the most torturous being malnutrition, dehydration, boils, lice, dysentery, fevers, and nausea. The sick could no longer take care of themselves, and a few didn't even try any more. Rutherford had known the voyage was going to be rough, but he had no idea the conditions on the ship were going to be this bad.

Luckily, he and Sally had stayed fairly healthy, mostly because he had enough money to bribe the crew for extra food and water.

Rutherford had tried to discuss the conditions with the crew a number of times, but they shrugged and replied that the voyage and condition of the ship were normal. After he made a few more inquiries, the captain's first mate told him to mind his own business and not stir up any more trouble if he knew what was good for him.

Rutherford had no choice, and he suffered silently along with everyone else. On the forty-first day, a little boy became the second passenger to die, and Sally cried for him the entire day. Rutherford tried to comfort her as best as he could, but it didn't seem to help much.

By the fifty-second day, ten adults and two children had died. There was nothing more horrifying than watching the crew drop the bodies over the railing into the cold, dark ocean. The horrible scene was made even more gruesome because the poor souls didn't even have time to sink before they were ripped apart by giant sharks that had started trailing the ship.

The days miserably passed by. And just when Rutherford thought it couldn't get any worse, he learned on the eighty-second day of the voyage why his father had always told him that the sea was a dangerous and fickle place.

Rutherford awoke early that morning and went onto the deck to eat his meager breakfast, which consisted of one moldy biscuit. Mercifully, they had only a couple of weeks of sailing left. And despite the awful conditions, he was happy. The end of the miserable journey was at least in sight.

The moment he climbed above deck, he knew something was wrong. The sky was cloudy, and even though the seas were relatively gentle, the crew acted nervous and fidgety. They ignored all the passengers and kept looking at the southern sky with great worry on their faces.

Sally came up on deck and walked over. "What's wrong, John?" she asked with concern in her voice.

He pointed towards the horizon. "The crew keeps looking at the sky. I guess they think there is a storm coming."

Sally's hair was blowing wildly in the ever-increasing winds, and he could tell she was nervous. Hell, he was nervous.

"Don't worry," he said weakly. "I'm sure the captain has sailed through worse weather. I'm sure this is nothing."

Rutherford was right about the concern of the crew being weather-related. What he didn't know was that the storm they were about to sail through was unlike any the crew had ever experienced. In fact, as he was to quickly find out, they were hours away from being directly hit by a full-blown hurricane.

With every passing hour, the sky became darker and darker, and the waves grew larger and more powerful. Rutherford had been seasick a few times at the beginning of the voyage, but now everyone aboard, including him, was green and sick from the beating the ship was taking.

The temperature felt like it had dropped at least twenty degrees in just the last hour, and thick sheets of horizontal rain pelted the ship. Rutherford stood frozen at the stern and watched as the crew frantically tied everything down. He wanted to help, but every time he offered, they rudely told him to stay out of their way.

Giant streaks of lightning cut across the sky, and deafening thunder reverberated from all directions. Most of the passengers had gone below because they were too weak to stand above deck and risked being hurled overboard by the large waves battering the ship. Rutherford held on tightly to a cable attached to the mast. He thought it would be pretty ironic if, after managing to escape Barrett, he met his fate at the bottom of the ocean.

The sky had grown a dark gray, and the wind was so strong that he had trouble even standing. Yet he couldn't bring himself to go below deck.

He could barely see past the front of the ship because a constant stream of mist flew over it as the bow dipped to fight each large wave.

Finally, the captain ordered the few remaining passengers to go back down into the hold. Reluctantly, Rutherford obeyed the order and climbed below. He took one last look back, and it was a sight he would never forget. The sky reminded him of a scene from Dante's *Inferno*. It looked as if hell was descending from the sky.

If Rutherford thought he knew what it was like to be afraid after his close call in Bristol, he was sorely wrong. Running from Barrett was terrifying, but at least then he had a chance of escaping or hiding from him. There was no running or hiding from this creation of the devil.

At six o'clock that night, the monster hit the ship with full force. The fury of the wind as it screamed through the wooden planks was the most horrifying sound that Rutherford had ever heard in his life. It was such a terrifying high-pitched roar that Rutherford swore only the devil himself could make such a noise.

Rutherford sat next to Sally and held her tightly in his arms. Neither spoke. The ship felt as if it had lost total control. It seemed as if it was going forwards, backwards, up, and down – all at the same time. The passengers were tossed around like rag dolls, and everything that was not secured became a flying projectile.

After a particularly nasty wave hit the ship, a metal can flew out of nowhere and hit Rutherford right above the eye. Sally tried to help him stitch it up, but with the blood and the ship being rocked so violently it was impossible. He pressed a towel to his eye and prayed liked he had never prayed before. More and more water started seeping through the ship, and soon the cold water was ankle high. Rutherford didn't know much about ships, but he knew enough to realize that this was not a good sign.

He was just about to go above deck to tell the captain about the flooding when the first mate came tumbling down the hold, along with a large supply of ocean water.

He struggled over to Rutherford. "We're taking on water!" he shouted at the top of his lungs. "Grab some men. I need to show you how to work the pumps."

Rutherford left Sally and recruited eight men to help him.

"How is the ship holding up?" Rutherford yelled to the mate.

He looked exhausted and scared to death. "It's hard to tell. I've never seen a storm as bad as this one. I don't think the ship can take much more."

The first mate showed them how to work the pumps, and with great effort, he climbed back up the ladder and disappeared onto the deck.

Manning the pumps was hard work, but Rutherford was at least glad to have something to do. The storm raged through the night, and on more than one occasion Rutherford thought the ship was going down for good. Time had all but ceased. Seconds were the equivalent of days and minutes were an eternity as everyone's life hung in the balance.

At some point, pretty close to morning, the men collectively stopped pumping and quit their fight in utter exhaustion. They had done all that they could do. It was time to accept whatever fate God had decided for them.

Total fatigue had overtaken Rutherford. He was so tired that he no longer had any fear of death, if that was at all possible to believe. He lay down next to Sally and wondered if he would ever see another sunrise.

Rutherford didn't know how long he had been asleep when he felt a hand rub across his face. He opened his eyes. Sally was sound asleep lying across his chest. He raised his head and looked around. It took a couple of seconds for him to realize where he was and remember all the events that had unfolded the previous night. He couldn't believe it. They had surviveed.

He reached inside his shirt, trying not to wake Sally, and pulled out his Saint Christopher's medallion that the young boy had sold him back in Bristol. It seemed like such a long time ago. He silently prayed to God for delivering the ship safely through the storm. Rutherford was convinced that the charm had protected the ship. He closed his eyes and wished he could somehow thank the little boy.

Sally started to stir. She sat up and looked down at him.

God, she is so beautiful, Rutherford thought.

"That wasn't too bad of a storm, was it?" she playfully asked.

"I told you Saint Christopher would be looking out for us," Rutherford answered.

They both laughed, and then their eyes locked. Rutherford reached over and kissed her gently on the lips. In that brief moment, something passed between them, and their relationship changed.

One by one the rest of the passengers started to move about. Rutherford sensed that everyone had awakend with the same unusual feeling that he had; a feeling that the ship had survived a storm it shouldn't have. There was no celebrating, only a quiet and solemn realization that their lives had been spared.

Rutherford heard someone coming down the ladder from above deck. It was the captain in his familiar black navy jacket. Close up he made a striking figure. He was in his forties and had a thick white beard and a leather face tanned brown from countless ocean voyages.

He made his way to the middle of the hull, where all eyes were on him. He stood and stared at the ragged group of passengers for a couple of seconds. Then slowly, almost in a whisper, he started to talk.

"Ladies and Gentlemen," he said, "I have been at sea my entire life. I have even sailed around the Cape of Horn three times. But never in my life have I ever encountered a storm like the one we have just been through. I appreciate what each and every one of you did. Every person played a part in saving this ship, and for that I am thankful. I know there are many different reasons why all of you are on this ship. Regardless of the how or why, everyone will be starting a new life when we arrive in Charleston.

"I believe God has given each us of a chance at a new beginning, a chance to redeem ourselves and live a good and prosperous life. Let's take this gift and use it well."

The captain shuffled his feet. He looked totally exhausted. There were dark circles under his eyes, and his skin looked unnaturally yellow. He cleared his throat before continuing. "We were blown a little off course, but God willing, we should arrive in Charleston in two to three weeks. Let's all pray for our deliverance and a safe remaining voyage."

The captain climbed back up the ladder to the deck. Slowly, one by one, the weary passengers followed him above. Rutherford climbed up behind Sally, and once on deck, he couldn't believe how clear everything had become. The sky, the sun, the water. Even the filth and stench in the hull had disappeared. The storm had cleansed everything in its path.

He took the words of the captain quite literally; he had been given a second chance, and he swore that he wasn't going to make the mistakes he had made in the past. He was more determined than ever to live life on his terms, not on someone else's. He had never felt more at peace with himself. Maybe that's what inner strength actually was: discovering peace within.

He smiled at Sally, and she smiled back.

"Sally," he said softly. "There is something I need to tell you. I'm sorry I didn't tell you earlier."

She looked confused. "What is it, John?"

I wasn't exactly forthcoming with you about what I did for a living in Bristol."

She shook her head. "It doesn't matter, John."

"It does to me. I should have told you this before, but I . . . I didn't want you to think poorly of me." He paused and looked at her.

He took her hand. "What is it, John?"

"I worked for Arthur Barrett."

She pulled away, and her face registered a look of surprise and confusion. "Did you do bad things for him?"

"No, I swear to you I didn't." Rutherford paused. "I took the job for money. I'm guilty of that! But I never did anything to hurt anyone."

"Why are you on this ship?"

"I discovered things about Barrett and Johnstone that I shouldn't have, and they tried to have me killed. I'm running away and hoping to start a new life. I'm sorry I didn't tell you this earlier."

Sally turned and walked over to the railing of the ship. Her back was to Rutherford.

He walked over and put his arm around her shoulder. "Do you hate me for not being more forthcoming?"

"John," she said, turning towards him. Her eyes were misty. "Of course not. Both of our lives have been turned upside down because of that man."

He wiped a tear from her eye. "I know," he replied gently, "but we're still here. Perhaps there's a reason for that."

She smiled and hugged him.

The next three weeks passed by swiftly and without incidence. Rutherford was on deck watching a school of Spanish mackerel crackling on the surface of the water when he heard the call of land ahead. He had never heard sweeter words in his entire life.

The ship slowly made its way into Charleston's harbor, and Rutherford was amazed at the number of ships. It was almost as busy as Bristol's port. The captain slowly navigated the ship through the harbor. The voyage was over.

XVIII

Charleston, South Carolina

Rutherford and Sally stood anxiously at the bow and watched as Charleston came into view. From the distance, the city appeared a good bit smaller than Bristol, and there were only a few buildings that stood taller than three or four stories.

A tall wooden wall surrounded the outskirts of the city, and palm trees lined the banks of the harbor. The most distinguishing feature of the skyline was the multitude of steeples that rose towards the heavens. In fact, there appeared to be more steeples than buildings.

The captain docked the *Sea Biscuit*, and Rutherford gathered the rest of his goods and happily departed the ship. He couldn't wait to spend the night in a comfortable bed and, more importantly, eat a decent meal.

Once he stepped on land, his relief of having escaped death not once but twice was overshadowed by losing Sally, at least for the time being. She would have to leave to fulfill her indentured service at the rice plantation across the Ashley River.

They stood together as a swarm of dock workers started to unload the ship. Neither one of them said a word. He knew it was a sad time for both of them, and he desperately wanted to tell her his feelings.

"Sally," he began.

She stood close, put her hand to his mouth, and stopped him. She leaned even closer.

Rutherford felt a lump grow in his throat.

She whispered, "This is goodbye, but only for now. Don't forget about me."

She lightly kissed his lips.

Rutherford watched stoically as she grabbed her few belongings and put them on the cart that would take her to her new home. He unconsciously pulled out the Saint Christopher's medallion and looked at it for a moment before hurrying over to her cart. He took the necklace off.

"Sally, I want you to have this." He handed her the necklace. "It's for good luck and so you won't forget about me."

"John," was all she managed to say as she took the necklace and cradled it to her chest.

The driver cracked the reins of the horses, and the cart began to pull away.

Rutherford walked alongside it and looked up at Sally. "I swear to you," he said, "I'll find a way to buy out your contract."

She waved goodbye, and Rutherford saw tears begin to run down her cheek.

As he watched the cart clatter down the dirt road, he swore he would keep his promise to her. No matter what it took, he would find a way to free Sally from the rice plantation. With great reluctance, he grabbed his bags off the dock and walked into town full of mixed emotions.

During the long voyage, Rutherford had learned a bit of history about Charleston from other passengers and crew. The town had been founded in 1670 after the two-hundred-ton frigate The *Carolina* arrived, having survived a brutal seven-month journey from England. The *Carolina's* voyage was plagued by storms, and two other ships that were making the same journey were both lost to the sea. Ninety-three passengers were onboard when the ship finally arrived and sailed down the Cooper River past Oyster Point and into the Ashley River.

Captain Joseph West sailed The *Carolina* down the first large creek he spotted off the Ashley River, and their long-suffering journey finally came to an end. The settlers cleared the land, built a defensive perimeter, and named their new home Albemarle Point.

Life was not easy for the first group of settlers, and after a disastrous couple of years, the town's very existence was in serious doubt. In a last-ditch effort, the settlers decided to move back across the Ashley River. The peninsula was better suited for a city because of its defensive position, and the ocean breezes thinned out the clouds of mosquitoes that had tormented the settlers night and day.

The new city was renamed Charleston in honor of the King of England, Charles II. When the town leaders laid out the plans for the city, they wanted to avoid the narrow and twisted streets of most European cities, so they set forth a checkerboard plan similar to the one used for the city of London after the great fire of 1666.

The plan for Charleston was to build broad, straight streets lined with beautiful homes. Next, a defensive wall was built around the entire town to protect the city from its many enemies, including the Spaniards, French, local Indians, and marauding pirates.

By 1718, Charleston's diverse population of English, Barbadians, Africans, and sailors of many different nationalities had grown to over five thousand. In a short period of time, Charleston had grown into one of the great colonial cities, rivaling Boston, New York, and Philadelphia.

Rutherford slowly walked along the dirt and cobblestone streets, taking in the sights and sounds of his new home. He was amazed that Charleston was considered to be a developed, prosperous city in the New World, when in fact, he thought it was primitive, dirty, and undeveloped.

He laughed. He had always thought it would be impossible for any city to have worse streets than Bristol's, but he had been wrong. Charleston's streets were packed full of animals and their waste, and from the amount of garbage in the streets, he reckoned it must have doubled as the local trash dump.

Rutherford passed an inn on East Bay Street and paid for a room for the night. It was getting late, and he was looking forward to his first real meal in months.

The **Moultrie Tavern** was already crowded by the time he arrived, but he found an empty table in the back. Most of the patrons appeared to be sailors, local shop owners, and dock workers. By the large crowd and noise, he knew Charleston had at least one thing in common with Bristol: its citizens liked to drink and have a good time after their work was done for the day.

A skinny waitress with huge brown eyes came to his table, and Rutherford ordered pork chops, collard greens, and fresh bread, along with a pint of beer. His mouth watered at the thought of the fresh meat.

During his short walk that afternoon he had learned the general outlay of the city, and tomorrow he would start looking for a job. He figured that if worse came to worst, he could always find employment down on the docks loading and unloading ships until he found something better.

"Excuse me, sir."

Rutherford looked up to see a wiry old man standing in front of his table. He was short, wore glasses, and had a few long strands of hair that were combed across in a bad effort to try and cover his egg-shaped bald head.

"Do you mind if I share this table with you? All the rest are taken."

Rutherford didn't mind the company. Perhaps the gentleman would be able to give him some useful information about Charleston. "Of course not. Have a seat. My name is John Rutherford."

"James Restin."

Restin sat down and ordered dinner. The two men talked about Rutherford's voyage from Bristol. Restin explained that he had come to Charleston seven years ago from London and that his wife had died during the trip from a bout of typhoid fever.

The skinny waitress appeared with both their dinners.

Rutherford greedily cut into the pork chops and took a large bite. "I cannot tell you how good this tastes," he said, his mouth half full.

Both men devoured their meals, and after dinner they ordered another round of beers.

Restin patted his belly contentedly. "You know, John," he said. "I have been looking to hire someone over at my store."

"Really? What type of store do you own?"

"It's an apothecary. I need someone to deliver goods, take care of customers, and keep the store clean. Any idea of what you're going to do in Charleston?"

"No. I had planned to start looking for a job tomorrow."

Restin thought about the situation for a second. "Why don't you consider coming to work for me? With your previous business experience, I think you would do a great job. There is even a small bedroom in the back of the store you can use for as long as you want."

Rutherford didn't have to think about the offer for long. This little angel of a man had just solved two of his most immediate problems. He couldn't believe his luck. A small salary was agreed upon, and Restin even paid for his dinner.

Rutherford started to work at Mr. Restin's store the very next day. It was located on the corner of a two-story faded brick building. A bakery was next door, and Rutherford licked his lips at the sweet aroma of the freshly baked breads and muffins. He passed the bakery and entered Mr. Restin's store, where he found a multitude of medicines, ointments, and everyday products neatly arranged on numerous shelves.

Mr. Restin was behind the counter sorting through a box of supplies. He looked up and saw Rutherford. "Ah, John, come on in. Let me show you the store."

They started in the back supply room, where wooden boxes were neatly stacked.

Mr. Restin opened a side door. "John, this is the room I mentioned. You can stay here as long as you like."

Mr. Restin lit a candle to show him the room. It was pretty bare, but it had a comfortable-looking cot, a little table, and a couple of chairs.

"Thank you," Rutherford replied. "I appreciate it."

"Think nothing of it."

Mr. Restin blew out the candle and led Rutherford to the back door of the store. Mr. Restin opened the door, which emptied into a little courtyard, where a thick horse was stabled.

Mr. Restin pointed towards a cart. "You will be making all the deliveries. And that's Sandy." He motioned towards the horse.

Rutherford walked over and patted Sandy on the nose. He didn't know what it was about him and horses, but the damn creature bit him on the hand.

Mr. Restin laughed. "I should have told you: Sandy is a bit ornery, but she'll get used to you."

They walked back inside, and Mr. Restin explained the rest of his duties, which were pretty straightforward and didn't appear to be all that demanding. Rutherford knew that his salary wouldn't be enough to buy out Sally's contract, but at least it was an opportunity to get back on his feet.

After two weeks of working for Mr. Restin, Rutherford had settled in fairly well and felt his luck might finally be changing for the better. He was stacking supplies in the back when he heard Mr. Restin call out his name.

"I'm in the back!" Rutherford yelled back.

Mr. Restin appeared at the closet door.

"John, tomorrow I need you to deliver supplies to the Smithwick Rice Plantation. They're one of our best customers, and I have reached an agreement to deliver supplies to them every two weeks. So I'll need you to plan on making the deliveries."

Rutherford couldn't believe his ears. What a wonderful piece of luck! That was the plantation where Sally worked.

"Yes, of course," he responded with a big grin.

Mr. Restin furrowed his brows. "Why do you seem so excited about the delivery?"

"Oh, I happen to know someone working there that I have been dying to see."

"This person wouldn't happen to be a woman, now would she?"

Rutherford smiled from ear to ear. He couldn't wait to see Sally.

"I thought so," Mr. Restin said, answering his own question.

Rutherford didn't sleep a wink the entire night. He couldn't wait to see Sally, and he wondered if she would be just as happy to see him.

The long night finally passed. Rutherford jumped out of his small straw bed barely after sunrise and quickly loaded up the cart with medicines, ointments, and health supplies. He had no trouble, except for Sandy, who wouldn't cooperate at all and nipped him twice before he finally managed to hook the damn beast up to the cart.

Rutherford sat impatiently on the cart and waited for Mr. Restin to show up. Mr. Restin had an amused look on his face when he arrived to see the cart already packed and Rutherford ready to go.

He walked over to the cart. "John, you must really like this woman."

If you only knew, Rutherford thought. "Just want to get an early start," he answered cheerfully.

"I'll bet." Mr. Restin gave him a knowing smile.

Mr. Restin gave him directions to the plantation for a third time plus a few ham sandwiches for the trip. The plantation was located about fifteen miles away, and the only way to get there was to cross the Ashley River by way of a little ferry barge. The trip would take most of the day.

Rutherford excitedly rode out of Charleston, hooting and hollering at the mass of chickens, dogs, cats, cows, and other assorted animals that perpetually clogged the streets.

He arrived at the river and saw the ferry operator, who was a tall and sun-tanned man about his age named Stuart. The river was only about a half-mile wide, but it was treacherous. The currents were extremely fast because the river emptied into the ocean less than three miles away.

Stuart safely navigated them across, and Rutherford had only twelve miles to go before he reached the plantation. He expected a bumpy ride on a primitive trail but instead was surprised to find that the trail was actually a smooth dirt road, and it was in excellent condition.

He found the cutoff that Mr. Restin had described and turned the carriage down the long sandy road that led to the plantation. The path was about three-quarters of a mile long, and hundreds of mammoth oak trees lined the road on each side. Masses of Spanish moss hung from their limbs created a natural canopy, and Rutherford rode through the broken streaks of late-morning sunlight and the dappled shade of the magnificent ancient trees.

Rutherford knew he was almost to the plantation when he spotted a series of small brick houses – the slave quarters, as he would later learn – off to the side of the road. Just then, the plantation house came into view. It was a massive white colonial house, with Roman columns in the front and a wrap-around porch. Rutherford guessed everyone must be at work in the rice fields because he didn't see a soul.

He stopped the horse and jumped down from the carriage. He then walked up to the front door and knocked a few times. Finally, he heard the shuffling of feet behind the door. When it opened, he couldn't believe his eyes.

"John!" Sally let out a muffled scream and threw her arms around him. "Oh, John! I can't tell you how happy I am to see you. I've missed you so much."

They held onto each other tightly.

"Sally," he said while running his hand through her thick hair, "I can't tell you how much I have missed you. How have you been doing?"

She giggled. "Come, let's talk out on the back porch. We can sit in the swinging chair and have a glass of cold lemonade."

She led him into the house. A huge spiral staircase wound its way up to the second floor. The ceilings must have been at least twenty feet high, and they were built out of the highest quality oak. The hardwood floors were immaculate. He guessed that someone must polish them every day to keep them that clean. And everything from the furniture to the fixtures had been imported from England.

He followed Sally down a long hall towards the kitchen. "Are you sure it's all right for me to be in here?" he whispered. "I don't want to get you in trouble."

"No, it's all right," she answered. "You could not have picked a better time. Everyone is out in the fields, and on Tuesdays the Misses goes into Charleston to shop. She spends the whole day in the city. They leave me here to polish the silver and look after the house."

Sally poured two glasses of lemonade from a crystal pitcher. "Let's go outside."

They walked outside to the back porch and sat down together on a large swinging chair.

He took a sip of the lemonade. "So how do you like it here?"

Sally shrugged and then frowned a little. "It's all right. The work isn't too hard, and Mrs. Pinckney is pretty fair with me."

She paused and looked out towards the marsh. "It's just not how I imagined my life turning out. I can't wait until my service is up. At least I can be free to do whatever I want."

"I hope that includes something with me," Rutherford blurted out, surprised that he had been so forward.

She turned towards him, her deep blue eyes reflecting the sunlight. "I want us to be together, too, John. I have fallen in love with you. I can't tell you how much I have thought about you."

Rutherford had never heard sweeter words in his entire life. "I love you, too," he responded.

They sat in the swinging chair, drank their lemonade, and talked.

Rutherford could have stayed in the chair with Sally forever, but he had to return to Charleston. He grabbed her hand. "I have to get back. Mr. Restin will be expecting me."

They walked back around the house, and Sally helped him unload the supplies. After they finished, Sally approached Sandy and started petting the horse on the nose. The horse licked her hand.

"Yes, you're such a nice, gentle horse," Sally cooed. "What's her name?" she asked, turning to Rutherford.

"Rotten," he mumbled under his breath.

"What?"

"Sandy." He smiled.

Rutherford hated to leave her. "I'll be back in two weeks," he said, kicking some dirt.

"I can't wait to see you again." She stopped petting Sandy and pulled out the Saint Christopher's medallion that he had given her. "Whenever I hold it, I think of you and know that one day we will be together."

They kissed goodbye, and Rutherford jumped into the cart, Charleston bound.

IXX

Edward Teach stood on the deck of his ship and watched as the sun disappeared into the ocean. It was a sight he never grew tired of. His mind drifted back to that fateful day in Bristol when he had swindled Arthur Barrett for enough money to buy a ship and crew.

He had made good use of Barrett's initial investment and bought a small sloop with ten guns and enough men and supplies to get him to the Bahamas. Once Teach had arrived, the first thing he did was plunder a French ship called the *Concord*. Not only did he steal the goods onboard, but he also set adrift her crew and took the ship for himself and renamed her *Queen Anne's Revenge*.

In a short period of time, Edward Teach, with his new and improved ship, had become the most feared man on the open seas. He was so feared, in fact, that he was no longer called by his Christian name. He was simply known as Blackbeard. From Boston to the Bahamas, the simple utterance of his name was enough to strike fear in the hearts of sailors.

He laughed and took a swig of rum as the glowing sun dropped below the horizon. Arthur Barrett – he couldn't believe his luck in tricking that old fool. Blackbeard had promised to give Barrett half of his profits and to protect his interests. It was a promise he never intended to keep, and of course, he didn't.

It was a cool night for May, and Blackbeard had an unusual but serious problem on his hands. A large number of his sailors were sick, and he needed to get them healthy fast. A long vacation down in New Providence had finally taken its toll on his crew.

He cursed under his breath. He couldn't understand why God saw to it that every pleasure in life also came with a price. If he didn't get his men proper medicines quickly, there would be no way he could continue on. His men wouldn't have the strength to attack, let alone defend the ship. The pirates were suffering with everything from yellow fever to alcohol poisoning, but what had afflicted them the worst was syphilis.

The women of the Caribbean had sent the pirates contently away, but their happiness would soon end. Most of the men were running high fevers and were extremely lethargic. It had gotten so bad that all of Blackbeard's attention had shifted from plundering vessels to finding medicine so he could treat the God-awful curse that had decimated his men.

But he had a plan to solve their painful problem. They were about three hundred miles south of Charleston. Blackbeard had done quite a bit of illegal trading with the colony and was familiar with the city. Thus, he knew that the city had a large supply of medicines.

His plan was to sail to Charleston and get the medicine using any means necessary. Sailing along with him was Captain Stede Bonnet, who Blackbeard thought was a dolt but a harmless one at that.

He had a soft spot for Bonnett because their upbringings had been similar. Like Blackbeard, Bonnett had left a comfortable existence to risk life and limb on the open seas. While in New Providence, Bonnett had pleaded with Blackbeard to take him along.

He had told Blackbeard that the reason he wanted to leave the Bahamas was that he was bored with life on the plantation and that if he spent another day with his wife, he would kill her. Blackbeard ended up agreeing to his request because Bonnett owned a ship and had an enormous amount of money. He decided to humor the man while it served his interest.

Blackbeard's loyal friend, Israel Hands, commanded another ship called the *Adventure*. All told, Blackbeard had three ships and over three hundred men at his command. Even though most of his men were sick, he had enough hands and bravado to get what he wanted from Charleston.

XX

As the weeks turned into months, Rutherford became more comfortable with his new home and missed Bristol less and less. It helped that he was fortunate enough to spend every other Tuesday with Sally at the plantation. She was required to work there for another two years, and then she would be free to go.

However, most indentured servants, even after their servitude had expired, continued to work for the people whom they were indentured to because they had no money and nowhere to go. Rutherford swore he wasn't going to let that happen to her.

During his biweekly visits, they had started to make plans for the future and even talked about the possibility of getting married. Mr. Restin told him that he had a friend who would be willing to rent them a small house until they could afford to buy their own place. All in all, things were going well, and Rutherford had even managed to save a little money.

But in life, unexpected turns were always right around the corner. And such was the case on that average day in May of 1718, when Rutherford's life was turned upside down, yet again.

Rutherford was busily sweeping the floor of the drugstore when Mr. Restin burst through the front door with a scared but excited look on his face.

"John, you're not going to believe who is anchored out in the harbor!"

Rutherford had never seen Mr. Restin so excited. "Who?" he asked.

"Blackbeard – that's who!" Mr. Restin practically screamed. "Evidently, those rascals have blockaded the harbor and have taken hostages from a ship whose passengers include Samuel Wragg and his son."

Samuel Wragg was a wealthy and influential man in the Carolinas. The local businessmen admired him because he tended to side with them concerning matters of commerce.

"What do they want?" Rutherford asked.

"I don't know, but a couple of Blackbeard's men have rowed ashore and are meeting with the town council and the governor right now."

Mr. Restin was a ball of nervous energy and he continuously looked out the window of the store, as if he expected Blackbeard to show up any moment.

Rutherford shrugged and went back to sweeping the floors. He felt bad for the hostages, although he had to admit it was kind of exciting to have the notorious Blackbeard in town. Regardless, he couldn't get as worked up as Mr. Restin was. The matter didn't concern him. His mind was focused on only one thing these days, and that was Sally.

After pacing for a few more minutes, Mr. Restin ran back outside without telling Rutherford where he was going or what time he would be back.

By lunchtime, Rutherford had pretty much forgotten the whole Blackbeard affair until Mr. Restin and a large group of men charged through the front doors of the store. No one paid Rutherford the slightest bit of attention as they scurried about, making a complete mess out of the floor he had just swept.

"Do you think you have enough medicine and supplies here?" one of the men hollered to Mr. Restin.

Mr. Restin looked around at the shelves. "I'm pretty sure we do. Thank God for that shipment last week."

Mr. Restin tripped over a box and fell into Rutherford, who was just trying to stay out of everyone's way.

"Oh, John, there you are," he said, as if Rutherford hadn't been in the store the entire day. "Get over here and give me a hand with this stuff."

"What's all this for?" Rutherford asked.

"It's for Blackbeard," Mr. Restin answered. "He is threatening to kill all the hostages and storm the city if we don't meet his demands for medical supplies."

A councilman named Peters added, "Those filthy damn pirates are the scourge of the earth. More than half of the bastards have some type of disease from exploits with unholy women. And all of them are raging drunks. It is a wonder they can function at all."

Rutherford burst out laughing. Peters was widely known for his excessive drinking and womanizing.

Peters gave him an ugly look. "We should consider ourselves lucky that all they want is medicine," he exclaimed to no one in particular.

Rutherford kept his mouth shut, but he was amazed that a town of thousands of able-bodied men would give in to the demands of a couple hundred sick pirates.

Rutherford helped the men load the supplies onto a large cart outside of the store.

"All right!" Peters hollered. "Let's get this stuff down to the boat so we can get those damn pirates out of our town."

Rutherford guessed Peters was in charge of the operation because everyone seemed to be following his orders.

They took the goods down to the dock and loaded them in a large old rowboat. The contingency of nervous men were standing around, staring at the supplies in the boat when Mr. Restin brought up an interesting point that none of the nitwits had even stopped to consider.

"Hey," he said hesitantly, "who is going to row this stuff out to Blackbeard?"

For the first time that day, the men who all liked to be heard on matters great and small became completely silent. And when the silence was finally broken, it was almost comical. One by one, the cowards all gave some wretched excuse, explaining why they couldn't row the supplies out to Blackbeard.

First, Peters chirped like a frightened schoolgirl. "I would love to gentlemen," he squawked, "but everyone here knows that I have a bad back. I couldn't possibly row all the way out to their ships."

His obvious lie opened the floodgates, and another called out, "Uh, my wife is pregnant and could go into labor any second. I'd better stay, too."

Rutherford had never heard so many ailments and excuses in his entire life. His favorite was from a portly old man who was the town's tanner. He explained that he couldn't go because he had eaten some bad oysters and was having severe stomach problems.

Not one second after he gave his wretched excuse he got a strange look on his face and said with pursed lips, "Oh, I'm having another bout." He promptly turned and ran down the street holding the back of his britches.

After every excuse in the book had been given, there was complete silence, and all the men stared down at their feet.

"What about you, Rutherford?" Peters asked. "You'd be doing the city a great service."

Everyone looked at him. Rutherford was under no obligation to help them out, but for some reason he didn't immediately refuse. He really believed that once the supplies were delivered, Blackbeard would release the hostages. Since everyone else was afraid to run the supplies out, Rutherford figured it might be worth some compensation if he volunteered his services.

"I'll go," he said flatly. As he was saying the words, he had a sudden premonition that he had just made a terrible mistake. "But I expect to be paid for my services," he quickly added.

Rutherford didn't know if his rash decision was inspired by the quest for adventure or the desire to take a risk, but it didn't really matter much at this point. What was done was done.

Mr. Restin approached him. "Son, you don't have to do this," he half-whispered. "It's not your responsibility."

"Don't worry. They just want the medicine. They will let the hostages and me go after I deliver the supplies to them. Anyway, I could use the money."

Rutherford smiled and patted him on the shoulder. "But you have to promise me to hold the money, and if I don't come back, I want you to give it to Sally."

Mr. Restin didn't look too happy about his decision. "Good luck, John," he said hesitantly. "And don't worry about the money. I always keep my promises."

The boat was an oversized piece of junk that must have been leaking from a half dozen places. Rutherford guessed the wealthy businessmen were afraid Blackbeard would also steal the boat if they sent a halfway decent one out.

He set off and had a clear passage out to Blackbeard's ship because no one dared sail in or out of Charleston with the pirate ships anchored in the harbor's entrance.

It was unseasonably cool for May, which was a lucky break, since it was going to take him a good hour to row out to Blackbeard's ship. The rowboat's condition didn't help matters. He had to stop every fifteen minutes to bail out water.

He was both nervous and excited to meet the famous pirate from his hometown. He wondered if all the stories he had heard about him were true. On second thought, he hoped all the stories weren't true, or he might never see Sally again. He wondered what Sally would think if she knew he was pulling this crazy stunt.

Blackbeard's ship, *Queen Anne's Revenge*, got closer and closer, and he could see a group of men standing on the ship. They kept a close eye on him as he slowly rowed closer.

As he approached the broadside of the ship, a ragged-looking pirate yelled down, "Pull that damn boat around to the stern, and hurry it up if you know what's good for you!"

Not exactly the welcome Rutherford had been hoping for, but at least they weren't shooting, at least not yet. He pulled the boat around to the stern, where three pirates were waiting for him in rope netting that hung down from the railing of the ship.

"About time you showed up," said a grumpy-looking fellow who was missing two front teeth and smelled like he hadn't bathed in a couple of weeks. "We were just about ready to have a little fun with the hostages."

Rutherford tied off the boat.

"Start handing up those supplies!" growled another.

It didn't take long for the ragged pirates to unload the supplies, and Rutherford wondered what was going to happen next. He didn't have to wait for too long to find out. After the last box was handed up, a pirate leaned over the railing with two cocked muskets aimed directly at his head.

"All right, you grubby little worm," the pirate said. "Get your ass up here now!"

Rutherford had no choice but to follow the order. He climbed the rope netting up to the deck of Blackbeard's ship. When he reached the top, a couple of pirates grabbed him and pulled him up over the railing.

An average-sized and handsomely dressed man approached. "Captain Stede Bonnett," he said, tipping his hat to Rutherford. "Glad to meet you. Thank you for bringing the supplies to us. It was very kind of you, indeed."

Rutherford shook his hand and tried to ignore the snickers of the other pirates. He decided it was probably in his best interest to play along and not get anyone riled up.

"Thank you, Captain," he said in a cautious manner. "I hope these supplies will help. I know a lot of people in Charleston were very happy to lend a helping hand."

"Well, that's very gracious of you," Captain Bonnett replied with an amused look.

Bonnett lit a cigar, and the other pirates, having grown bored with their conversation, started to drift off.

The captain seemed like a reasonable enough man, so Rutherford thought it might be a good time to request that the hostages be released. "Captain Bonnett, it's getting late," he said confidently. "Can you release the hostages so we can get back to shore before dark?"

Bonnett blew out a great puff of smoke and gave another amused look. "Well, son, let me tell you about that. Blackbeard's the captain of this ship, so you're going to have to ask him." Bonnett took another puff from his cigar and smirked. "However, whatever you say to Blackbeard, I would choose my words carefully, or you might never see Charleston again."

Rutherford had been wondering where Blackbeard was, and he guessed he was going to find out soon enough.

The notorious pirate must have been down in the hold of the ship; because when he came up on deck, there was no doubting his identity. He was a giant of a man who stood at least a half-foot taller than anyone else and was built as solid as a rock. He wore black trousers that were tucked into tall black leather boots, and his black coat covered a set of thick, broad shoulders. There was no doubt that physically he was an enormously powerful man.

Blackbeard slowly strode across the deck towards Rutherford. His presence was so intimidating Rutherford now cursed himself for volunteering.

With a confident smirk, Blackbeard looked him up and down. "So you are the errand boy who has brought our supplies," he said, his voice resonating with authority.

Rutherford was determined not to show his fear. He cleared his increasingly dry throat. "Uh, yes, sir. Everything that you asked for has been delivered."

Rutherford didn't want to come out and ask Blackbeard to keep his end of the bargain and release all the hostages. Rather, he hoped the pirate would just decide to do so. However, as Rutherford would later realize, nothing with Blackbeard was that easy.

"So what's your name, errand boy?"

"John Rutherford," he answered nervously.

"Well, John Rutherford," Blackbeard replied, "how did you get tricked into coming out here? Or is it . . . ," he began, smirking at his crew, "is it that you are just plain stupid?"

The men roared with laughter, and one of the pirates called out, "He just looks plain stupid to me!"

Rutherford had nothing to lose, so he just told Blackbeard the truth. "They promised me money to deliver the goods out to you."

Blackbeard laughed. "Ah, I see a man of principle. I like that."

"I also wanted to meet you," Rutherford foolishly continued.

Blackbeard gave him a disgusted look and yelled to Bonnett, "Get those coward bastards above deck! Now!"

Bonnett nodded and climbed down into the hold of the ship. A few minutes later, the disheveled hostages emerged from the galley of the ship. They looked a little shaken, but didn't appear to have been treated too badly.

Blackbeard swaggered over to the hostages, who had stopped in the middle of the ship. They huddled together like a group of scared ducklings who had lost their mother.

Blackbeard pulled his huge cutlass out of his belt and pointed it at Rutherford. "Look here," he said to the hostages. "This errand boy has delivered the goods needed to secure your release. I appreciate your stay on my ship as my guests, but I'm afraid our time together has come to an end."

Blackbeard sounded as if he were a mild-mannered innkeeper, bidding goodbye to his overnight guests. But then the real Blackbeard thundered, "And if you are not off my ship in two minutes, I'll slice everyone of you to ribbons and feed your remains to the sharks!"

That was all the encouragement the hostages needed to get their butts moving. They practically ran to the end of the ship where Rutherford stood, and they began to hurriedly climb down the netting in a none-too-orderly fashion. In their panic to get away from Blackbeard, they became entangled in the rope net that hung off the ship. The harder they tried, the more they became entangled. They looked liked a swarm of flies hopelessly trying to free themselves from a spider's web.

The pirates were laughing so hard at the spectacle one would have thought it was the funniest thing they had ever seen.

Even Rutherford had to struggle to keep his composure because the group of men looked so ridiculous. Eventually, they managed to untangle themselves and board the boat.

Rutherford then turned to face Blackbeard. "Thank you for everything. It was a pleasure meeting you."

He turned to climb down the netting and into the boat with the hostages.

"Hold it, errand boy," Blackbeard growled. "Where do you think you are going?"

Rutherford's heart skipped a beat. "I'm going to row everyone back to shore," he stammered.

"I don't think so," hissed Blackbeard. "I haven't killed anyone in a few days, and I'm really feeling bad about that."

In the only display of anything remotely called courage from the hostages, Samuel Wragg yelled up, "Blackbeard, the supplies have been delivered, just like you requested. Please release this man and keep your end of the bargain."

Blackbeard walked over to the railing and gazed down at the men in the boat. "I'm keeping my end of the bargain. The deal was when the supplies were delivered, I would release the hostages. And, as you can plainly see, I am doing that. John Rutherford was not included in that agreement." He turned and gazed at Rutherford with a sneer. "Anyway, I have some plans for him. My men are a little rusty, so I think we may have a little target practice later."

Rutherford's head began to spin. Did Blackbeard really intend to kill him? What the hell should he do now? The only thing Rutherford could think of was to make a run for it and jump over the deck and take his chances in the water. But before he could even get his legs to move, he was grabbed from behind by a couple of pirates. Blackbeard laughed while he struggled against their hold.

Blackbeard then turned and looked down at the ex-hostages, saying, "Now get the hell out of here before I decide to change my mind and use all of you for target practice."

Rutherford watched in disbelief as the men he had just saved simply shrugged and began rowing towards the distant shore. Judging by the speed that they were rowing, he had no doubt that they were on pace to set a record for the fastest-ever boat crossing of Charleston Harbor.

Rutherford felt a pang of despair grow in his belly. Why did he have to open his big mouth?

XXI

The pirates released their hold on Rutherford.

"Mr. Rutherford," Blackbeard began in a less threatening tone than the one he had used with the hostages present, "is that a Bristol accent I detect?"

"Yes, it is." He hoped that Blackbeard might show a little compassion towards a fellow Bristol citizen.

"How did you get to Charleston?"

Rutherford didn't know what came over him, but he told Blackbeard the whole story of his employment at Barrett Trading and his escape after Johnstone had tried to kill him. Rutherford was surprised because Blackbeard listened intently without saying a word.

When Rutherford had finished his story, Blackbeard let out a huge roar of laughter and grabbed a bottle of rum from one of his mates. He took a huge swig from the bottle. "Well, I'll be!" he cried out, as rum poured from the corners of his mouth. "We have something in common after all!"

Rutherford wasn't sure what he was talking about, other than the fact that they were both from Bristol.

"Mr. Rutherford, I'm in a generous mood, so I am going to make you an offer, and I will even give you two choices. We need an extra man on this ship, and I think you would fit in just fine. Your duties would be pretty basic: you would be the lowest ranking man onboard, and thus you would be required to perform all the duties that no one else wants to do. And, of course, you would be expected to fight like the devil when the time comes. And trust me, the time will come.

"Now, being a generous man, I will give you a second option. If you don't want to join us," he said, looking around the ship and then glaring back at him, "then I will kill you. The decision is yours, and you have one minute to decide."

In a way, Rutherford guessed he was lucky. At least he had a choice. It really wasn't a difficult decision to make. He would accept Blackbeard's offer and could always try to escape later. Of course, he realized there was a pretty good chance he would die from disease, in battle, or at Blackbeard's hands, but he didn't have much of a choice at the moment. Either way, he didn't want to use up the whole minute he had been given for fear that Blackbeard might change his mind.

"It would be my honor to join and serve upon your ship, sir," he replied.

Rutherford didn't think Blackbeard expected to hear a different answer, but he acted like Rutherford had just given him a huge surprise. He broke out in a grin from ear to ear and called out, "Tonight we celebrate our successful trip to Charleston and the addition of our new crew member!"

Blackbeard turned towards Bonnett and waved his cutlass in the air. "Captain, break out the rum! Tomorrow we sail to Nassau, but tonight we celebrate!"

Everyone let out a holler that Rutherford swore could be heard all the way back in Charleston. Despite the various illnesses that plagued so many of the men, they consumed more liquor that night than he thought was humanly possible. Rutherford tried to pace himself, but his new friends would have none of it, and they practically forced rum down his throat at every possible opportunity.

As the party continued late into the night, the motley band of pirates continued to drink and listen to old war stories, mostly told by Blackbeard.

Despite the pleasant feeling from all the alcohol, Rutherford swore that he would escape at his first chance and return to Sally. He just hoped she would wait for him, since it looked like it might be a while before he saw Charleston again.

Blackbeard, meanwhile, was a master storyteller and kept everyone entertained with great adventure tales. As the party started to wind down, Blackbeard told one last story about how he had tricked the wealthy trader Arthur Barrett into funding his first ship.

Rutherford couldn't believe it. Not only was Blackbeard from Bristol, but he also had business dealings with Barrett. Now he knew why Blackbeard had told him that they had something in common. Rutherford had just thought he was talking about the fact that both of them were from Bristol. He now realized how lucky it was that he had spilled the beans about Barrett and Johnstone to Blackbeard. In the back of his mind, he wondered if Blackbeard would have killed him if he had not told him the story of his falling-out with Barrett.

The last thing about the night that Rutherford would remember was falling down on the deck of the ship and not being able to get back up.

Rutherford awoke feeling disoriented and in extreme pain. He was only half-awake, and he felt horrible. Where was he? In a haze, he felt like someone had beaten him over the head with an iron rod. After trying hard to get his eyes to focus, his vision finally started to come around, and then everything that had occurred the previous day and night came flooding back to him.

For the first time, he realized he wasn't back home in bed in the back of Mr. Restin's store. He was on Blackbeard's pirate ship. Rutherford's head felt so bad he wished that Blackbeard had just killed him instead.

His brain felt like an overripe watermelon. His tongue was dry and swollen. And his throat – Dear God, Rutherford thought – it was closing up. Was it possible to die from this? If it was, he just wished it would happen quickly and end his misery.

He was curled up in a ball on the deck of the ship, and he had stopped trying to open his eyes because the sunlight felt like tiny glass shards piercing his pupils. In his pain and agony, Rutherford didn't hear anyone approach, and he was startled out of his tortured malaise when someone gave him a swift kick in his backside.

"I hope you had a good night's sleep because it is time to get to work. We have a two-week sail down to Nassau, and you have a lot to learn."

Rutherford couldn't see who had kicked him, but it sounded like Blackbeard. He rolled over and opened his eyes. Blackbeard was indeed standing there.

"This is Jack," Blackbeard said.

Rutherford's right eye must have been stuck shut, because he couldn't see the man Blackbeard was motioning towards.

"He is going to show you the ropes."

Rutherford turned but still couldn't see anyone.

What happened next, however, got his attention awfully quickly. A bucket of cold ocean water was dumped on his head. It momentarily took his breath away, and when he wiped his eyes, he finally saw Jack. He was standing over him, laughing hysterically with an empty bucket in his hands.

It was hard to tell how old he was – probably about Rutherford's age – but his face looked like he had already lived a hard life. Jack had wrinkles around the corners of his eyes and mouth, and one of his front teeth had been knocked out, probably during a fight. He was thickly built and had long, stringy hair that had been tied off with a ribbon.

Jack didn't bother to exchange pleasantries. The heartless bastard threw a mop down so hard that the handle hit Rutherford right in the center of his forehead, shooting an explosion of pain through his alcohol-swollen head. It hurt so bad that Rutherford thought for sure that sweet Jesus was calling him home.

Jack smirked at his obvious discomfort. "All right, you lazy pig. Get up and mop this whole deck till there isn't a speck of dirt anywhere. And when you've done that, mop it again."

Rutherford staggered to his feet and started mopping, despite the fact that his head felt like it could split open at any moment.

After an hour or two, he started to feel a little better. Actually, the mopping was probably the best cure for his hangover because the physical exertion helped sweat out some of the evils he had consumed the night before. Rutherford continued to mop, all the time marveling how, in the space of twenty-four hours, he had gone from being a clerk to a pirate on Blackbeard's ship.

After the ship had sailed a good distance from Charleston, Blackbeard reappeared on deck. "Tend the mast!" he barked. "We sail for Nassau."

Sailors jumped and scurried about. It looked like mass confusion, but as Rutherford would learn later, there was a method to the madness. He stopped his work and stood off to the side. He watched the activity until someone knocked him in the back of the head.

Rutherford didn't even have time to yelp before Jack grabbed him by the arm. "Come on and follow me," he ordered. "Time to make a sailor out of you."

His first day of sailing had already been a hard one, and it wasn't even noon yet. He followed Jack to the mast on the bow.

"All right, follow me up the mast. I'm going to show you how to tie off the sails."

They climbed up the tall mast with no problems. Rutherford kept his eye on Jack's foot right above him the whole way up. Jack scooted across the top beam of the mast and started to arrange the sails. Rutherford began to follow him across.

He had been looking skyward the entire time and didn't realize how high up they actually were, and that's when he made a big mistake: he glanced down, and it hit him. He completely froze with terror and fear. Rutherford had just discovered that he was terrified of heights.

The only support that was kept him from falling to the deck below was a thin rope underneath his feet and the mast that his hand was now clenching.

Rutherford stood locked in place. The deck seemed like it was a thousand feet below. His legs felt like warm jelly, and his heart was beating so fast he could feel the blood coursing through his veins.

"What the hell are you doing?" he heard Jack yell. "Get your ass over here so I can show you how to tie off these sails."

Rutherford heard him, but he couldn't make his legs move. He couldn't even breathe because his body was completely frozen in terror. He was frankly surprised he hadn't already passed out and fallen to the deck below.

The next thing Rutherford knew, Jack was standing next to him. He was paralyzed, but he could still hear. "John, listen to me," Jack said. "John, if you can hear me, which I know you can, shake your head."

Realizing that Jack was probably trying to help him, Rutherford managed to feebly move his head.

"All right, that's good. Now listen to me. There are only three outcomes in this situation. The first is you fall and die. The second, you stand here like a frozen crab, and after Blackbeard and his boys have their fun with you, you'll wish you had fallen and died. Or the third, you act like a man and snap out of it."

Jack stuck his face right into his. "I don't think you want to die. That is, at least not until after we have some fun in Nassau. So here is what we are going to do. First, I want you to look me in the eyes."

Rutherford somehow managed to turn his head a little. He couldn't believe the son of a bitch was smiling at him like this was all some big joke.

"That's good, John. You know you're not the first person to get the willies from being up this high. It even took me a little while to get used to it, but you're not going to have that luxury."

The smile never left Jack's face. "First thing you have to remember is to never look down, because that will always get you in trouble. Look at the mast, the horizon, or the sails. Look anywhere you want, but don't look down.

"Next, always have both of your feet and at least one hand secured onto something to keep your balance. Lastly, I want you to whistle your favorite song until you get back on the deck."

Rutherford couldn't understand why in the hell Jack wanted him to whistle, but he was desperate at this point, so he began whistling an old fishing song his dad had taught him.

Jack smiled. "Now I am going back to finish tying off those sails. I want you to watch how I do it, and when I come back, we're going to climb back down the mast together."

Rutherford did exactly as he was told. When the time came, he somehow managed to unlock his frozen body, and they climbed back down safely. He was so happy to be back on the deck that he felt like getting down on his hands and knees and kissing the dirty wooden planks.

"You can stop whistling now, you idiot!" Jack snapped. Jack's smile disappeared, and he pointed a finger at Rutherford's chest. "Every morning and every afternoon we're going to climb those masts until you are not afraid of doing it. The only way to overcome fear is by forcing yourself to do it. Very shortly you will have to do this by yourself, and do you remember what I told you up there about the three possible outcomes?"

Rutherford nodded.

"Well, about two years ago a new guy just like you froze up there. Do you know how they got him back down?"

"How?" Rutherford asked, not really wanting to hear the answer.

"Blackbeard and Israel Hands went to the stern and had a contest to see who could shoot him off. The dumb bastard never moved an inch the entire time."

"Who won?" Rutherford asked in jest, not happy at the thought of being used for human target practice.

"Blackbeard. His first shot hit him square in the stomach. The unlucky bastard was still alive, even after he fell to the deck."

Jack was telling him more than he wanted to know.

"His blood and guts oozed out of his stomach, and the guy kept asking us why we had shot him." Jack paused and looked around. "Blackbeard heard him and walked over, and I swear, I couldn't believe it myself, but he kicked him right in the stomach and yelled down at him that this ship is only for real men and real men are not afraid.

"After he kicked him one more time, he stormed off, and a couple of the guys picked him up and threw him overboard while he was still alive."

Jack looked at Rutherford with an expression of disgust. "Do you even know how to use a sword or shoot a gun?"

"I used to be pretty good at fencing when I was younger."

"Pretty good at fencing?" Jack repeated in a mocking tone. "That's make-believe. Fighting with swords is a whole different matter when your life depends on the outcome." Jack shook his head. "Looks like I am going to have to teach you how to fight, as well. We'll practice that, too."

"Hey, Jack," Rutherford called out as Jack started to walk away. "Thanks for helping me out up there."

Jack didn't turn around. He shook his head, waved an arm in the air, and climbed down into the hull. After Jack's story, Rutherford knew he would never freeze up on the mast again. He couldn't afford to.

XXII

It was a blustery night as Rutherford sat on the deck of Blackbeard's ship and hungrily ate his dinner of salted pork. For the first time that day, he realized that the other two ships that had helped blockade Charleston were not in sight and that Captain Bonnett was not on board anymore.

"Hey, Jack, what happened to Captain Bonnett and the other two ships?"

Jack swallowed a chunk of spit-fired chicken. "It took you this long to notice this?"

"Well, with my hangover and trying not to get killed the first day, I guess I wasn't paying much attention."

Jack threw the remains of his dinner overboard and sighed. "I guess it wouldn't hurt to tell you, since Blackbeard let you come with us in the first place. The other two ships and Captain Bonnett are headed back to North Carolina to receive pardons from Governor Eden."

Rutherford was confused. "You mean the governor can grant pardons to pirates, and they will be free from future prosecution?"

"Yes. As long as they don't commit any more crimes, they're safe from prosecution."

"Then why don't Blackbeard and the rest of you go to North Carolina and get pardons as well?"

Jack didn't answer the question immediately, but then he must have figured it was all right to let him in on the plan. "Blackbeard pulled a fast one," Jack answered. "He convinced the men on the *Revenge* and the *Adventure* to go to North Carolina and take their pardons. They believe that's where we are heading after we take a slight detour to the south."

"Slight detour? Aren't we going to Nassau?"

"Yes, we are, but they don't know it. Blackbeard wants to have one last adventure, and he doesn't want to split the profits with so many people. He has something up his sleeve. I'm not sure what it is, but it must be big.

"Anyway," Jack continued, "after this last trip down to Nassau, the plan is to head back to North Carolina and get our pardons while we still can."

The ship sailed uneventfully for the next couple of days, and every afternoon Jack spent hours teaching Rutherford how to fight with both a sword and a gun. It amazed Rutherford how much there was to learn, but Jack was an excellent and patient teacher, and Rutherford began to feel that he could hold his own with anyone. He quickly began to fit in and learn his new duties as a pirate aboard *Queen Anne's Revenge*. And he soon discovered that the notion that a pirate's days were filled with murder, mayhem, and robbery and that the nights were spent drinking, gambling, and sleeping with women was not entirely accurate.

Actually, there was an orderly routine and regimen that the pirates followed, most of which involved a lot of hard work in the blazing hot sun. The ship demanded constant attention. Something always needed to be washed, cleaned, or fixed. Everyone aboard worked hard, but to say that these men aboard were a bunch of hard-working, God-fearing teetotalers was not exactly accurate, either.

Blackbeard's men were not saints, but there was a discipline that Rutherford hadn't expected. Of course, that discipline came from the mutual desire to get rich plundering goods and the equally strong desire not to get killed in the process. And in order for the pirates to achieve those two equally important tasks, there had to be a certain level of cooperation and trust. An honor code among thieves, Rutherford mused.

Over the passing days, Jack and Rutherford slowly became friends, and they would watch the sun fall into the ocean after their work was done. It was during these peaceful nights that Rutherford learned a lot about Jack, Blackbeard, and a pirate's way of life.

After ten days of sailing, *Queen Anne's Revenge* passed the southernmost part of America called Florida. From his studies, Rutherford had been taught that Florida had been discovered by Ponce De Leon in the early 1500's and had been firmly in Spain's control ever since.

After questioning Jack about it, Rutherford learned that England had never made it a point to take Florida away from Spain, although they had tried a few times in the past. Francis Drake looted and burned Saint Augustine, but it seemed that England, at least for the time being, was content to settle more to the north.

Jack and Rutherford had finished eating their fish dinner and were relaxing at their familiar spot at the stern of the ship.

"So, Jack, where are you originally from?" Rutherford asked, realizing he didn't know much about his new friend's past.

Jack took a draw from his pipe and let the ocean breeze steal the smoke from his mouth. "I was born in London. But when I was a boy, my parents came to America for a better life."

"And did they find it?"

Jack thought for a second. "In London, both my father and mother worked sixteen hours a day in a filthy factory. We lived in a slum in the manufacturing district, and our one-room apartment was barely big enough for the three of us. As it was, I slept on the floor. Our condition was pretty ironic."

"Ironic?" Rutherford asked.

"What I mean is that people were born, lived, and died in those conditions because they never knew anything better. If my dad hadn't believed that there was a better life out there for us, then I would probably be working in some God-awful factory sixteen hours a day just so I could afford a piece of bread and a mug of beer for dinner."

"What happened to your parents when you came to America?"

"After we left London, we sailed aboard a ship destined for Virginia. What I remember most about the trip was how excited my father was. It was like he, all of a sudden, became a new person. He wasn't the beaten-down man I had grown up with. He had a spark in his eyes that I had never seen before. It was a tough journey across the Atlantic, but we arrived in Virginia in good health. Somehow my dad acquired some land outside of Roanoke, and we farmed and hunted in order to support ourselves. I'm not saying it was an easy life; we had our share of hardships. In fact, the first winter we almost starved to death. But somehow we managed to survive, and eventually we were living in a pretty comfortable fashion."

"Well, how in God's name did you wind up with Blackbeard?"

"We lived and worked on that farm for five years. It was the happiest time in my life. One day, my dad gave me some money and told me to go down to the town and get some supplies. I took my horse Charley."

Jack paused, smiling as he recalled the memory of the horse of his youth.

"I rode him into town, and when I returned home . . . " He paused again, and Rutherford could see a pained look in his eyes. "I found both Ma and Pa had been murdered."

"Murdered!" Jack had said it so casually that Rutherford was honestly shocked and wasn't quite sure what to say. "That's awful," he blurted out. "What happened?"

Jack refilled his pipe with fresh tobacco and then lit it. "There was a tribe of Indians called the Powhatans. One day, out of the blue, they went on a murderous rampage, killing any white person they came across, including women and children."

"What happened to the Indians after their attack?"

"A town militia was put together, and they hunted the Powhatans down. Most were killed, and I guess the survivors left for good."

"Well, at least they paid for what they did," Rutherford said, thinking Jack must have hated those Indians.

Jack didn't even look at him. He continued to stare out at the ocean. "I hated those Indians and what they did for a long time, and my hatred almost destroyed me. Night and day, it was all I could think about. Why would they do that to innocent people? My parents never did any harm to them. Later I learned the reasons why the Powhatans went on their murderous rampage."

"Why?"

"The Powhatan Indians were a large coastal tribe that had lived in the Virginia area for as long as people had lived in England. The tribe lived in relative peace because the land and ocean provided them with everything they needed to survive. They loved and respected the land and nature around them. One day a boat came with settlers from England. They settled in Jamestown, and at that time the Powhatan tribe numbered fifteen thousand. At first the Indians trusted and even helped the settlers. Have you ever heard the story of Pocahontas?" Jack asked.

Rutherford nodded.

"Pocahontas was a member of the Powhatan tribe. If it hadn't been for her and her tribe, those settlers would have never made it through the first winter. At first the English tolerated the Indians because they had no choice. They needed the Indians to help them survive. Over the years, more and more ships came, and as the English population grew and their dependence on the Powhatans lessened, so did their tolerance. The tribe didn't understand the rules of the English. They didn't understand about land ownership and imaginary boundaries dividing one piece of land from another.

"The settlers got together and started complaining about the Indians hunting on their property. Eventually they told the Powhatans that they would have to leave."

"And did they?" Rutherford inquired.

Jack shook his head. "Of course not. They didn't understand why they should be the ones to leave. The tribe stayed and continued to live the way they had for countless generations. That is until one day when a large group of the settlers banded together and attacked one of the tribe's villages early one morning. They slaughtered men, women, and children. Anyone that crossed their path was cut down.

"After the massacre, the Powhatans numbered less than two thousand. It took the English only a few years to wipe out an entire civilization that had been around for thousands of years. In one last-ditch effort to reclaim their stolen lands, the Powhatans regrouped and attacked every white man in sight. Unfortunately, my parents happened to be at the wrong place at the wrong time."

"How did you find all this out?"

"From a surprising source," Jack replied. "Blackbeard."

He looked around before continuing. "When we first got to know each other, I was a very bitter and angry person. Blackbeard, in his usual straightforwardness, asked what in the hell was wrong with me. I told him my story, and in typical fashion he started laughing at me. I couldn't understand why he would be laughing about my parents' death, and it was all I could do not to take a swing at him.

"But he explained that if I was going to blame anyone, I should blame England. After years of hating the Indians, I came to the realization that I could hate their act but I couldn't blame the Powhatans for what they did. They were just trying to protect what was theirs. They would have shared the land, but the greed of the English settlers knew no boundaries."

"Damn, that's awful about your parents. I guess it would have been better if they stayed in London after all, huh?"

"Damn, you are pretty stupid, aren't you?" Jack cursed. "Have you not listened to a word I have said? For five years my parents were the happiest they had ever been! Just to be alive does not mean you are living, John. I know if my parents had a choice between having those five years on their farm or being slaves back in London, they would do it all over again."

Jack got up and left without saying another word.

Rutherford sat there for quite some time watching the ship skim the calm ocean surface.

The closer the ship got to Nassau, the more restless and excited the crew seemed to get. Only one more day of sailing remained, and the anticipation had grown to a fever pitch.

Blackbeard gathered the crew together to inform them of his plan. "Gentlemen, tomorrow we land in Nassau." His words generated a lot of whooping and hollering from the crew. Blackbeard raised his hand and waited for the noise to die down.

"I know a lot of you have been wondering why we're heading back to these waters. I'm sorry I haven't been able to give you the details. But I promise, if you can bear with me a little longer, I guarantee you will not be disappointed."

Rutherford guessed the crew liked what they heard because there were shouts of approval. The only consistent thing he had learned about Blackbeard's crew was that they would have followed him straight to hell if he had told them it was a good idea.

XXIII

The next morning, *Queen Anne's Revenge* sailed into Nassau, and the excitement of the crew had taken hold of Rutherford as well. He couldn't believe the beauty of the Caribbean waters. He had never seen anything like it. The shallow waters alternated between shades of blue, green, and aqua. He didn't even know if some of the colors he saw had names.

Like both Charleston and Bristol, Nassau was bustling with shipping activity. Vessels of all different sizes, shapes, and nationalities were anchored in its port.

Nassau was technically under British rule, but the little island actually acted more like a free trade zone. Everyone, regardless of nationality, had one goal in mind, and that was to make money. And of course that took precedence over minor details like country loyalty.

Blackbeard gave the order to drop anchor, and he gathered the men together. He was dressed in his finest outfit. He wore a long black overcoat over a fine white silk shirt. Two pistols were tucked into the front sides of his black trousers, and his cutlass shined from a recent cleaning. His long black boots had been freshly polished, and even his black mustache was trimmed and waxed. Blackbeard definitely commanded respect.

Having spent the last few weeks with the notorious pirate, Rutherford could now understand how he was able to recruit so many men to blindly follow him. He was a born leader, with a magnetic personality that cast a spell over anyone he came in contact with. He led men as if it was somehow predetermined that he was going to lead and all others were going to follow – all without question.

Blackbeard studied his band of men. "Gentlemen, we are only going to be in port for two or three days, and then we sail off to find the glory and riches that I have promised."

A loud cheer went up, and Blackbeard waved his arms. "I know we have been at sea for a long time, and you have not had a proper rest in months. So I want us to have a little fun before we set sail on our last journey together, and I think this should help us achieve that goal."

Blackbeard reached inside his jacket, pulled out a sack of gold coins, and started to hand them out to the crew. The unexpected gift brought an even louder cheer as the men realized how much liquor and women they could now afford.

The crew anchored the ship in the harbor and took turns rowing into port. Rutherford, Jack, and Blackbeard were the last group to leave the ship, and as they approached the docks, people took notice.

Rutherford was sitting next to Jack and asked quietly, "Does everyone here know who Blackbeard is?"

"Of course they know who Blackbeard is, you idiot," Jack said.

"Don't the authorities mind?"

"The authorities?" Jack said, laughing. "Everyone here is a pirate or at least engaged in some type of scheme. Blackbeard is a very respected man here."

Jack smirked at Rutherford's ignorance and gave him a painful jab in the ribs.

After reaching the docks, the crew split up from Blackbeard, who left to tend to some business matters.

The group of pirates explored the city, taking in its sights and sounds. Later that afternoon, they went to a tavern called, appropriately enough, **The Pirate's Den**. There was one large table left, and they sat down.

"Why does everyone call you Fat Stan?" Rutherford asked, because the man didn't have an ounce of fat on him.

His question brought a whale of laughter from everyone at the table.

"I'll tell you how he got that name!" Jack yelled from across the table. "Fat Stan has what you would call unnatural urges."

"They're natural enough to me," Fat Stan blurted out in his own defense.

"You see," Jack went on, trying his best not to laugh, "Fat Stan only likes woman that weigh at least three times more than he does."

"That's because there is more to love," replied Fat Stan.

"Anyway," Jack continued, "he got his name in Philadelphia a few years back. We had all gone out drinking when Stan, as he was known at that time, started soliciting the fattest lady I had ever seen. I mean, she was as big as a blue whale.

"One thing led to another, and the two of them ended up in bed together. Well, the next morning Stan comes back to the ship, all doubled over and moaning in agony.

We asked him what was wrong, and do you know what he told us?"

Rutherford shook his head while the others, except for Fat Stan, were in tears because they were laughing so hard.

"Well, the lady was so fat the only way they could consummate their union was for her to get on top. At the moment of her ecstasy, she collapsed onto Stan and broke three of his ribs. From that moment on, he was known simply as Fat Stan."

At that point everyone, including Fat Stan, was in hysterics. Beer was followed by rum, which was followed by more beer. The pirates were having a grand time telling stories and listening to each other's lies. The day had run into night, and Rutherford had completely lost any sense of time. All he knew was it had to be getting late, because more and more people began passing out from too much alcohol. The inebriated patrons would fall either on the floor or collapse in their chairs. And if an unlucky sod collapsed in an inconvenient place, a group of men would carry him out of the bar and throw him out on the street.

Rutherford was pretty drunk himself when he felt a hand grab his shoulder and spin him around. He thought it was one of the crewmembers playing around with him, but much to his dismay, he received the shock of his life.

"Well, well, look what we have here. I thought that was you."

Rutherford couldn't believe who was standing in front of him. It was Samuel Johnstone. His face brought back memories of a time and place he had almost succeeded in forgetting. What in the hell was he doing here?

Rutherford stared up at him with his mouth wide open.

"So, what have you been doing with yourself, Mr. Rutherford?" Johnstone asked sarcastically.

Rutherford was too shocked by his sudden presence to answer.

"I'll have you know," Johnstone continued, "we were a little disappointed that you quit your position and left without informing us. As a matter of fact, I spent two days looking for you." He smiled broadly. "I was going to try to persuade you to come back to work for the company."

Rutherford's blood began to boil. "Oh, I'm sure you and Barrett would have welcomed me back with open arms, just like you did with Allen Lawrence."

Johnstone laughed. "No, I can't fool you, Rutherford. You're right: I was going to kill you. You know, I just missed you at the dock in Bristol. If your ship had left just a little bit later, well, let's just say if that had been the case, we wouldn't be having this conversation now. But anyway, here we are, so why don't we step outside and finish this like gentlemen?"

Rutherford had no doubt that in a hand-to-hand fight Johnstone would kill him. But what choice did he have?

Rutherford stood up just as Blackbeard walked into the front of the bar. The bar quieted down when the drunken patrons realized who had just entered. Everyone wanted a glimpse of the famous pirate. Johnstone turned to see why the bar had suddenly quieted down.

Blackbeard stopped dead in his tracks when he saw Johnstone. Slowly, a smirk came across his face as he strolled over to the table. "My, my, if it isn't good old Samuel Johnstone," Blackbeard said in a condescending voice. "Barrett must have sent his little puppy dog out on another errand."

Rutherford saw Johnstone's body tense. "Teach, I told Barrett from the beginning that he was making a mistake by trusting you, but we both know how unreasonable the old man can be."

Johnstone looked at Rutherford and then back at Blackbeard. "Anyway, I don't care that you swindled Barrett. My quarrel is not with you. I'm just going to step outside with this gentlemen, and you can carry on with your business."

Blackbeard peered around Johnstone and saw he was talking about Rutherford. Blackbeard pointed. "You have a quarrel with this man?"

"Yes, I do, but it is nothing to concern you, so we will just be on our way. Come on, Mr. Rutherford. Let's step outside."

Rutherford had completely sobered up with the realization that he was going to have to fight Johnstone and would probably get killed in the process. He slowly started to leave when Blackbeard violently grabbed Johnstone by the arm.

"Listen here, you little rat bastard!" Blackbeard sneered at Johnstone. "This man is with me. If you have a problem with him, then you have a problem with me. You will have to fight me first. And I tell you what, Johnstone, I would love for you to try so I could have the pleasure of sending your head back to Barrett."

Johnstone looked shocked and for once seemed to be at a loss for words. He stood there, as if he wasn't sure what to do next. It had never occurred to him that Rutherford was with Blackbeard.

Blackbeard didn't wait for Johnstone to gather his wits. "I'm going to give you ten seconds to get your ass out of this bar, and if you don't, I will cut your head off right here."

Before Rutherford had even blinked, Blackbeard had drawn his cutlass and had it pressed against Johnstone's neck. Johnstone might have been a cold-blooded murderer, but he wasn't stupid. Without looking at Rutherford, he turned around and left the bar.

So many emotions poured through Rutherford, he wasn't quite sure what he felt.

Blackbeard turned and winked. "Listen, Rutherford," he announced loud enough so that the other men could hear. "Don't be angry with me. I know you wanted to go outside and kill the bastard, but I have a personal issue with him that I need to settle later."

Blackbeard then whirled towards the bar and shouted to the barkeep, "Don't just stand there, you lazy pig! Bring us another round! We're thirsty!"

After a new round was brought, Rutherford drank half of his beer in one swig. He realized that Blackbeard had not only saved his life but had also preserved his honor in front of the other men. He didn't know if that was what Blackbeard had intended, but it didn't really matter. Rutherford knew from that moment on he would be loyal to him no matter what.

The rowdy pirates continued their drinkathon until Blackbeard finally decided to let them in on his plans. The men gathered around Blackbeard as he began to explain his plan.

"A merchant ship is due to arrive in San Salvador in the next couple of days. As you are well aware, France and England have been battling for years over territories in the Caribbean, and recently England has gained the upper hand." Blackbeard gave a coy smile. "I have learned from my sources that France, in a desperate attempt to level the playing field, has sent a merchant ship to Salvador with thousands of pounds of gold bars and coins aboard."

Israel interrupted Blackbeard. "But why would France send so much money on an unprotected merchant ship with no guard whatsoever?"

"Because no one is going to think twice about a single merchant ship coming into port. The French are trying to maintain an element of surprise. They don't want the British government to know what they are up to."

Blackbeard drank the rest of his rum and motioned for a refill before continuing. "The French intend to use the money to buy vessels and arms in an attempt to reinstate their dominance in the region. The reason for their deception is that if England were to get wind of it, the British would have the entire fleet out searching for this ship to see that it never arrived. So the French are taking a calculated gamble. They're trying to sneak it in, right under everyone's noses."

"It still seems like a stupid plan to me," Israel replied.

"What can I say?" Blackbeard replied. "They're French. But this is the best part of it." He turned and looked directly at Rutherford. "You, especially, are going to like this, Rutherford," he said, winking. "The ship that the gold is on is owned by Barrett."

"Owned by Barrett!" Rutherford called out in shock.

"That's right."

"But why would Barrett be escorting gold for the French, especially to be used to finance war operations against England?" Rutherford asked.

"Very simple: the English won't attack a ship flying the Union Jack, and the French know to let the ship pass without interference. And for escorting the gold for the French, Barrett and Johnstone get a third of it."

"That greedy bastard is also a traitor!" Rutherford interjected.

"Traitor is a loose word that doesn't really apply to this part of the world," Israel responded.

Rutherford supposed he was right, but he couldn't believe how far Barrett would go to build his trading empire. The thought of stealing money from Barrett was a delightful proposition, and it overshadowed any sense of danger that Johnstone had posed.

"That's why Johnstone is in this area," Blackbeard commented. "He's going to meet the ship and take the gold back to England." He turned to Rutherford and flashed a devilish grin. "I bet you can't wait to have the pleasure of finally screwing Barrett."

Rutherford smiled back. Blackbeard was right: he couldn't wait.

Blackbeard laid out the plans for the attack. It seemed like a pretty straightforward plan, and he didn't expect much resistance from the ship. The now intoxicated crew finished the last round of drinks and staggered back to the ship to sleep off their excesses.

XXIV

After two more days of drinking and debauchery, Blackbeard's crew sailed out of Nassau with one objective: to seize Barrett's ship and steal the fortune in gold. Rutherford was more than a little nervous about his first battle as a pirate, although from what Jack told him, it would be unlikely they would see much resistance.

Queen Anne's Revenge sailed the short journey over to San Salvador and patiently waited for the arrival of the disguised French ship. For three days they sailed in a circle about three miles offshore, and on the fourth day the spotter up in the crow's-nest saw a ship approaching far off in the distance. It was about six miles away and sailing straight for them.

Blackbeard grabbed his scope and aimed it at the approaching ship.

"This is it!" he yelled in a calm but excited voice. "Get your weapons and gear together."

Rutherford was handed two single-shot pistols and a sword. Hopefully his fencing expertise from school and his intense lessons from Jack would pay off. He stuck the guns in the front of his pants and carried the sword. He wanted his share of the loot as badly as everyone else, but he hoped he didn't have to fight anyone for it.

Blackbeard gave the order to sail directly at the approaching ship. Stalking the deck like a caged lion, the man was a sight to behold. He had two pistols tucked into the front of his pants, and four more were attached to a bandoleer that he wore over his coat. Two large knives dangled from his side, and he carried a large cutlass in his right hand.

Besides the arsenal of weapons, Blackbeard lit slow-burning matches and stuck them in his hair. With all the weapons, his all-black outfit, and the dark black smoke curling off his head, the man looked like the devil himself.

Rutherford stood next to Jack and watched the approaching ship with growing trepidation. He could feel knots forming in his stomach. He didn't have the foggiest idea of what to do, so he decided to just follow Jack and try to stay out of harm's way.

"Something's wrong," he heard Jack say to no one in particular.

"What do you mean?" Rutherford asked nervously.

"That ship has to know there are a lot of pirates in these waters. They've seen us approaching them, yet they haven't made any moves to avoid us."

"Maybe they think we are just another merchant ship."

"No, if you had that much gold aboard and it was largely unprotected, the captain would play it safe. He would at least tack to a different course to see if we followed."

"What do you think it means?" Rutherford asked.

Jack continued to stare at the rapidly approaching ship. "I think it means we may be in for a much harder fight for that gold than we first thought. Obviously, the captain believes he can fight off any attack. Only that can explain why they have continued to sail directly towards us."

The knots grew tighter in Rutherford's stomach, and he could feel his heart doing flips, it was beating so fast. He hoped Jack was wrong, but for some unexplained reason he knew he wasn't. The pirates aboard *Queen Anne's Revenge* were about to have a battle on their hands.

The two ships slowly approached one another, and Blackbeard shouted the order to tack directly into the other ship. Quicker than Rutherford thought was possible, *Queen Anne's Revenge* headed directly for Barrett's ship.

There was no way the two ships could avoid each other now, and Rutherford braced for the collision. The two ships slammed into one another on their starboard side, and all hell broke loose.

A group of pirates led by Israel Hands hurled grappling irons at Barrett's ship, and they quickly climbed over to the other deck. But as soon as they reached the other side, a large group of French sailors stormed out of the galley with their pistols blazing. A hail of bullets sailed through the air, and the French sailors kept streaming up from below deck, where evidently they had been waiting to ambush them.

The unexpected hail of gunfire cut down almost the entire initial assault. Rutherford knew that Blackbeard hadn't expected this, but he also knew that Blackbeard wasn't going to be denied his gold, or at least they were going to die trying to get it.

Blackbeard climbed up onto the railing and yelled with a mighty roar, "All men of *Queen Anne's Revenge*, attack!"

Blackbeard led the way. Everyone was whipped into a murderous frenzy, and the entire crew charged the French sailors, who were reloading their pistols.

As was his plan, Rutherford stayed right with Jack, and they were the last two to jump over to the French ship. Mass confusion now reigned aboard Barrett's ship. Pistols had given way to knives and swords, and the shooting battle had turned into bloody hand-to-hand combat. Occasionally, Rutherford heard a random shot, but the fighting was too close and confusing for anyone to use their pistols effectively.

As Rutherford jumped across, he landed on top of a blood-soaked body. He couldn't tell whom the body belonged to because a bullet had destroyed the center of its face. Rutherford didn't know what Jack's plan was, but his strategy was to stay alive, and he especially hoped to avoid any form of combat.

However, it quickly became evident that Rutherford's plan was not going to work. He was going to have to fight if he was going to have any chance to live through the battle. The events were happening so fast that his body was reacting to instincts that Rutherford didn't even know he possessed.

Since he and Jack were the last over to Barrett's ship, all the fighting was in front of them, and he was pressed up against the railing. The close-quarter combat had spread out along the entire deck, and he reluctantly followed Jack down the railing to the stern of the ship.

Rutherford hadn't moved more than five feet when, out of the corner of his eye, he caught a glimpse of a Frenchman coming straight at him with his sword raised. It was time for him to join the fight. The sailor took a big swipe at Rutherford's midsection, but he misjudged the distance between them and missed.

Rutherford's old fencing lessons came back to him, and with a quick thrust he jabbed his sword forward, aiming directly at the sailor's midsection. The Frenchman easily deflected his advance. He stepped back and grinned while uttering something in French.

Rutherford didn't understand the man's words, but he understood the meaning. The French sailor knew he was fighting a novice. He was coming to kill Rutherford, and he didn't think he would have much of a problem doing so.

As quick as lightning, the Frenchie faked an advance and then swung his sword at Rutherford's neck in one fluid motion. Rutherford ducked and felt the blade of the sword pass right over the top of his head.

Rutherford gripped the handle of his sword as hard as he could and rammed it with all his might upward towards the Frenchman's ribcage. The steel blade drove straight through him with almost no resistance. As their bodies came together, they stood face to face, only inches apart.

The Frenchman's face registered a look of surprise and then shock, followed by immense pain. Blood trickled from the corner of his mouth, and Rutherford drew back on his sword. It made a sickening noise as he pulled it out. The entire blade was covered with thick blood and fragments of ribs, cartilage, and organs.

The Frenchman stood there for a moment with a stunned, uncomprehending look on his face, and then his eyes rolled back in his head. He fell backwards, dead before his body even hit the deck. For a long time afterwards, Rutherford would think about that look he saw in the Frenchman's eyes.

The French sailors had gained an initial advantage with their surprise attack, but the battle was slowly turning in Blackbeard's favor. Blackbeard had a lot to do with that. Rutherford watched him kill at least half a dozen men. He fought with a cocked pistol in one hand and his huge cutlass in the other. After he fired his pistol, he would toss it away and grab a loaded one from his bandoleer, all the while slashing anything that moved with his huge cutlass.

The ebb of the battle continued to push Rutherford along the rail towards the very back of the stern. Along the way, he engaged in a few light skirmishes that mostly involved slashing his sword in defense and moving on. Luckily, after his initial confrontation, he was able to avoid any prolonged fights.

The smell in the air was pungent. Gunpowder, blood, sweat, fear, and death. The deck of the ship was soaked in blood, and it had become a slippery mess. Rutherford almost fell a couple of times, but luckily he was able to regain his balance in time. He knew a fall in a battle of this nature would surely lead to a quick and painful death.

The battle cleared somewhat in front of Rutherford, and he saw that Fat Stan had become cornered by two French sailors, who were trying to wear him down before closing in for the fatal blow. Despite his ferocious defense, Fat Stan wouldn't be able to hold them off much longer. Without considering the ramifications of his actions, Rutherford, with his sword raised, ran over to where they had cornered Fat Stan. He hoped to kill at least one of them by surprise.

The nearest Frenchman must have sensed he was coming because he whirled around just in time to avoid Rutherford's blade. The Frenchie countered with a swipe that cut Rutherford's left forearm.

Rutherford cried out. He had been cut, but he didn't know the extent of the wound. With his adrenaline flowing, he really didn't feel any pain, only a stinging sensation and a desire to not end up like the Frenchie he had just killed. Regardless, he didn't have time to feel pain; he was locked in a struggle for survival. The French sailor seemed to take his fighting abilities more seriously than the last, and they alternated attacks, each trying to find the other's weakness. Every attack was repelled with a counterattack, and neither could find an advantage.

Rutherford knew his life was on the line, but he felt an immense urge to scream out, "All right! Enough! Let's call it a draw and go home." But he knew he couldn't, so the two battled on.

Rutherford could feel his strength starting to drain. The Frenchie was wearing him down, and he had gained the offensive. Gradually, he had pushed Rutherford backwards until he had no more room left to retreat.

Rutherford was utterly exhausted, but he knew he had to try to gain a little distance between them so he could at least maneuver some. Somehow, he mustered a last batch of reserve energy and made a series of offensive attacks that pushed his combatant back just enough so he could swing around to his left side. However, as he swung around, Rutherford made a near-fatal mistake.

He had kept his eyes on the Frenchman and failed to see a dead sailor to the side of him. As he moved, he tripped over the body and ended up flat on his back staring straight up at the Frenchman, who was standing over him with his sword raised.

Rutherford couldn't believe this was it; his life was about to be over. He closed his eyes, not wanting to see the deathblow he was about to receive. He was amazed at how many thoughts were able to pass through his mind in those few short seconds. He saw his parents, Bristol, Mr. Livingston, Anne, Mr. Restin, and Sally – all the people and places that had been important to him. He didn't want to die, but in that briefest of moments, he had accepted his fate.

He was prepared to meet his Maker when a loud pistol-shot rang out from nearby. Then a body fell across his chest with a loud thud. Rutherford let out a sigh of relief. Someone had shot his executioner.

He slowly opened his eyes to see Blackbeard standing over him with a huge grin on his face.

"Rutherford, that's the second time in one week that I've saved your life. You'd better not forget it."

Blackbeard rolled the dead Frenchman off of him, grabbed his good arm, and hauled him straight up like he was a rag doll. Rutherford was dazed, but he was alive.

The battle for control of the ship was almost over. Of the forty or so French sailors, all were dead, except for a handful that had thrown down their weapons and surrendered when it had become obvious they had no chance.

Blackbeard had won, but the battle had taken its toll. Thirteen of Blackbeard's pirates were dead, and just about everyone had some sort of injury. Everyone, that is, except Blackbeard. He didn't even have so much as a scratch on him. Rutherford truly wondered if the man was indestructible.

Blackbeard put his arm around Rutherford. "Let's go see what these smelly Frogs have left for us."

He led Rutherford towards the front of the ship, stepping over dead bodies along the way, some of which had been Rutherford's friends not an hour ago. The dead bodies didn't seem to faze Blackbeard in the slightest, and Rutherford followed him, trying not to look down at the faces.

Thank God. He spotted Jack. Except for a black eye and some scratches, he had emerged relatively unscathed.

Most of Rutherford's adrenaline had dissipated, and his arm was starting to hurt like hell. It was a deep cut, but it would heal. He wrapped a handkerchief around the wound as Jack approached with a big grin on his face.

"Well, I see you survived your first battle," he said. "Good thing I taught you everything I know about fighting."

Rutherford smiled, more so from relief than anything else. They followed Blackbeard as he descended into the hold of the ship, and it didn't take them long to find what they had risked their lives for. Right in front of their eyes, hundreds of huge oak trunks were stacked one atop another. The trunks stretched the entire length of the ship.

"Rutherford!" Blackbeard called out. "You and Jack pull one of those trunks down. Let's have a look."

The damn trunk was so heavy it took a few more men to help them get it down.

Blackbeard pushed a handful of the greedy pirates out of the way and stood next to Rutherford and Jack. "Well, don't just stand there," he said impatiently. "Open the damn thing up."

Rutherford felt every eye upon him in anticipation. He undid the latch on the trunk and slowly opened the lid, praying that the contents were what Blackbeard had expected.

A stunned silence took hold of the crew as everyone fought to gain his breath. Even in the dark hull of the ship, the gold shined like a thousands suns. There must have been a fortune in gold coins just in this one trunk alone. No one uttered a word.

The silence didn't last long. A collective roar went out, and grown men started jumping up and down like school kids, hugging and dancing with each other.

After a few minutes of unadulterated joy, Blackbeard broke up the victory dance, partly because there was still a lot of work to do. "Settle down, you bunch of girls," he jokingly called out. "There will be time for celebrating later. Let's get these trunks out of here and over to *Queen Anne's Revenge.*"

Over the next two hours, the pirates transferred the trunks of gold from Barrett's ship to *Queen Anne's Revenge.* It was backbreaking work, but no one was complaining. Rutherford took special joy in knowing that Barrett and Johnstone were finally getting a taste of their own medicine.

After they had completed the transfer of the gold, there was still the question of what Blackbeard was going to do with the French prisoners. The French sailors stood together in a tight circle, none of them so much as moving an inch. Of course, they had no choice in the matter because they had pistols aimed at their heads. Rutherford didn't know what Blackbeard was going to do with them, but he hoped that he had seen enough bloodshed for one day.

Blackbeard walked over to the prisoners. "Any of you dirty Frogs speak English?"

With no hesitation or fear, a Frenchman from the back pushed to the front and answered in a heavy accent, "Yes."

He was middle-aged and had a stout body, along with the biggest pair of hands Rutherford had ever seen. Rutherford was glad their paths hadn't crossed during the battle.

Blackbeard looked him up and down. "What's your name?"

"Jacques Boulier."

"Well, Jacques, if you had just surrendered in the first place, no blood would have been shed today."

Jacques thought about Blackbeard's statement, and he didn't seem the least bit afraid or intimidated. The stout Frenchman replied while looking Blackbeard directly in the eyes, "Our orders were to protect the gold from pirates."

"Well, you didn't do a good job of following those orders, did ya?" replied Blackbeard as a howl of laughter went up. "Well, Jacques, let me ask you a question," Blackbeard continued. "What should I do with you and your friends now?"

Jacques looked surprised by the question. He appeared to be judging his words carefully, because what he said next would probably mean the difference between life and death for him and his friends.

"Sir, as you can see, we are unarmed, and we presently do not pose a threat to you," he responded in halted English. "You have acquired what you set out to possess. If you release us, I can only promise you one thing."

Rutherford thought for sure he was going to beg for their lives to be spared, but instead the bold Frenchman surprised him.

"If I ever get the chance to do battle with you again," the sailor said, "I would love to fight you one to one."

Rutherford couldn't believe what the Frenchman had said. The fool had actually threatened Blackbeard. Did he not realize he had just signed not only his own death warrant but those of his friends as well?

Rutherford was shocked further when Blackbeard laughed out loud and then walked over to the Frenchman and threw his arm around his shoulders. "I'm sure you would, Jacques," Blackbeard replied. "And perhaps someday you'll get the chance. I am going to let you live because I want you to give a message to someone."

Blackbeard glanced at Rutherford and then back at the Frenchman. "Be sure to tell Samuel Johnstone that John Rutherford and Edward Teach very much appreciate their gold, and we'll be thinking of them as we spend it on liquor and women."

Blackbeard removed his arm from the sailor's shoulder and called out to his men, "We sail now! Let them go!"

They set the Frenchmen adrift in a rowboat. Then they set Barrett's ship on fire, just out of spite, and waited for it to sink.

Rutherford stood next to Blackbeard as they happily watched the ship sink into the ocean. Rutherford turned and asked, "What would you have done if the Frenchman had begged for mercy instead of showing defiance?"

Blackbeard didn't answer his question directly but responded instead, "A man never has to fear a brave, honest man because he will fight you face to face.

Only cowards will stab you in the back, and those are the ones you have to fear the most."

Blackbeard turned and gave the orders to set sail for the Carolinas. Their destination: Ocracoke Inlet, North Carolina.

XXV

Johnstone threw the plate of food across the room in utter disgust after Jacques Boulier gave him the news regarding the gold. "Blackbeard!" Johnstone cursed. "What's wrong with you bloody cowards?" he yelled at the Frenchman. "I should have known not to trust the French to protect anything."

Jacques looked at Johnstone with an angry sneer. "You should have put more men aboard, and you'd best not question my honor again."

Johnstone couldn't believe it. He had had it all worked out. After the French had given him his split of the gold, he was going to retire in luxury to Jamaica and spend his days drinking rum and frolicking with the young island girls.

Blackbeard and Rutherford had put an end to that dream, at least for now. Johnstone's hatred of the two men had reached a level that he had never felt before. The money was important, but not as important as his desire for revenge and to personally see both men die.

"Any idea where they're headed?" Johnstone asked in a more civil tone.

"I overheard the crew talking about getting fresh provisions back in Nassau before sailing to a place called Ocracoke Inlet."

North Carolina, Johnstone thought after regaining some of his composure. The thought of killing both Blackbeard and Rutherford calmed him down further.

"Jacques," he said, "get the sloop and men ready. We're sailing first thing tomorrow morning."

Jacques nodded and left to make the arrangements.

Johnstone knew that Blackbeard only had a day's head start, plus he had to stop in Nassau for provisions. In the much faster sloop, he would be able to get to Virginia and back to Ocracoke Inlet about the same time Blackbeard would arrive. Then he could exact his revenge.

Williamsburg, Virginia

Johnstone had pushed the crew of the small sloop to the limit and had arrived in Williamsburg in record time. He knew that Blackbeard would be taking his time getting back to North Carolina, so he still had plenty of time in which to lay his trap. He walked into Governor Spotswood's office and took a seat.

Alexander Spotswood was in his first term as regent's governor of Virginia, and Johnstone knew things were not going well for him at all. He had barely managed to get himself appointed to the position, despite bribing and making outlandish promises to everyone who had anything remotely to do with the appointment.

Even with all his promises and bribes, it finally took Arthur Barrett's influence to secure the post for him. And needless to say, Spotswood had entered office with a lot of enemies waiting to seize on any mistake he might make. Spotswood owed a lot of promises and money, and he was having a hard time delivering.

Johnstone had waited for ten minutes when he stood up and walked over to Spotswood's office door.

"Excuse me, sir," his secretary timidly called out. "He will be with your shortly. He's very busy."

"I don't give a damn!" Johnstone said as he pushed open the door.

Spotswood looked up. "What in the hell do you think you are doing?" he called out angrily.

Johnstone walked into the office and threw his hat on a chair. "My name is Samuel Johnstone, from Barrett Trading."

Spotswood's demeanor quickly changed. "Oh, of course, Mr. Johnstone," he replied in a more accommodating tone. "Have a seat. I didn't know it was you, or I certainly wouldn't have kept you waiting."

"Certainly not," Johnstone replied icily.

Spotswood motioned to his secretary, who was standing at the door. "It's all right. You can shut the door."

She nodded and followed his instructions.

Johnstone sat down and watched as Governor Spotswood nervously played with a corncob pipe.

"What can I do for you, Mr. Johnstone?"

"I need your help. I need to borrow a warship."

Spotswood laughed. "A warship – that's a good one."

"I'm not joking."

Spotswood looked confused. "How can I possibly get you a warship?"

"The *Pearl* is already anchored in your harbor. I just need you to sign the proper documents giving me control of it for a few days."

"The British warship captained by Lieutenant Maynard?" Spotswood asked incredulously.

"That is correct."

"But Maynard would never agree to such a thing," Spotswood stammered. "Not to mention the British Government. I want to help, but–"

Before Spotswood could finish, a knock came from the office door. "Governor," his secretary called to him. "Lieutenant Maynard is here to see you."

Spotswood looked at Johnstone with confusion. "Send him in," he responded.

The door opened, and the British lieutenant walked stiffly into the office. He was well over six feet tall and had wide shoulders and a barrel chest. His face appeared to be chiseled directly from granite, and his naval uniform was clean and crisp.

Johnstone pointed to Spotswood. "Lieutenant Maynard, this is Governor Spotswood."

The two shook hands, and Maynard sat down next to Johnstone.

"You two know each other, I take it," Spotswood surmised.

"We go back," responded Johnstone.

"Well, what can I do for you, then?" asked Spotswood.

"We need you to sign an executive order authorizing the *Pearl* and Lieutenant Maynard to attack another ship in North Carolina waters."

"What ship?"

"Blackbeard's."

"What makes you think I have the authority to do that?" Spotswood asked.

"Because you're governor and, as governor, you have the authority to commandeer other nations' vessels to protect your state. Don't worry, Lieutenant Maynard is going to fully cooperate."

"What makes you think Blackbeard is back in the Carolinas?" Spotswood asked.

Maynard spoke for the first time in a crisp military fashion. "After holding Charleston hostage, Blackbeard ditched that fool Stede Bonnett and his other two ships. He then took about forty men and sailed to Nassau for what I believe was one last plunder before returning to Carolina to take advantage of King George's offer of a pardon."

Spotswood sat back in his huge black leather chair.

Johnstone knew Spotswood despised the governor of Carolina, because for years pirates had been using Carolina as a base to attack vessels, especially ones from Virginia.

"Listen, Spotswood, you have a chance to kill two birds with one stone. First, by killing Blackbeard you'll be doing Arthur Barrett an enormous favor, one that he would greatly appreciate. Secondly, it would show Governor Eden that you are not a man to be taken lightly."

Spotswood put down his pipe. "Why is it so important to you to kill Blackbeard?"

A typical politician, Johnstone thought. He knew financial arrangements were eventually going to be brought up.

"That doesn't concern you. But I would be willing to offer you a rather nice payment in gold for the necessary authorization."

Spotswood put down his pipe and stood up. "Of course I would be willing to help."

Lieutenant Maynard and Johnstone immediately departed Williamsburg for North Carolina. Johnstone was more than confident in Lieutenant Maynard's ability to make good on his promise to destroy Blackbeard. His ship, The *Pearl*, was one of the largest, fastest ships ever built. Its twenty large guns would overpower what Blackbeard had onboard *Queen Anne's Revenge*.

Maynard had personally recruited sixty highly-trained sailors, and from the reports Johnstone had received, his crew would outnumber Blackbeard's by almost two to one. It would be no contest if he could find him in time. He just had to get to him before the governor of North Carolina granted the scoundrel a pardon.

It was only a day-and-a-half journey from Williamsburg down to Ocracoke Inlet, Carolina. When they arrived, Lieutenant Maynard moored his ship, and Johnstone sent spies ashore with orders to report back once they had discovered that Blackbeard had arrived.

XXVI

The journey back to North Carolina was a relaxing affair. They had favorable weather, and everyone – including Blackbeard, who sometimes had a tendency to be foul and moody – was in an exceptionally good mood.

Queen Anne's Revenge leisurely sailed up the Carolina coast. No one aboard was in any big hurry, and most of the crew, including Blackbeard, had decided to accept the King's pardon by surrendering to Governor Eden of North Carolina.

With the amount of gold they had stolen, everyone could now afford to retire comfortably. Rutherford didn't know how the gold was going to be divided, but he had learned firsthand there were a lot of misconceptions about how pirate ships operated, especially when it came to Blackbeard's. The ship was actually run in a democratic way. Of course, Blackbeard was the undisputed leader. But ultimately, he had to have the support of the crew to get anything accomplished.

Accordingly, Blackbeard would get the largest share of the gold, but the rest would be divided up according to various factors, such as length of service, a man's worth to the ship, and of course, his fighting ability. Regardless, even the lowest-ranking man on board was going to receive a large sum of money.

The day before they were due to arrive in Ocracoke; Blackbeard divided up the gold. As Rutherford had anticipated, he received the smallest share of the treasure. But he was ecstatic, because his share was still a small fortune.

With so much free time, he found himself thinking about Sally constantly. He knew in his heart that he loved her more than anyone else in the entire world. And with his share of the gold, he could buy out her contract, and they could afford to settle down in Charleston. He was probably the only person aboard *Queen Anne's Revenge* that was anxious to get the trip over with. He just wanted to get back to Charleston as fast as possible.

It was unbelievably warm for November, with the temperature hovering in the low eighties. The sky was a brilliant color of deep blue, the seas were calm, and the winds were light.

Since the ship was going to be disbanded, there wasn't a lot of work to do. Rutherford sat on the deck with his feet dangling over the side as they sailed the last few miles into Ocracoke Inlet outside of Bath, North Carolina.

Although he couldn't believe it, his stay aboard Blackbeard's ship had worked out far better than he could have ever anticipated.

Blackbeard and the crew decided that once they reached Ocracoke Inlet, they would go into Bath, meet with Governor Eden, and accept the pardons that were being offered, before it was too late. It appeared Blackbeard's pirating days were over. He said he wanted to move back to his house in Bath and spend the rest of his days drinking, gambling, and carousing with young women. Rutherford found it hard to believe that a man of his spirit would be able to quietly retire.

Blackbeard told Rutherford that when he met with Governor Eden, he would explain that Rutherford had been taken hostage in Charleston and forced to sail to Nassau. Blackbeard was going to get the governor to issue Rutherford an official document stating the facts so he wouldn't have to worry about any future legal reprisals. Then Blackbeard was going to have one of his smaller sloops that he had harbored in the inlet take him back to Charleston.

Rutherford would be back home in less than a week, and he couldn't wait. After paying off Sally's contract at the plantation, Rutherford was going to ask her to marry him. With his share of the loot, he had enough money to pay off Sally's debt, buy a nice house, and perhaps even help start a small business.

Jack spotted him and sat down next to him. "What are you thinking about, Rutherford? It looks like you're a million miles away."

Rutherford smiled. "Just looking forward to going back to Charleston."

Jack gave him a sly grin. "Aye, I bet the first thing you are going to do is find that girl you keep talking about."

Rutherford didn't even bother to deny it. "So what's next for you, Jack?"

"I think I am going to go back up to Virginia, buy a piece of land, and find me a nice lady to settle down with."

"Sounds like a good plan. Are you sure you won't miss sailing the ocean?"

Jack stared out at two seagulls flying low over the ship. "I love the sea, but I think my luck has run out. This was going to be my last trip with Blackbeard anyway. I've had a feeling for a while that it's time to get out while I still can. I'll miss the adventure, but it's time for me to move on."

That afternoon *Queen Anne's Revenge* sailed into Ocracoke Inlet and dropped anchor. Blackbeard pulled out his best barrels of rum, and everyone drank as much as they could. Rutherford, as usual, was the first to pass out, and he was sleeping at his usual spot on deck when he was rudely awoken by a swift kick in his behind.

He groggily opened his eyes, expecting it to already be morning, but instead was somewhat confused to see that it was still dark outside.

He felt a hand go over his mouth. "Be quiet, and follow me." It was Jack's voice.

Jack led Rutherford down to the stern of the ship and told him to climb down into a boat that was anchored next to the ship. Rutherford saw a shadowy figure sitting in the boat, but in the darkness, he couldn't make out who it was. He tried to ask Jack for an explanation, but Jack just pushed him over the railing and said he would explain everything later.

Rutherford climbed down the net, wondering if he was making a big mistake. He quietly jumped into the boat and was surprised to see that the mystery person was actually Blackbeard. He was drinking rum from a huge bottle.

He handed Rutherford the bottle. "Glad you could make it, John. We have a little work to do tonight."

Rutherford took a swig of the rum, and when he handed the bottle back, he noticed the trunks at the front of the boat. He decided not to ask any questions. He would let them explain everything later.

Jack jumped in right behind him, and he started rowing toward the distant shore. The half moon shined on the tranquil water and provided a spotlight for them all the way to shore.

After they had rowed out of earshot of the ship, Blackbeard finally spoke again. "I guess you would like to know what you are doing out here in the middle of the night rowing all this gold to shore."

"Well, the thought did cross my mind," Rutherford replied.

"It's simple, John. I don't really trust anyone. However, some I trust more than others. Jack has been with me from the beginning, and he is almost like a son to me. While you were sleeping, we loaded up my share of the gold, and now you are going to help us take it to land and hide it properly."

"But why me?" Rutherford asked.

"Because after we get our pardons tomorrow, I am shipping you immediately back to Charleston. So if you did get any funny ideas about trying to get your hands on our loot, it would be too late by the time you got back up here."

Rutherford started to protest, but Blackbeard laughed, saying, "John, I'm just having a little fun with you. We need some help moving all this gold inland, and we trust you. Don't we, Jack?"

Jack punched him in the shoulder. "Not really, but everyone else was too drunk to help."

They laughed and took turns rowing and sharing the bottle of rum. When they were about two hundred yards from shore, Rutherford saw a fiery glow from a torch on the beach.

"There he is," Blackbeard said as they rowed towards the light.

They pulled the boat up onto the beach. The man who had been holding the torch walked over, and the light from the flame shined on his face. He was quite old. He went over and hugged Blackbeard, who affectionately returned the hug. Rutherford was surprised at Blackbeard's display of affection towards the man.

"I've done just like you said, Edward," the old man said. "I looked every day for the arrival of your ship, and, praise the Lord, was I excited to see you back again!"

That was the first time Rutherford had heard someone other than Johnstone call Blackbeard by his real name.

"You did real good, Hank," Blackbeard responded. "Did you bring those two old mules of yours?"

"Yes, I did." He pointed to a group of trees off the beach. "They're tied up over there."

"Good. Bring them over."

Hank ran off to fetch the beasts. When he returned, they loaded the gold onto the mules, and Hank led them to a trail that left the beach and snaked through thick underbrush. Rutherford had no idea where they were going, and he walked behind the mules and kept his mouth shut. After about three miles of walking, Hank held up his hand, and they all stopped.

"There it is, Edward. Just like I told you."

"I don't see it," Blackbeard said.

His statement seemed to delight Hank, who was giggling. "I know you can't see it. That's why it's such a great spot to hide your gold!"

"Yes, it is." Blackbeard laughed. "So where is it?"

Hank led them about ten yards and pointed to an outcrop of trees. They walked behind the trees and came up against a rock ledge. Hank pointed towards the ground. Rutherford still couldn't spot the hideout.

Blackbeard walked over to where Hank was pointing, and he motioned for Rutherford and Jack to come over. The three men moved a large rock that Hank pointed out, and a narrow entrance appeared that opened up into a small cave.

"You did good, Hank," Blackbeard said, obviously happy with the hideout. "This place is perfect. C'mon, boys. Let's get it unloaded."

They unloaded the trunks of gold, said goodbye to Hank, and made the long journey back to the ship. By the time they got back, it was almost sunrise. Rutherford was exhausted from the exertion of the trip, way too much alcohol, and lack of sleep. He went down into the hull and immediately fell into a deep sleep. He slept almost the entire day, and when he awoke, his shipmates were busily preparing for a big celebration.

"What's going on?" Rutherford asked Israel Hands, who was dancing in a circle like a crazed chicken while Fat Stan played the fiddle.

Israel flashed him a crooked smile and flung his arms around his shoulders, exclaiming happily, "Why, laddy, tonight is our last night together, and we are going to celebrate one last time! Blackbeard went into town, and he is buying every scrap of food and alcohol that he can find."

From the smell of his breath, ol' Israel had already gotten a head start on the celebration.

Blackbeard showed up an hour later, and he didn't disappoint anyone. His boat was so overloaded with food and drink that Rutherford couldn't believe it hadn't sunk on the way back. Blackbeard returned with kegs of beer, rum, and wine, plus quail, venison, lobster, fish, potatoes, and boxes of fat cigars. Israel was right: they were going to have a feast.

Minutes after all the goodies had been unloaded, the drinking began in earnest. Rutherford was drinking a beer, trying to pace himself somewhat, when Jack forced a huge glass of rum down his throat. There was no point in fighting it; it was going to be a long night. Anyway, Rutherford didn't really care that he was going to feel horrible tomorrow. After all, this was his last night as a pirate, and he intended to enjoy it.

The happy crew ate and drank all night. Somehow, Blackbeard had even convinced a couple of townsfolk to come aboard and keep them entertained with music. It was a party to end all parties. Rutherford knew he would remember his adventures aboard Blackbeard's ship for as long as he lived.

Long after the sun had set and the moon had risen high in the sky, Rutherford knew he was blind drunk. Everything was blurry, and he had to shut one of his eyes to keep from seeing double. He stumbled towards the stern of the ship with a bottle of rum and fell asleep next to an empty keg of beer.

XXVII

As the party aboard *Queen Anne's Revenge* continued late into the night, there was a much different atmosphere aboard Lieutenant Maynard's warship. Johnstone ordered the Lieutenant to anchor in a little tributary about ten miles north of Ocracoke Inlet, where they waited patiently for the time to strike Blackbeard.

Johnstone had sent two sailors into the town to act as spies and to report back when Blackbeard showed up. After three days, they returned and gave Johnstone the information that he had been hoping for. The spies told him that Blackbeard was anchored at Ocracoke Inlet and that he had gone into town and bought an enormous amount of alcohol and food.

Johnstone knew Blackbeard had become complacent and that he didn't have the least bit of suspicion about their presence. If he did, the rascal certainly would not be planning such a grand party. This was good news. Not only would they have the element of surprise on their side, but Blackbeard's crew was going to be either drunk or hung over.

Johnstone turned to Maynard. "We attack at first light."

Maynard gathered his officers together and gave them the news. "Gentleman, after sunup we are going to give those savages a taste of their own medicine. We're going to strike so hard and so fast they won't even know what hit them. The element of surprise is totally on our side, not to mention that we have more guns and manpower than Blackbeard does. I expect to win and to win quickly."

Maynard looked at Johnstone, who nodded his approval. Maynard dismissed the crew, and he and Johnstone went down to their cabins to get some rest. Before retiring, the two men enjoyed a nightcap in Maynard's cabin.

Maynard poured two glasses of brandy and raised his glass. "To Blackbeard's demise."

Johnstone raised his glass in a mock salute. "To killing the bastard and getting back my gold."

They drank their brandy in silence.

"One more thing, Maynard. There is a man onboard named John Rutherford. I want you to instruct your crew to spare him. Leave him to me."

Maynard nodded, and Johnstone left to return to his cabin.

The morning could not have come fast enough for Johnstone, and well before sunrise, knowing that sleep wouldn't come, he got up and started preparing for the early-morning attack.

One by one, Maynard's officers and crew joined him on deck for coffee and biscuits. Maynard sailed the *Pearl* out of the tributary before sunrise and headed down the coast to Ocracoke Inlet.

At the mouth of the Inlet, Maynard stopped and waited patiently for the sun to rise. Their timing was perfect, and Johnstone wouldn't have to wait long to exact his revenge. A few minutes after they arrived, the first rays of light poked out of the sky, revealing Blackbeard's ship starboard, about a mile away.

Maynard looked through his scope. "No one appears to be on watch," he said to Johnstone.

Johnstone grabbed the scope and peered through it. The deck of Blackbeard's ship was a mess: food, bottles, and bodies were lying everywhere. The savages must have slept where they had fallen.

Johnstone smiled. His plan couldn't have worked out more perfectly. With any luck, he would be able to sneak to within a couple hundred yards of Blackbeard's ship without the pirates even knowing it.

Johnstone couldn't figure out whom he wanted to kill the most – Rutherford or Blackbeard. Maynard sailed to within firing range of *Queen Anne's Revenge*.

Rutherford was deep in alcohol-induced sleep when, for some reason, he felt the need to wake up. Something was not right. He opened his eyes and saw that the sun had just started to rise. His back was stiff from having slept in an awkward position on the hard wooden deck. He reckoned he must have passed out after relieving himself off the side of the ship.

He slowly stood up, trying to get the kinks out of his back. Damn, he needed some water! His mouth and throat felt like he had walked through a desert for a week without anything to drink.

He turned, and a ghostly apparition appeared in front of him. He wondered if he was actually still asleep and just having a nightmare. A huge British warship was just off portside. Heavily-armed sailors lined the entire deck.

Then he saw his nemesis and knew he wasn't dreaming. Johnstone stood on the deck and stared at Rutherford. He smiled broadly and saluted.

No one else on Blackbeard's deck was even stirring. It seemed like a lifetime as Rutherford stood there staring at the motionless navy sailors lining the deck of the warship. Rutherford caught a glimpse of movement by one of the cannon guns.

"Goddamn it!" Rutherford yelled at the top of his lungs. "The bastards–"

Before he could get the words out, a huge blast rang out from one of the cannons. The violent explosion broke the quiet morning calm. Their aim was slightly off, and the cannonball sailed over the bow of the ship and harmlessly landed in the harbor.

The explosion from the cannon was all that was needed to wake even the drunkest of Blackbeard's crew. Men hurriedly scrambled to their feet, unsure of what was happening. Mass confusion reigned on the deck of *Queen Anne's Revenge* as the British warship unleashed a hail of rifle fire.

Israel Hands ran past Rutherford while trying to pull on his pants.

"Get the anchor up!" roared Blackbeard, who had appeared out of nowhere.

Rutherford, Jack, and Israel managed to get the anchor up before the British warship could finish them off. Rutherford knew Blackbeard was in his home waters, and even though he had been taken by total surprise and was outnumbered and overpowered, Rutherford was sure the pirate had a few tricks left up his sleeve.

"Set course for the Ocracoke Island beach!" yelled Blackbeard.

They set tack and headed on a course directly for the beach. Rutherford had no idea why Blackbeard had ordered them to sail directly towards the beach, because if they got stuck in the shallow waters, they would be sitting ducks for the warship's cannons.

"What the hell is that bastard doing?" cursed Lieutenant Maynard. "Is he still so drunk that he would ground his ship on the beach?"

"Just set course and follow him," shot back Johnstone, who could only think of exacting revenge upon Blackbeard and Rutherford.

Just when it seemed that *Queen Anne's Revenge* was about to come to a grinding halt on the sandy bottom, she slipped though a shallow channel. The *Pearl*, meanwhile, was closing fast, and just when Maynard was ready to unleash another round of cannonballs, his ship abruptly hit the sandbar that *Queen Anne's Revenge* had just escaped. The warship ground to a dead halt.

Johnstone knew they had been tricked.

Maynard barked out orders and looked at Johnstone in contempt. "Any brilliant ideas now?"

For the first time, the possibility of defeat and even death crossed Johnstone's mind. The warship was trapped on a sandbar, and he could see Blackbeard's ship maneuvering to get in position to unleash its cannons upon them.

Rutherford turned and saw that the warship was stuck. He felt a rush of exhilaration, and he couldn't wait for Blackbeard to give the bastards a taste of their own medicine.

Blackbeard maneuvered *Queen Anne's Revenge* to within striking distance of the *Pearl* and gave the order to fire. Great explosions sounded from the cannons as pillows of white smoke rose up and drifted into the morning sky. The cannons found their marks with destructive force. The first cannonball hit the stern of the warship, killing at least three men, and the second tore through the middle of the hull, destroying three cannons.

Blackbeard barked out orders to get *Queen Anne's Revenge* back in position for another round of firing. Rutherford knew the British ship would be able to withstand only a few more rounds from their cannons.

The cannons fired a second time, inflicting a tremendous amount of damage. Blackbeard's crew reloaded the cannons for a third round when the unspeakable happened. Just when it looked as if the warship was doomed, Blackbeard's luck ran out. The tide had risen just enough, and the battered warship had freed herself. Blackbeard's cannons had inflicted a lot of damage to the *Pearl*, but not a fatal blow.

"Damn you, Fates!" Blackbeard yelled towards the heavens. "Why have you forsaken me now?"

Now that the warship was free, and even though it was considerably weaker than before, it still had more cannons and more men at its disposal than Blackbeard did. The inlet was too small for Blackbeard to try and outrun the warship, and anyway, Rutherford knew it wasn't in Blackbeard's nature to run from anyone, despite the odds.

"Gentlemen!" Blackbeard called out calmly. "Prepare yourselves. We're going to ram her."

Queen Anne's Revenge gathered speed and rapidly approached her target.

Rutherford checked his pistols and grabbed a cutlass. Every man on both ships now knew it was going to be a bloody hand-to-hand battle.

Jack came over to Rutherford. "Good luck, John." He smiled broadly.

Rutherford nodded and said, "Same to you."

The two great ships collided broadside, wood and metal grinding in a shrill chorus. Gangplanks and grappling irons were thrown to each other's deck, linking the two ships in a dance of death.

As usual, Israel Hands led the charge. Israel's initial assault was met with equal fury and determination. Of the men who led the initial charge across, not one was left standing, including Israel, Blackbeard's loyal first mate.

The well-trained British sailors, including the officers, stormed aboard *Queen Anne's Revenge*. It was difficult to tell who was who, with so many men fighting each other in close proximity. Rutherford had been pushed back to the stern of the ship during the initial onslaught and reluctantly was forced to fight for his life once again.

He clutched his cutlass in his right hand and a single-shot pistol in the left. It was the only pistol he had, so he had to make good use of its only shot. The battle was ferocious, and the deck quickly became smeared in blood. As the number of men standing dwindled, the fighting got more personal.

After a short period of time, it was clear the British were winning the battle. Rutherford retreated to the very stern of the ship, where he came across Blackbeard. He hadn't seen him during the chaos, and Rutherford actually thought he might have been killed in the initial assault.

He was alive all right, but he had a multitude of injuries. There was a slight pause in the action around them, as the British seemed to be concentrating on surrounding a small group of pirates at the bow of the ship.

Rutherford looked at Blackbeard and couldn't believe he was still standing with as many wounds as he had suffered. He had been shot twice in one arm and once in his chest, and Rutherford counted multiple stab wounds across his torso.

Blackbeard smiled at him. "Well, John, they sure have a funny way of granting pardons in North Carolina, don't they?"

Rutherford laughed and marveled at his sense of humor in light of the dire circumstances. As the fighting continued in front of them, Blackbeard pushed him back against the railing of his ship.

"Listen, John. We've been set up, and this time there is no escape. You owe me a favor for saving your life. I want you to sneak off the ship and swim back to Ocracoke Island. Go back to Hank's farm and give him my gold." Blackbeard winced. "You can take your share out of that."

Rutherford was shocked at his request. "But what about you and the rest of the crew?" he protested. "I just can't leave now!"

A bullet whizzed by his head, and Rutherford ducked instinctively, as if it would have even mattered.

Blackbeard grabbed him by the lapels of his coat and pulled Rutherford towards him until they were touching noses. "It is more important to me that you give Hank the gold than it is for you to die here. If you don't go now, I will kill you myself."

He turned around to survey the battle and then let go of Rutherford's coat.

"I owe Hank," Blackbeard solemnly explained, "and I want you to see that it's done. Anyway, you didn't ask for this type of life. I forced it on you."

"You didn't force me into anything," Rutherford said weakly, wondering if perhaps he should accept Blackbeard's offer after all.

For the first time, Rutherford saw Blackbeard wince in pain.

Blackbeard looked at him with a gentle sadness in his eyes. "Please, John, I don't have time to argue with you. Go back to your woman in Charleston, but make me a promise."

"Anything," Rutherford answered.

"Johnstone won't be done with you after this is over with. He'll find you back in Charleston."

"I know."

"Don't take the easy way out and hide from him. You're going to have to settle up with him once and for all."

"I know."

"Good luck!" Blackbeard pushed him back, gave a wry smile, cocked a pistol, and ran straight into the heart of the battle with his cutlass swinging.

As he watched Blackbeard run toward a group of British sailors with a pistol firing in one hand and his cutlass swinging in the other, Rutherford couldn't believe what was transpiring. He had been two days away from being a free man back home in Charleston. But instead, if he didn't do what Blackbeard asked, he was probably going to be killed in battle or hung later.

Blackbeard had given him a chance to live, and Rutherford decided to take it. He had to swim for it and take the risk of being shot or drowned. He climbed over the railing and took one last look back at the battle on board *Queen Anne's Revenge*.

There was no doubt the pirates had lost. Only a few men remained fighting, one of whom was the great Blackbeard. Out of the corner of his eye he caught his last image of Blackbeard. He had been shot at least five times, and God knows how many times he had been cut. Yet he fought on unfazed by his wounds.

Blackbeard had used up all of his pistols and was just flailing away with his cutlass at anything that moved. Rutherford knew he should get into the water, but he couldn't take his eyes off the battle. Blackbeard's wounds were bleeding everywhere, but no one could stop him. Perhaps he was the devil, like everyone had claimed.

Six British sailors had circled him, obscuring Rutherford's vision somewhat. But he would never forget what happened next. Four or five British sailors in front of Blackbeard distracted his attention with a feigned attack while Johnstone sneaked up from behind and with one swipe of his sword decapitated the great Blackbeard. Blackbeard was indeed human after all; his head hit the deck with a sickening thud and rolled backwards.

Blackbeard's words to Rutherford had been right all along: the cowards were the men who one had to fear the most. It was evident that Johnstone had stayed onboard the *Pearl* until it was safe, and then he had killed Blackbeard from behind, like a true coward.

Rutherford took one last look back, and the mighty pirate saved one last surprise for him. His decapitated head rolled to a stop with his face looking directly at Rutherford, who couldn't believe the great Blackbeard was actually dead.

Then it happened. Blackbeard's eyes opened, locking onto Rutherford's. Blackbeard smiled directly at him, and then he winked. And his eyes slowly closed for the last time.

It was time for Rutherford to go. As he climbed down the netting, he heard Johnstone call out, "Mr. Rutherford, where are you? I bet you are hiding down in the hull like a frightened schoolgirl. Get ready. Here I come!"

As quietly as possible, Rutherford slowly lowered himself into the water. It was freezing cold, but luckily the currents weren't too strong. He started to swim as quickly and quietly as possible. He could still hear random shots being fired, but he knew the battle was over. Every one of Blackboard's men was either dead or too wounded to fight on. He had to forget about them for now if he was going to save himself.

Once Rutherford reached what he thought was a safe distance from the ships, he turned and started swimming directly towards the shore. It was only about two-thirds of a mile away, but he started to have serious doubts about whether he could make it. He had never been much of a swimmer, and he was already tired from the exertion and the cold water. His arms and legs felt like they weighed a ton each, and his fear of being spotted and subsequently shot gave way to the realization that he was probably going to drown.

As he struggled towards the shore, Rutherford started having trouble keeping his body afloat. He couldn't stop his teeth from chattering, and he started to lose feeling in his hands and feet. He wasn't going to make it. He had absolutely no strength left. Rutherford turned and started to float on his back. He could no longer paddle with his arms or legs.

What a beautiful morning, he thought as he stared up at the sky. He drifted into a state of semiconsciousness, and the bright blue sky disappeared and he was with Sally.

They were walking hand in hand out in the country. Rutherford felt as happy as he had ever been in his entire life. Sally stopped and turned towards him. She put her arms around his neck and pulled him close. She whispered in his ear, "I'm waiting for you to come home, John. I love you."

Rutherford abruptly came to his senses and realized that he wasn't out in the country with Sally. He was still in the icy water, and he was close to dying.

"No!" Rutherford screamed. "Not now! Not like this!"

Somehow, with Sally as his only thought, he mustered a reserve of energy and began to swim again. After a long struggle, he managed to get to shore.

Rutherford dragged himself onto the sandy beach, spitting up what seemed like a gallon of salt water. He crawled under a palm tree and shed his wet clothes. He was shaking uncontrollably, but luckily, even though the water was freezing cold, it was reasonably warm outside. He sat naked in the sun, thinking about how he would never take a nice, warm fire for granted, ever again.

Johnstone stood at the bow of the ship and looked out over the water. He looked down and saw a red scarf lying next to the railing. He bent down and picked it up. Netting hung off the railing down to the water. He looked more closely at the scarf. It was the same one that Rutherford had been wearing.

"Damn it!" Johnstone cursed. The bastard had escaped from the ship.

Johnstone surveyed the inlet and the beach. There was no sign of him. The coward must have jumped ship when the fighting began. Johnstone scanned the tranquil waters. He had probably drowned in the cold waters, but Johnstone had to be sure. He knew that if Rutherford had survived, he would be going back to Charleston.

After sailing the warship back to Virginia, Johnstone would head to Charleston. He hoped that Rutherford had survived so that he could have the pleasure of killing him personally.

XXVIII

After an hour or two of warmth and relaxation, Rutherford had regained enough strength to force himself to get up and put on his partially dried clothes. He headed straight back to Hank's house.

He was starving and dead tired, but after a two-hour hike, he found Hank's little house. He knocked on the door, and after a few seconds Hank opened the door. Hank took one look at him and nodded. Without saying a word, Rutherford walked into the old man's house.

He sat down at the table, and Hank disappeared into the kitchen. He returned a minute or two later with a bowl of hot soup and a bottle of brandy.

Rutherford greedily ate the soup, and Hank poured two glasses of brandy. They both took a sip, and finally Rutherford told Hank how they had been ambushed and what had happened to Blackbeard and the rest of the crew.

When he finished, Hank poured another round. He raised his glass. "To Blackbeard. He was a true sailor and a lover of life."

They toasted Blackbeard and drank down the brandy. "Why didn't you take all the gold for yourself?" Hank asked. "I would have never known."

Rutherford was surprised by his question, mainly because the thought had never entered his mind. "Blackbeard saved my live in more ways than one," he replied. "He asked me to keep a promise, and I'm doing that."

Hank seemed to accept the explanation, and Rutherford finished off another glass of brandy. He struggled to keep his eyes open.

Hank got up from the table. "Come on. You need some rest."

Rutherford obediently followed him to a small bedroom that was dark and musty. He fell asleep as soon as his head hit the pillow, and he didn't wake up until late the following morning. It took him a couple of seconds to regain his senses and realize where he was.

A wave of sadness swept over him as he thought about Blackbeard, Jack, and the rest of the crew. He somehow managed to drag himself out of the bed. He was still fully clothed. Hank must have taken his shoes off, because they were lying next to the bed. He slipped them on and went out to find the gentle old man.

The house was quiet and dark. He walked into the kitchen and looked out the small cracked window. It was a cloudy, nasty day, mirroring Rutherford's mood. He saw Hank out by the barn putting a shoe on a horse. He walked out and sat down on an old tree stump and watched Hank finish shoeing the horse.

"You know it probably isn't safe for you to stay around here," Hank replied to Rutherford.

Rutherford knew he was right. He stood up and stroked the horse's neck.

"I'm leaving for Charleston, but first let's go get our gold."

Hank smiled, and they set off to find the spot where they had hidden Blackbeard's gold, not two days before. Rutherford opened up one of the trunks, and the gold gleamed as bright as the day they had taken it off Barrett's ship.

"Listen, Hank, I'm going to need to take that horse of yours to get back to Charleston."

Hank never took his eyes off of the gold. "I figured you would. That's why I was putting new shoes on her. Her name is Betty."

Rutherford nodded and patted the horse's neck. "Let's get my gold back up to your house. And if I was you, Hank," Rutherford cautioned, "I would keep your gold hidden here where no one can steal it."

They rode side by side on the way back to the farm. "You're also going to need a strong pack mule. That gold is too heavy for just one horse. You can take ol' Whiskey. That damn beast is stronger than an ox. Won't have no trouble hauling that gold down to Charleston."

"I was wondering bout that. Thanks." Rutherford replied.

Hank pulled out a pouch and stuffed a wad of tobacco in his mouth. "We also got to figure out a way to hide that gold of yours. They're a lot of robbers and thieves on the trail."

"Any ideas?" Rutherford asked.

He chewed the tobacco loudly and spit out a stream of brown juice. "Since I'm a wealthy man now, I can spare plenty of satchels of rice and corn. We'll split up the gold into a dozen or so large grain bags. Unless someone cuts them open and looks through the grain, they won't spot the gold."

Rutherford grinned broadly. Hank's plan was a good one since most thieves in the area had no desire to risk a hanging over a few bushels of grain.

"I could kiss you Hank."

Hank laughed. "Save it for your woman."

Once they got back to the farm they loaded the animals with the gold hidden in the grain satchels. When they were finished Hank disappeared into the barn and returned carrying a pistol.

"Just in case." He handed the pistol to Rutherford who tucked it into his pants.

"And remember," Hank warned sternly. "Follow the trail. But if you get lost, head east until you find the ocean, and then head directly south and you will eventually run into Georgetown. It's over two hundred miles from here, but take your time and use your head. From Georgetown you'll be able to find someone to give you a boat ride down to Charleston."

Hank's expression grew more serious. "But remember, don't under any circumstances travel through the swamps."

"The swamps?" Rutherford asked nervously.

"I don't mean to scare you, but if you get lost in one," he said, swatting at a large horsefly, "you'll never come out alive."

Rutherford mounted Betty and tied off the rope to the mule. He waved goodbye to Hank, and headed off to Georgetown. He took Hank's warning seriously. He had heard that the Carolina swamps were filled with huge alligators, poisonous snakes, and massive swarms of biting insects. He decided that he would avoid the death swamps, even if it meant that he had to travel fifty miles out of his way.

After finding the trail that Hank had told him about, Rutherford headed south, and with every mile that passed, his spirits steadily improved.

The trail was actually in better condition than he had expected, and he made pretty good time the first day, traveling sixteen miles at a leisurely pace. Late in the afternoon, Rutherford found a nice little site underneath a crop of pine trees to pitch a camp and spend the night. He fed and watered Betty and the mule, and then built a fire. Rutherford sat in front of the smoldering fire and nibbled on smoked fish as the giant orange sun dipped beneath the horizon.

After the sun went down and darkness surrounded him, it finally hit him: he was completely alone. For the first time in his life, there was absolutely no one around for miles and miles. Even though Sally had his Saint Christopher's medallion, he hoped the saint was still looking out for him. Not only was he completely alone in the woods, but he also had no wilderness experience at all. What if he got lost or was injured?

Rutherford started to get a little panicked. He took a large swig from a bottle of rum to calm himself down. It seemed to do the trick. The strong alcohol threw some liquid courage into him, and he quickly fell asleep, exhausted from the day's journey.

He awoke the next morning feeling refreshed and relaxed. He shared his breakfast with Betty until the damn horse showed her gratitude by biting his hand. He punched the miserable beast on her shoulder, and she whinnied, as if mocking his feeble attempt to punish her.

He cursed the horse again, gathered his belongings, and hopped on the ungrateful animal. But as soon as he jumped onto her back, the wretched animal bucked and threw him off.

Rutherford hit the hard ground with a loud thud, and he prayed that he hadn't broken anything. He looked up and the pack mule was staring down at him with what appeared to be a grin.

"You both are miserable beasts." He swore in disgust.

Luckily, for his sake as well as Betty's, he hadn't broken anything. Only after apologizing and feeding Betty some corn biscuits did he manage to get back into the horse's good graces.

As the miles passed, he became more comfortable alone in the wilderness. For five days he rode all day and camped out at night. Rutherford's provisions started to run low, but he wasn't worried. There were plenty of streams and creeks for water, and if his food ran out, he could always fish or hunt deer.

After nine days, he knew he had to be getting fairly close to Georgetown. He had perhaps another day or so at the most. Finally, on the eleventh day of the journey, he ran into the first group of people he had seen in over a week. He had stopped on the side of the trail to fix lunch and rest Betty when he heard the sound of wagons approaching.

The wagon got closer, and a group of travelers finally came into view.

"Good afternoon!" he shouted out to make sure they knew his intentions were peaceful.

A huge man on the lead horse rode over to where he was standing, and the whole group stopped behind him.

"Afternoon," the rider replied while tipping his hat. "Where you heading to?"

"I'm going to Georgetown and then down to Charleston. Do you happen to know how far Georgetown is from here?"

The man took off his hat and pointed behind him. "Five miles. Straight ahead."

His words were music to Rutherford's ears. The travelers wished each other luck, and Rutherford continued on his way.

Georgetown was not as large a city as Charleston, but it was still impressive. The Spanish had originally settled the area in the 1500's, but they had failed miserably as farmers. After a few disastrous years, they left and went further south to Florida and to the spice islands of the Caribbean.

The English eventually settled the area in the 1600's and never left. The Spanish were dreamers of treasure, gold in particular, and they didn't realize what they had abandoned in their greed.

After the Spanish deserted the area, the English resettled there, and in a span of one hundred and fifty years the land created unimaginable wealth for its owners. The wealth was generated from gold, but not the type of gold the Spanish were seeking. The entire area was perfect for growing rice, and eventually the British cleared over forty-five thousand acres of land and dug eight hundred miles of canals to create one of the largest rice cultures ever known.

The rice that was grown in the area was known worldwide for its quality and abundance. In fact, its reputation was so prestigious that the rice was called "Carolina Gold" throughout the world. At its peak, over fifty-six million bushels were harvested and sold. The plantation owners became some of the wealthiest people in America.

After another hour of riding, Rutherford left the path and followed the dirt trail into town. He didn't expect to find much of a town but was actually surprised to see that it was a well-developed little city. He rode Betty down the main street, passing shops of every type along the way.

There were a good many people out conducting their daily activities, and no one seemed to pay him the slightest bit of attention, which suited him just fine. Rutherford spotted a little inn, guided Betty and the mule over, and tied them off. Despite their initial problems with each other, they begrudgingly got along now, so long as Rutherford remembered to feed her two corn biscuits in the morning.

His first order of business was to get cleaned up and then get a good hot meal. He paid for the room and hauled his belongings, including the gold, up to his room. After cleaning up, Rutherford went back outside and walked around the little town. The innkeeper had directed him to a little restaurant down by the harbor, and he headed in that direction.

Rutherford found the restaurant without a problem and sat down by a window that overlooked the harbor. He couldn't wait to have a nice meal. His meager travel rations left much to be desired, and he wouldn't have cared one bit if he never tasted a piece of dried fish for the rest of his life.

Rutherford ordered as if he hadn't eaten for a week. The waiter brought plates of venison, duck, lobster, and some of the sweetest oysters he had ever tasted. He washed everything down with large quantities of beer.

After he paid for the meal, which four people could have shared, he decided to take a walk down to the docks to see if he could walk off some of the massive quantity of food he had just consumed.

Right next to the restaurant was a little tobacco shop, and he stopped in and purchased enough cigars to last him until he got back to Charleston. Aboard Blackbeard's ship, he had developed a taste for tobacco. The sun was starting to go down, and he was glad he had decided to wear his jacket because it was going to be a chilly night.

He walked leisurely down to the docks while smoking his cigar. A group of river barges were tied together at the far end of the dock, and the larger ships were harbored out in the port. He passed a few sailors, but no one seemed to pay him much attention.

Rutherford strolled down to the end of the dock, where a kid was loading rice onto a flat barge.

"Good evening," he said. "How are you doing?"

"Fine, thank you," the young boy replied without looking up from his work. He continued to pile the rice sacks onto the barge.

"Where you headed to?"

The kid thought about it for a second before responding, "Charleston."

Rutherford's luck seemed to be improving by the day. "Who takes the rice to Charleston with you?" he asked, hoping to perhaps get a ride with them.

"My father."

"What's his name?"

"Bill McCuddy."

"How long a trip is it?"

The kid threw down his last bag. "About two days. Depending on the weather."

"When are you leaving?"

"Tomorrow."

"Listen," he said excitedly, "I am headed to Charleston myself. How much would you charge if I hitched a ride with you?"

The boy shrugged and they proceeded to haggle over a price for the ride. Finally they agreed to a price for him and his cargo of grain. The boy told Rutherford to meet him and his father at the dock at sunrise.

The next morning Rutherford met them down at the dock as planned. The kid's father was a pudgy man with a ruddy complexion and a fat red nose – no doubt from too much drinking and too much time spent in the sun. Both the father and son were in jovial moods. Rutherford was sure it was from the grossly overpriced fee the two had charged him for the ride. But he didn't mind paying. He just wanted to get to Charleston as fast as possible.

They transferred his supplies from the horse and mule onto the boat. The innkeeper appeared just before they were to set off.

"Here you go." Rutherford said as he handed him the reigns. "They're all yours now."

The innkeeper grinned. "You must be crazy to give me two fine animals for free."

"Can't take them with me."

Rutherford smiled as he watched the innkeeper lead the two animals back down the dock. Then they set off. Rutherford sat on top of his grain sacks and relaxed. He smoked cigars, and watched the riverbank sail past.

Tomorrow, he would be back in Charleston, and he couldn't believe it. This wasn't how he had originally expected to return to Charleston. Nonetheless, he was going to finally make it back home. Rutherford didn't think he would have any problems once he arrived in Charleston. The entire town knew he had been taken hostage by Blackbeard, and he was going to stick to that story.

But he still had a big problem: Johnstone. He had tried not to think about it, but he knew that eventually Johnstone would come looking for him.

The day passed quickly as Rutherford lazily fell in and out of a comfortable sleep. They passed a couple of small ships and a few barges, but that was about it. Around four o'clock in the afternoon, Bill steered the barge over to the riverbank, and they tied the barge down for the night. It was going to be a cold night, so the three travelers left the barge and built a large fire to keep warm. For his part, Rutherford didn't think that Bill really needed a fire to keep warm. He had been chugging down corn mash like it was water ever since they had docked.

His son ignored him and sat by the fire whittling a bear out of a block of wood. The boy was actually quite good at it. The bear wasn't finished, but one could tell the boy had some talent.

Rutherford went over and sat down next to the boy. "You're pretty good at that," he said, pointing to his wooden bear.

"Thanks." He continued whittling.

Rutherford had no one else to talk to, so he tried the kid again. "How long have you been whittling?"

"Ever since I can remember."

"Are animals your specialty?"

"Animals and ships."

Rutherford felt sorry for the kid. He started to ask him if he had a mother but was interrupted by a loud shout from Bill, who had fallen down the riverbank while trying to get another bottle of whiskey mash from the barge.

Rutherford didn't know it was possible to say complete sentences using only curse words. Old Bill had fallen and gotten stuck in the mud. It was actually a pretty funny sight.

Finally, after it was apparent that Bill wouldn't be able to free himself, Rutherford and the boy went down to the bank to help. After some considerable effort, they managed to pull the fat drunk free.

He mumbled something under his breath, which Rutherford didn't believe was a thank you, and then proceeded to get his second bottle from the boat. Rutherford returned to the fire. He couldn't care less if Bill got himself totally smashed as long as he delivered him to Charleston the next day.

Rutherford gathered his blankets from the barge and settled into bed next to the fire. Thankfully, Bill had had his fill of alcohol and passed out without causing too many more problems.

Rutherford awoke early the next morning as excited as a little kid on Christmas day. They were just hours away from Charleston.

It was a cool, crisp morning, with just a touch of frost coating the ground. Rutherford was surprised to find that he was the last one up. Bill and his son had already prepared the barge for the trip into Charleston.

He went over to see if he could give them a hand. "Good morning, gents. Anything I can do?"

Bill just grunted something he didn't understand, and his son said nothing. Rutherford was glad he only had to spend one more day with this pair of misfits. The three of them ate some hard rolls for breakfast and then shoved off. Rutherford knew there were going to be some surprised people when he arrived back in Charleston.

After drifting down the slow, meandering river for about five hours, they saw the outskirts of Charleston slowly come into view. Rutherford couldn't believe he had actually made it back. The last hour of the journey had seemed to last longer than the entire six months he had been away.

Bill docked the barge, and they said goodbye.

Charleston looked exactly the same. Even in early winter there were a large number of ships in the harbor. Rutherford hired a driver and a cart to help haul his belongings. He followed the cart down the busy dock over to East Bay Street and down to Mr. Resin's Apothecary store.

IXXX

Rutherford slowly walked through the town. He passed by a few of the merchants who had been there on that fateful day when he had agreed to deliver Blackbeard's ransom supplies. No one even gave him so much as a second glance. Rutherford guessed he had long since disappeared from their memories.

He walked into the apothecary, and Mr. Restin saw him immediately. Mr. Restin's face registered so many different emotions that Rutherford wasn't sure whether he was happy or sad to see him. Finally, the frail little man smiled and gave Rutherford a great big bear hug, nearly crushing his ribs in the process.

"John, I can't believe you're here!" Mr. Restin pulled back from their embrace. "I thought for sure you were dead. I cannot tell you how happy I am to see you."

"Not as happy as I am to see you," Rutherford said, laughing as they hugged again.

"What happened? Where have you been? I heard that Blackbeard and his entire crew were killed up in North Carolina."

"News travels fast," Rutherford responded, saddened over the memory of his friends who hadn't made it. "It's a long story. First, can I ask you a favor?"

"Anything my boy!" He responded cheerfully.

"Can I store my goods down in your underground storage room?" Rutherford asked. He had spent considerable time thinking about it, and Restin's underground room was probably the best place in the entire city to hide his gold."

"Of course. Of course. You can keep it there as long as you need to." Restin answered.

After his supplies were safely stored. Mr. Restin shut the front door and put the *Closed* sign out. "Come on back. Let's hear about your adventures."

For a straight hour, Rutherford told his story. Mr. Restin listened with his mouth open. He asked several questions, and Rutherford answered them as truthfully as possible.

Rutherford finally decided he had talked enough about his time away from Charleston. He had more important matters to discuss.

"Did you talk to Sally after I left?" he asked.

Mr. Restin nodded. "After the hostages came back, they told us that Blackbeard had refused to let you go and that they were planning on killing you. I was devastated, and I blamed myself for letting you go out there."

"It was my decision," Rutherford interjected, feeling guilty at having caused both Mr. Restin and Sally pain because of his greed and thirst for a little adventure.

Mr. Restin waved his hands in the air. "I shouldn't have let you go. Anyway, I waited for a day or so, praying that Blackbeard would change his mind. But when you didn't show up, I thought you were dead for sure. I rode out and told Sally exactly what you told me to say."

"How did she react?"

"What do you mean, how did she react?" bellowed Mr. Restin. "She was upset as hell. That girl loves you. She told me that she didn't believe that you were dead and that you would be back one day."

"She really said that?"

"Yes, she did. I didn't want to give her any false hope. But she was so upset, I just agreed with her, although I didn't hold out much hope for your return. Every time one of the servants from the plantation came into town, she had them come over here and ask if I had heard any news about you."

"Hey, I almost forgot!" Mr. Restin jumped up and went over to his safe by the wall. He opened it up and brought a bundle over to him.

"What's this?"

"It's your money that you asked me to hold for you. You still want it, don't you?" he asked with a teasing grin.

"Of course," Rutherford said, grinning. "I earned it."

They talked late into the night about pirates, Charleston, and Sally. Mr. Restin agreed to let him have his job and his old bed back. But it was only temporary, because Rutherford was going to start his own business and ask Sally to marry him.

Late into the night after they had talked themselves into exhaustion, they bid one another goodnight. Mr. Restin agreed to let him borrow one of his horses so he could ride out to the plantation the next day. Rutherford didn't think he would be able to sleep in anticipation of seeing Sally, but once he lay down, it only took a few seconds to fall asleep.

The ride out to the plantation was exhilarating. Rutherford was ecstatic to be able to once again travel underneath the huge oak trees with Spanish moss clinging to their limbs. He savored the familiar smell of the vast marshes.

Upon reaching the plantation house, he jumped off the horse and knocked loudly on the front door.

A servant greeted him. "How can I help you?"

"Colonel Pinckney, please."

"Can I ask what this matter refers to?" the butler asked rather coolly.

"It's a financial matter."

The butler made Rutherford wait outside, and after about ten minutes, a distinguished-looking gentleman opened the door and walked out. He was dressed in high English fashion. It was obvious he had come from many generations of wealth.

"Good afternoon," Pinckney said in a genteel voice. "What can I do for you today, sir?"

Rutherford cleared his throat. "I am inquiring about an employee of yours named Sally Weston. She works here as a lady servant."

"Yes. What about her?" Pinckney asked somewhat defensively.

"I understand she is working off an obligation." Rutherford didn't want to get Pinckney the least bit upset, so he didn't mention the fact she was practically forced by one of his own relatives into virtual slavery. "I have come here to pay off her debt."

Pinckney appeared to size him up, and Rutherford had no doubt that he was a smart businessman. Pinckney had something Rutherford wanted, and the man knew it was a seller's market.

"I'm sorry. What is your name? We haven't been properly introduced."

"John Rutherford."

"Mr. Rutherford, I appreciate your offer, but Sally is a tremendous asset to my wife. She absolutely adores her, and I don't think we could possibly part with her services at this time."

It had never crossed his mind that Pinckney would refuse his offer, but he had no doubt it was just a matter of offering him the right price. The two men went back and forth for a while – in a civil fashion, of course – and eventually Rutherford agreed to a price three times his original offer. But the money didn't matter one bit. He would have spent every last penny he had to free her.

He paid Pinckney with Barrett's gold, the irony of which delighted him to no end.

"Where can I find her?" he hastily asked after their business transaction had been completed.

"Out back, by the creek," Pinckney responded curtly.

The colonel turned and walked back into the house, and Rutherford walked around the back of the house and across the yard.

The creek was down a small hill, and when Rutherford reached the top of it, his heart was beating faster than the time he had been frozen on the top of the mast. He immediately saw Sally standing next to two other women. They were bent over, washing sheets in the creek with soap. He leaned against a tree and stared at her. Her long blond hair hung over her face, shimmering in the sunlight.

Suddenly, she turned toward him, as if she knew someone was watching her. He saw her eyes squint from the sun, and she raised her hand to shield the sunlight. Like magic, the sun ducked behind a cloud, and she was able to see him clearly.

"Oh, John!" Rutherford saw her mouth the words as she stood up and started to run up the hill toward him.

They met halfway and embraced each other tightly. Sally was crying, and they held on to each other for a long time.

"I'm sorry I left you, Sally," he whispered into her ear. "If you give me a second chance, I promise I will never leave you again. I can't tell you how much I missed you."

She hugged him tighter. "I knew you would come back to me."

Naturally, she had dozens of questions about what had happened to him and how he had acquired enough money to pay off her debt. Rutherford told her he would explain everything later. They gathered her few possessions and left the plantation for good.

They moved into a little brick house located off East Bay Street down by Oyster Point that Rutherford had purchased. Rutherford had discovered that, in another unusual twist, Captain Bonnet, who Rutherford had first met aboard Blackbeard's ship, had been found guilty of piracy and hung in the gardens a month before Rutherford arrived back in Charleston.

Rutherford continued to work for Mr. Restin while he kept an eye open for business opportunities. He didn't want to raise any eyebrows with his newfound wealth, so he spent the money modestly.

Sally stayed at home and took care of the household duties. And every once in a while Rutherford would walk down to the edge of the docks and watch the ships come in and out of the harbor. He didn't do it often because it reminded him too much of Blackbeard and Jack. It also reminded him of Johnstone, who was still out there.

One night, being a touch restless, he decided to take a walk along the harbor and then stop in at his favorite drinking spot, the **Moultrie Tavern**. Rutherford had asked Sally if she wanted to go, but she shook her head and replied that she had some things to do. He always asked out of habit, knowing full well that she would say no. She didn't have much of a taste for liquor, nor did she care for the atmosphere of the local bars and taverns.

Rutherford knew she would rather stay home and read one of her many books. She loved reading, and her favorite author by far was William Shakespeare. He had learned the best gift he could give her was any book or play written by him. Earlier that day, he had surprised Sally by bringing an early birthday present home. Rutherford had found a tattered but readable copy of Hamlet at one of the local bookstores. He was certain that when he came home later that night, she would still be up reading by candlelight. Once she started reading Shakespeare, she wouldn't quit until the book was finished.

It was a brisk evening as Rutherford slowly made his way down to the tavern. He had made friends with two brothers who ran a hardware store. They were regulars at the tavern. And like most nights, Rutherford knew they would be sitting at their favorite table drinking and telling lies.

The streets were filled with people milling about, finishing up the last of the day's chores. The sun was beginning to set. Twilight was his favorite time of the day. There was something magical about the color of the sky as the day turned into night. As he walked near the water's edge, the sun slowly fell below the horizon, creating a wonderful aura of colors and patterns.

Stray clouds hurried by, losing their usual white color as darkness started to take over the sky. The fading light turned the clouds into huge pink puffs of cotton, and part of the sky was a light iridescent blue, while another part turned a deep purple. One of the things Rutherford loved most about Charleston was its beautiful skyline, especially in the winter.

The tavern door was always open, and he strolled in. As expected, Rutherford saw the familiar faces of his two friends sitting at their favorite table.

He grabbed a beer and walked over to the table. "What a shock to find you all here," he said in jest. "Do you mind if I sit down?"

Jacob, whose favorite pastime was to give Rutherford grief, slid a chair out for him. "Sit down, young Rutherford. I see the little lady let you out for the night. How nice of her."

Rutherford smirked at the friendly barb and joined in the general discussion of the group. It seemed the boys were a little mad at the town government, in particular Governor Johnson, who, with the help of the city's new pastor, had instituted new laws cracking down on prostitution, public intoxication, curfews, and, God forbid, alcohol sales on Sunday.

Rutherford listened and agreed with them and their complaints, when in reality he thought a lot of the governor's plans were probably not such bad ideas. As the number of ships increased, so did the number of sailors and people of dubious backgrounds. Charleston had earned a much-deserved reputation as a bawdy city.

Sailors ran around drunk at all hours of the night, harassing people and vandalizing businesses and homes. Prostitution was widespread, with women of all ages realizing that men who had been at sea for a long time were willing to pay a lot of money for their companionship.

But Rutherford couldn't blame anyone for their indulgences. People in Charleston lived a hard life and suffered many hardships. Understandably, they liked to live it up when they got the chance.

The night wore on, and the group of friends became louder and louder with each additional round. Rutherford had drunk more than he had originally planned, but when hadn't that been the case? He was seated facing the front door, and as he was getting ready to say goodnight to his buddies, his worst fear walked into the tavern. With a grin only the devil could appreciate, Johnstone stood at the entrance. For the third time in six months, in three different locations thousands of miles apart, their paths had crossed yet again.

Johnstone was accompanied by a couple of rough-looking men who looked like they knew how to use their fists. He sauntered over to the table, and the smile never left his face.

"So . . . we meet yet again, Rutherford. It is a very small world, isn't it?"

The drunken babble at the table stopped.

"Yes, it is a very small world," Rutherford replied in utter disbelief.

Johnstone looked away from Rutherford and seemed to be sizing up his friends at the table. "Gentlemen, do you know with whom you are sharing beers?" Johnstone asked, pointing towards Rutherford. His tone was neither hostile nor friendly.

Michael, who had a bit of a temper, looked at Johnstone. "Yes, we do. What's it to you?"

Johnstone maintained his pleasant demeanor and without raising his voice replied, "Well, I don't think you gentlemen do, because obviously law-abiding citizens such as yourselves wouldn't have anything to do with a wanted pirate, thief, and murderer."

Johnstone paused slightly and then continued, raising his voice. "Not to mention the fact that he was a conspirator with Blackbeard, the very man who held your town hostage!"

Jacob stood up. "That's pure rubbish. Everyone knows that John was kidnapped by Blackbeard, and not only that," he said, his face turning beet-red, "he secured the release of twelve people, who owe their lives to his bravery."

Johnstone smiled broadly. "Maybe I can enlighten you with a few facts you may not know about your friend," he interrupted.

Rutherford didn't know what Johnstone was up to, but he knew the bastard had something up his sleeve.

"First of all, did you know that Blackbeard and Mr Rutherford are both from Bristol?"

"So," responded Jacob. "That doesn't mean a thing."

Johnstone raised his hands. "If you will allow me to continue, I think you will see my point."

No one raised an objection.

"Not only are Blackbeard and John from the same city, but they both were employed by Barrett Trading. That was, of course, before Blackbeard left to become a pirate and John ran away because he stole company funds and was wanted by the local authorities."

Rutherford angrily pounded his fist on the table. "I didn't steal any funds from Barrett! That's a damn lie, and you know it!"

Johnstone ignored his outburst and continued to address his friends. "Why do you suppose John would so readily risk his life to bring out Blackbeard's ransom supplies? I'll tell you why. Because he knew that no harm would come to him. He knew Blackbeard wouldn't harm an old friend. Now you can say that these are just a lot of unusual coincidences, but did John tell you what happened to him in Nassau?"

No one was drinking anymore. Rutherford realized he was helpless to stop Johnstone.

"I happened to be in Nassau on business when I ran into John at a local bar. I approached him because I wanted to confront him about the funds he had stolen from my boss. Before I even got a chance to ask him for his side of the story, Blackbeard walks in and grabs me. He tells me if I ever dare talk to one of his friends again, he will kill me."

Jacob interrupted with not a lot of conviction in his voice, "That still doesn't prove he was in cahoots with Blackbeard."

Johnstone smiled at Jacob. "Well, what if I told you that two days later Blackbeard attacked and plundered an innocent merchant vessel?"

Jacob responded, "I say, good for Blackbeard."

That seemed to lighten the mood a bit, as everyone laughed in agreement.

Johnstone smiled. "Well, I don't necessarily disagree with you, but John Rutherford not only was with Blackbeard, but he also helped in the attack and even killed two French sailors."

There was complete silence around the table, and Rutherford could feel his friends trying to wrestle with the possible notion that he was a pirate and murderer. Just when Rutherford thought Johnstone couldn't possibly have more to say, he fired the biggest salvo last.

"I can prove all of this, gentlemen. It just so happens that a man named Jacques Boulier was aboard that merchant vessel that Blackbeard and Rutherford plundered. He escaped and sailed with me from Nassau, and he is here in Charleston."

Rutherford couldn't believe it. He wanted to just get up and run out of the bar. He could tell that Johnstone was having a good time, because he was setting everything up perfectly, all at Rutherford's expense.

"I'm sure Jacques won't have a hard time identifying Rutherford as one of Blackbeard's crew."

Rutherford sat in stunned silence. Neither Jacob nor Michael came to his defense this time.

Johnstone bent down and whispered in his ear so that only he could hear, "John, I was just going to kill you myself, but I've decided watching you hang in front of your friends is going to be even better."

Johnstone stood up and addressed the table one last time. "Goodnight, gentlemen. I will report what I have told you to the governor tomorrow, but in the meantime, if I were you, I would watch my back."

Johnstone and his cronies turned and left the tavern.

Rutherford's friends were completely silent. He supposed they were waiting for some type of denial or explanation from him. But he didn't know what to tell them. His head was pounding. He had to get out of the noisy tavern to think about what he was going to do. He knew that Johnstone wouldn't make an empty threat, and he was in serious trouble.

He looked at his two friends who had remained silent. He didn't have the time or the patience to tell them his side of the story. "Listen," he addressed them meekly, "that man is a murdering liar and has twisted the facts to suit his purpose. Don't believe his version. I promise I will explain everything later."

They shook their heads, but that was all the support he received from them.

Rutherford left the tavern in a hurry. Once outside, the cold air felt good. It helped to clear his mind so he could think about what to do next. He knew if he was arrested, he would have to stand trial and would probably be hung like Bonnett down at Oyster Point.

The most damaging evidence against him would be from Jacques and Johnstone. He would have to somehow convince a jury that he was not in cahoots with Blackbeard and had killed the Frenchmen only in self-defense. The bottom line: he had better come up with a good plan and quick, or he risked putting his fate in the hands of people who wouldn't know who to believe.

On the way home, Rutherford decided his best bet was to be proactive. Instead of waiting for the authorities to come looking for him, he would go see the governor tomorrow and explain his side of the story and what he knew about Barrett and why Johnstone had wanted him dead.

Rutherford had heard that Governor Johnson was a fair and honest man. Surely he would be able to see his side of the story. He walked home, wondering if he was ever going to rid himself of Johnstone and Barrett.

Johnstone banged on the door as loud as he could. He knew the governor would be mad as hell to be awakened this late at night. He looked through the window and saw the governor walking down the stairs. He appeared to be cursing.

The door opened, and Johnstone smiled broadly.

"What the hell are you doing back in Charleston?" the governor asked in a none-too-friendly tone.

Johnstone knew that the governor hated both him and Barrett, but since Barrett was practically responsible for Charleston being a city, he had to accommodate them. After a hurricane, a bad harvest, and a malaria outbreak, the population of the city had been cut in half.

But Barrett hadn't wavered in his belief that Charleston would become a major trading hub, and he had pumped enormous amounts of money into the city when no one else had been willing to do so. Johnstone knew the governor was well aware that if it weren't for Barrett, he would still be a minor politician back in Lincolnshire.

"You don't sound too happy to see me, Gov'nor," Johnstone replied in a mocking tone.

"Good evening, Mr. Johnstone," the governor responded in a more civil manner. "I'm just surprised to find you at my door this late at night. What I can I do for you?"

"I need a few minutes of your time. There is some business I need to discuss with you."

"Can't it wait until tomorrow?"

Johnstone shook his head. "No, it can't."

Without being invited in, Johnstone walked into the house and headed straight to the study that the governor used for house calls. The governor entered as Johnstone poured himself a large snifter of brandy.

"Well, since you're here, what can I do for you?" the governor asked as he sat down in his brown leather chair.

Johnstone raised the glass to his nose and smelled the brandy before taking a large swallow. "There is a man named John Rutherford in Charleston. He is wanted in Bristol for embezzlement from Barrett Trading, and he is also wanted for acts of piracy committed while aboard Blackbeard's ship."

"Well, if what you say is true about this Rutherford fellow," the governor responded, "we have a legal system here, and I am confident that if a case can be made against him, justice will be done."

Johnstone set down his brandy glass and walked over to the governor. "This man, as I explained, has stolen from Mr. Barrett. I don't want to hear about justice and due process. I want him arrested and then hung, and I want you to make sure this happens, and I want it to happen immediately." Johnstone took another sip of the sweet brandy. "Mr. Barrett would be very happy to learn of your cooperation in this matter, so please see that it is done."

The governor looked tired. "All right," he responded. "I'll have him arrested tomorrow."

Johnstone smiled. "Good. But remember, I want him hung."

"Fine. Now, do you mind? I have a busy day tomorrow."

Johnstone left the governor's house. He couldn't wait to see the look on Rutherford's face as he was being led to the gallows.

XXX

Rutherford tossed and turned in his sleep. He couldn't bear the thought of losing Sally after everything they had been through. He prayed that after he told his side of the story, the governor would exonerate him.

Finally, after what seemed like the longest night ever, the morning sun started to rise. Rutherford got up and did some chores around the house, mostly in an effort to keep his mind off the problem at hand and to kill some time before he went to go see the governor.

During breakfast, Sally stopped eating and looked at him. "Are you all right, John? You seem a little nervous. Is something bothering you?"

She could always sense what he was feeling. Rutherford guessed there was such a thing as a woman's intuition.

He half smiled at her. "No, I'm fine. I am just a little tired. I didn't sleep very well last night."

He felt guilty about not telling her about his run-in with Johnstone, but he didn't want to needlessly worry her. He was halfway thought breakfast when an enormous crash came from the front door.

Sally gasped, and Rutherford stood up and ran to the front of the house to see what the hell was going on. He reached the living room, where he was met by a large force of the town's militia.

"What is this about?" Sally demanded, sounding part mad, part scared.

Rutherford, on the other hand, knew exactly why they were here. He just couldn't believe that Johnstone had been able to act so quickly.

A medium-sized man dressed in his dark gray militia outfit parted the soldiers and walked up to Rutherford. He wasn't carrying a rifle but was obviously in charge. "Are you Mr. John Rutherford?" he asked in a calm voice.

Rutherford nodded.

"I have a signed warrant from Governor Johnson for your arrest on charges of piracy, conspiracy, robbery, and murder. Will you please come with me?"

Sally stepped in front of him like a mother protecting one of her children. "Sir, there must be some mistake here. John didn't commit any of those crimes, and as a matter of fact, he was kidnapped by Blackbeard only after he helped win the release of hostages."

Rutherford was amazed at how strong and calm her voice was.

"Ma'am, I am here just to serve the warrant. It is up to the court to decide guilt or innocence. Come on, Mr. Rutherford. I don't want any trouble now."

Rutherford grabbed Sally's hand. "Don't worry, honey," he replied dejectedly. "It will be all right. Go get Mr. Restin. He'll know what to do."

Sally looked dazed and gave him a hug. Rutherford was escorted out of his house at gunpoint, and he seriously wondered if he would ever see Sally again as a free man. There was no telling what Johnstone had told the governor.

Rutherford was taken to Charleston's only jail, which actually was more of a dungeon. The jail was in the exchange house, and the cells were in the basement, below sea level.

Rutherford had always imagined dungeons as dark, wet, dreary places, and he now knew that his imagination was accurate. He was thrown into a little cell that couldn't have been more than eight feet by eight feet. The dingy room contained only two items: a straw cot and a bucket. The stench in the place was noxious due to the fact that the buckets were collected only every other day. It didn't help that every night hordes of drunken sailors were thrown into the dungeon to sober up.

Two days passed, and Rutherford thought he was on the verge of going mad. The guards wouldn't tell him anything, and no one had been allowed to visit him.

Finally, on the third day, one of the guards came down and took him into one of the interrogation rooms. The guard let him into the room, and he saw Mr. Restin sitting at a small table with a worried look on his face.

Mr. Restin stood up and shook his hand. "John, I'm sorry it took so long to see you. They wouldn't allow me to see you until now."

"That's all right. How's Sally holding up?"

"I can't lie to you, John. She is scared and upset. They would only allow one of us to see you, and she sent me because I'm in a better position to help you. She's outside right now. She wanted me to tell you that she loves you."

"Tell her I love her and miss her, too."

Mr. Restin nodded in acknowledgement.

"How do things look?" Rutherford asked.

Mr. Restin outlined the situation. "Evidently, your old boss Arthur Barrett has considerable influence in Charleston, and he wants you done away with. The most damning evidence against you is the French sailors, but we could probably make a reasonable argument of self-defense. I have talked to a lot of the merchants, and most have agreed to testify that you volunteered after we asked someone to take the medical supplies out to Blackbeard in exchange for the hostages. Even Samuel Wragg agreed to testify that you were taken against your will, and you know he carries a lot of clout in the city."

"Not as much as Barrett," Rutherford replied.

He knew it all came back to the original problem. If his case went to trial, Barrett would use all of his legal and illegal resources to secure a guilty verdict, and that meant he would be hung. So Rutherford had only two choices: either make sure the case never went to trial, or try and fix the outcome himself.

"How long till the case goes to trial?" Rutherford asked, not at all happy with Mr. Restin's news.

"I have been talking to the attorney I told you about, and he said it really depends."

"Depends on what?"

"The governor. He sets the date for the trial, but it could take up to three months."

The news shocked him. Rutherford didn't think he could keep his sanity for three months while being confined in that hellhole.

The guard pounded on the door. "You have two minutes!"

"Let me think for a day or so," Rutherford said, shaking his head wearily. "I have to come up with some kind of a plan."

Mr. Restin stood up and reached into his jacket. "Here, John. Sally wanted you to have this."

Mr. Restin handed a note over, along with the Saint Christopher's medallion. It broke Rutherford's heart to take the necklace, but he understood why she had given it back to him.

Mr. Restin left, and Rutherford was escorted back to his cell. He lay down on the uncomfortable straw cot and stared at the wet ceiling, trying to drown out cries of the other prisoners. He had to think of a plan – and fast. He pulled out the letter from Sally and read it.

Dear John,

I miss you so much. The last few days have been extremely painful. I am trying to put up a brave front, but it is so very hard to do. Mr. Restin is trying everything he can, and I pray for you every single hour.

I wanted you to have the Saint Christopher's medallion because it has brought us such good fortune in the past.

We will get through this. We just have to remain strong and keep our faith. I know it is difficult for you confined in that awful place, but always remember I am here for you. We will figure a way out of this together.

I love you,

Sally

Sally's letter had an unexpected effect on Rutherford, it snapped him out of his feelings of self-pity and made him mad as hell! Mad at Barrett and Johnstone for repeatedly trying to ruin his life. The bastards must have thought that he was no better than an insect they could just step on whenever they pleased.

He pounded his fist against the wall in anger and swore that he was going to get out of here. He was going to get even with both Johnstone and Barrett, no matter the cost. He had come this far against all odds, and he wasn't going to let Johnstone win.

Rutherford sat in his cell with a fire of hatred boiling inside of him. Never before in his life had he felt such a burning hatred towards someone. He didn't know it at the time, but it was the best feeling he could have had. His hatred kept his mind focused on revenge rather than the circumstances of his confinement.

Late in the afternoon of his eighth day confined in his own personal hell, Rutherford was allowed to see Mr. Restin for a second time.

Since their last meeting, he had spent every waking hour trying to figure a way out of the mess he had gotten himself into. He finally came up with an idea. He didn't know if it was going to work, but it was his only chance. He had racked his mind with every conceivable possibility, from trying to bribe Johnstone with his gold to just hoping the jury would understand his side of the story. The one thing he knew for certain was that if his case did go to trial, he was done for. Johnstone would see to that. Rutherford had to assume that everyone from the judge to the jury would be in some way bribed or threatened by Johnstone. Somehow, he had to get Johnstone to get the charges dropped before he went to trial. The scheme he had devised was his only hope.

Rutherford was led to a table in an empty room and sat down across from Mr. Restin.

Rutherford skipped the pleasantries. He didn't have time. "I need you to get Johnstone to come here and meet with me."

"How?"

"Tell him I'm willing to tell him where my the gold is hidden in return for my freedom."

Mr. Restin shook his head and sighed deeply. "Johnstone is a liar. Even if he agreed, once you told him where the gold was hidden, he would renege on his word."

"I know that. I just need you to throw out some bait and get him to come visit me. I have another plan in mind once he gets here."

Mr. Restin smiled. "I hope whatever you have up your sleeve works."

"Me, too."

They hugged goodbye. Rutherford would find out in the next couple of days if he was going to be a free man or a dead man.

XXXI

Two days passed. Rutherford was asleep on his straw cot when he was awoken by a loud noise.

"Wake up!" yelled a guard as he pounded on his cell door. "You have a visitor."

Rutherford rubbed his eyes, jumped up from the cot, and tucked in his shirt. This was it. His life depended on the next couple of minutes. It was all or nothing.

The guard opened his cell door, and Rutherford followed him to the interrogation room. He ushered Rutherford in and quickly shut the door, leaving the two men alone.

Johnstone was sitting in a chair, smoking a cigar. He had a smug look on his face.

"All right, Mr. Rutherford. Where is my gold?"

"I'm not going to tell you where the gold is hidden," he shot back.

Johnstone's expression didn't change. "I have had enough of your shenanigans. I hadn't really thought about hurting your beautiful young wife, but since you are being difficult, I may just have to consider it. So I will make you one last offer. Tell me where the gold is, and I will promise not to make your wife or Mr. Restin pay for all the troubles you have caused me."

"And what about me?"

"Oh, you are going to hang, regardless. Your death is more important to me than the gold. But if you persist in being stubborn about it, I'm sure that pretty little wife of yours knows where it is hidden."

Rutherford had expected this type of conversation, and now it all came down to whether or not Johnstone fell for his bluff.

"How well do you know Barrett?" Rutherford asked, trying his best to ignore Johnstone's threats.

"What the hell is that supposed to mean?"

"I bet you didn't know that he is an excellent record keeper. He keeps detailed logs of all business activities, one of which includes the fact that you murdered Allen Lawrence. Another, details how you shipped defective beams to a mine in order to collect insurance money, and how the subsequent collapse of the mine resulted in the deaths of twenty-eight innocent miners. And, of course, let's not forget the funding of pirate activities throughout the colonies."

Rutherford paused to let Johnstone digest what he had just said. "Do you want me to continue?"

Johnstone glared at Rutherford. "This dungeon has turned you into a madman!" he barked. "You don't know what you are talking about. You cannot prove

142

one thing you have just said."

"I have documents in Barrett's own handwriting on your company's letterhead that would prove otherwise. If the charges are not dropped, I am prepared to turn those documents over to the proper authorities to see that you and Barrett are brought to justice."

"You're lying!" Johnstone said, clearly agitated now. "First of all, those documents don't exist, and even if they did, there is no way you would have them in your possession."

Rutherford gave Johnstone a sly grin. "That is where you are wrong. I am not as dumb as you think. After your failed attempt to kill me, I decided I might need a little insurance. Later that night, I broke into Barrett's office and stole the documents from his safe."

Rutherford grinned. "Yes, you remember his safe. The big brown one right behind Barrett's desk. The one with the silver turnstile. The one you question Barrett about every year. The one you've always worried might contain incriminating information."

Rutherford could tell by Johnstone's expression that he had struck a nerve. Perhaps his bluff would work after all.

"I want to see those documents," Johnstone demanded.

Rutherford grinned with newfound confidence. "Do you think I am that stupid? The documents are in a safe place, and they're going to remain there."

Johnstone stood up and walked over to the room's only window and stared outside. He turned back towards Rutherford. "Let's say we did come to an agreement," he said, his tone becoming friendlier. "What's next?"

"Simple. You can explain to the governor that new information has come to light exonerating me. And that you feel it is your duty to report it rather than allow an innocent man to dangle from the gallows. You will look like a true gentleman."

"I will give you my answer in three days," Johnstone quickly replied.

Rutherford knew he was going to try and stall for some time. "No. You have until noon tomorrow to deliver a full pardon signed by the governor. If you don't, I will see to it that those documents are turned over to the proper authorities. We both know that not everyone is on Barrett's payroll and that he has quite a few enemies who would love to see him destroyed."

"It still won't change the outcome, John. I'm still going to kill you – sooner or later."

"We'll see about that. You have until tomorrow, or those documents will be delivered." Rutherford stood up and walked over to the door.

Johnstone laughed. "I do have to say, Rutherford, you certainly have surprised me. I thought you were nothing but a weak sap."

Rutherford smiled. "Not as much as you have surprised me, Johnstone. I can't believe you have allowed Barrett to amass so many incriminating documents on you. If it comes down to his hide or yours, obviously Barrett is prepared to sell you down the river." Rutherford hoped his last lie would help further convince Johnstone of the legitimacy of the documents.

"Well, I am still going to kill you when this is all over."

Rutherford pounded on the door. "Guard!" he called out.

He turned to Johnstone, who had remained seated. "We'll settle our differences when I get out of here."

The guard unlocked the door and escorted Rutherford back to his cell.

XXXII

Johnstone's deadline had passed, and the uncertainty of the situation was killing Rutherford. Doubts raced through his head. Did Johnstone know what was really in the safe? Did he even care? Was he calling his bluff?

Rutherford paced his small cell, and every second seemed slower and more unbearable than the last. He threw himself down on the small straw cot and lay there, staring at the wet ceiling.

Just when he thought all was lost, the main cell door clanked open, and a group of four men walked down the stairs and into the dungeon. Rutherford stood up to see who they were, but he couldn't make them out in the dim light as they walked down the stairs.

The group reached the bottom of the stairs, and they turned out to be two guards with two men dressed in civilian clothes. They passed all the cells until they were in front of his.

One of the civilians stepped forward. "John Rutherford?"

"Yes," he replied in a hushed tone. There was barely enough saliva in his throat to speak.

"I am William Golden, assistant to Governor Johnson." He paused and unrolled an official-looking document. "By order of Governor Johnson," he read aloud, "you have been fully exonerated of all charges related to piracy and robbery on the high seas. You have also been exonerated in the death of two French sailors that occurred on the merchant ship the *Lady*.

Rutherford felt like screaming out in joy. His bluff had worked!

The bureaucrat rolled up the document and spoke directly to Rutherford. "New evidence has come to the governor's attention that proves your actions were committed only upon coercion and in self-defense. You are hereby granted a full pardon and are a free man."

One of the guards opened the cell door, and Rutherford stepped out. He took one last look at his cell and vowed he would never go back to jail under any circumstances, no matter what the price.

Rutherford was escorted through the jail and led upstairs to freedom. The guards stopped at the front door, and the governor's aide handed him the pardon and left without saying another word.

Rutherford opened the door and saw sunlight for the first time in almost two weeks. The light was so bright, and his eyes had become so accustomed to the dark, that he could barely open them. He shielded his eyes, and someone tenderly wrapped their arms around him. Rutherford knew who it was immediately. Her smell, her touch – he would know her anywhere.

"John!" Sally cried into his ear.

Rutherford took her into his arms and kissed her tear-streaked cheeks. He had thought just minutes ago he would never hold her again.

His eyes gradually adjusted to the sunlight, and he saw Mr. Restin standing by himself with a big grin on his face.

Rutherford walked over to him and shook his hand. "You pulled it off."

Mr. Restin gave him a surprised look. "Damn right, I did. Were you ever in doubt?"

They laughed together.

"Let's celebrate!" Mr. Restin announced.

Rutherford couldn't wait to have a good meal and a beer. The group headed to the **Moultrie Tavern** for a night of food, drinks, and catching up.

Later that evening, Sally and Rutherford walked home hand in hand. He couldn't wait to get back to their home. They walked through the front door, and Sally led him to the bedroom. Neither one of them said a word. They didn't have to.

The next morning, they slept in late. It felt good to be home, but Rutherford knew he still had a big problem: Johnstone. He wasn't going to let Rutherford get off that easily. It might be tomorrow or a year from now, but he knew Johnstone would come for him.

Rutherford had sworn in his cell that he wasn't going to live in fear of the man anymore. He remembered what Blackbeard had told him during his final battle, and he knew he had no choice. The burning hatred he felt towards Johnstone hadn't diminished with his freedom. He loved Sally, but his desire for revenge burned in the pit of his belly.

He wanted to kill Johnstone and was willing to die trying. He had no choice but to act immediately and not wait for Johnstone to come to him. There were just too many dangers in that. Johnstone might even try to hurt Sally, and he wasn't going to let that happen. There was going to be a showdown, and he knew only one of them was going to live through it.

Rutherford devoted a considerable amount of sleepless nights to considering what he should do about Johnstone. Every day that passed without resolution became more and more dangerous for both Sally and him. Late one night, Rutherford committed to the only outcome that he knew was acceptable. It had to be done. Tomorrow, he would challenge Johnstone to a duel.

Duels in Charleston were not an everyday occurrence, but they weren't rare either. A year could go by without a single challenge, and then three could take place in the span of a month.

In Charleston, men of honor settled their differences in this manner. The weapons of choice were pistols. He knew Johnstone was a good shot, but what Johnstone didn't know was that Rutherford was, too. He had learned a lot while he was on Blackbeard's ship.

Rutherford left early the next morning and walked down Meeting Street toward Barrett's warehouse. It was a beautiful day outside, but he hardly noticed. His mind could only focus on the duel. He had to challenge Johnstone in a way that he could not refuse. That's why he decided to go to his warehouse and challenge him in front of his own men.

There was never a quiet moment at Barrett's warehouse, and today was no exception. Dozens of men worked outside, loading and unloading supplies.

Rutherford walked over to a cart where half a dozen men were working. "Excuse me," he said to the group. "Is Samuel Johnstone here today?"

No one looked up from their work, but one of the men shouted back, "He's in his office!"

This was it: the point of no return. Once he said the words, there would be no going back, no backing down.

He cleared his throat and addressed the men in a loud voice. "Would someone please go tell that murdering, lying bastard that John Rutherford is outside to see him?"

He waited for the words to sink in, and they quickly did the job. Johnstone's men suddenly stopped, and all eyes stared at him.

Rutherford continued, "And if he refuses to see me, then all his men will know what I have known for a long time: that he is a sorry coward."

A hulking Irishman with flaming red hair jumped down from one of the carts and walked over. "Did I hear you right?"

Rutherford stepped forward so only a few feet separated them. "Yes, you did. And if you wouldn't mind, please go tell Johnstone what I have just said."

The Irishman smiled in anticipation of the impending conflict and left to go find Johnstone. No one went back to work, and the Irishman reappeared a few minutes later with Johnstone, who followed close behind.

Rutherford stood his ground as Johnstone walked right up to him.

"What the hell do you want?" Johnstone asked in a venomous voice.

"It is time to settle things between you and me, you lying coward!"

Rutherford could see the anger beginning to build, but Johnstone also looked hesitant. Johnstone had never expected him to show up here. Rutherford had taken him by complete surprise, and his face showed it.

"Tomorrow. Ten o'clock. Cumberland Street."

"What are you talking about?"

Rutherford heard the murmurs from Johnstone's men, who were shocked by his audacity. "Do you agree to my request?"

Everyone in Charleston knew about Cumberland Street. It was commonly referred to as Duelers' Alley. If one's presence was requested on the street, one had been challenged to a duel with pistols.

Johnstone's initial anger gave way to a look of shock and disbelief. As Rutherford had planned, Johnstone was stuck. He had no choice but to accept the challenge. If he didn't, he would lose all respect and honor from not only his men but from all of Charleston.

Johnstone looked around at his men, who were waiting to hear his answer. He stared back at Rutherford with a cold, murderous look in his eyes. "Ten o'clock," he growled before turning and walking back inside the warehouse.

Rutherford took one last look at Johnstone's men and then walked away. It was done.

Rutherford sat outside a little outdoor café and watched life pass by. It was difficult to think that at this time tomorrow he might not be part of it anymore.

He ordered roast beef and a pint of beer. The food arrived, and surprisingly, he still had an appetite. The food was delicious, and Rutherford couldn't remember the last time a beer had tasted so good. Maybe everything tasted so good because he knew it might be one of his last meals.

There were no customers in Mr. Restin's Apothecary when Rutherford walked through the front door.

Mr. Restin was stocking medicines on the shelves when he saw Rutherford. He stopped what he was doing. "Well, well. Look who it is: Blackbeard's best friend."

Rutherford smiled.

Mr. Restin wiped his hands on the front of his apron. "Now, to what do I owe the pleasure of this visit?"

"I need to ask you if you will do me another favor."

Mr. Restin chuckled. "Haven't I done enough favors for you already?" he asked lightheartedly.

Rutherford didn't see the point of beating around the bush. "I am dueling Johnstone tomorrow, and it would be my honor if you would agree to act as my second."

Mr. Restin's jaw fell open, and his mouth tried to form a sentence. But nothing came out. Finally, he regained his tongue. "What? Are you crazy? You're going to get yourself killed! What the hell is wrong with you?"

"I'm sick of living in fear. Better to face him directly and have a chance than to be stabbed in the back one day."

"But–"

"Trust me. There is no other way."

"What about Sally?" Mr. Restin inquired.

"It's for her sake as well. Who knows how low Johnstone will stoop? He might even try to harm her just to get back at me."

"I suppose you're right, John, but I still don't like it."

Rutherford smiled weakly. "Don't worry. It's for the best. But whatever you do, don't tell Sally. She would never let me go through with it."

Mr. Restin nodded. "I'll see you tomorrow."

Rutherford left the store and went down to the market to pick up something for dinner. He decided to make a seafood feast because, although Sally didn't know it, it could very well be their last meal together.

When Rutherford arrived home, Sally was still out running some last-minute errands. She got home about an hour later as he was preparing their supper.

He heard the front door open. "Hello, John," Sally called out as she walked into the kitchen. "Wow! What's the occasion?"

Rutherford gave her a kiss on the cheek. "Just wanted to fix us something nice for dinner, that's all."

He had splurged. They had tuna steaks, oysters, crabs, and a nice bottle of wine. They ate, drank, and talked for hours. The food was great, the company was wonderful, and Rutherford was literally savoring every second of it.

After dinner, they had coffee and split a dessert cake that he had bought at a pastry store on Queen Street. Together they cleaned up the dishes, a monotonous task that took on new meaning for Rutherford, who was not sure if he would ever get a chance to do them again.

They retired to the bedroom, and he held Sally tightly the entire night.

XXXIII

Rutherford hadn't expected to get much sleep and was surprised to wake up and see the sun rising outside the bedroom window. Sally continued to sleep peacefully in his arms, and he slowly stroked her long hair, wondering what she was dreaming about.

He held her for another hour before she finally left her peaceful dream world. She slowly opened her eyes and caught him staring at her.

A faint smile appeared on her lips. "Good morning."

"Morning," he replied as he continued to weave his hand through her hair.

She smiled, and they quietly lay together in bed a while longer before Rutherford reluctantly forced himself to let go of Sally and get out of bed.

She watched him as he got dressed. "Where are you going?" she asked.

Rutherford hated lying to her, but it had to be done. "I promised Mr. Restin I would give him a hand unloading some supplies today."

"When will you be back?"

"Later this afternoon."

He finished dressing and kissed Sally goodbye on the forehead. "I love you," he said. "And no matter what happens; don't you ever forget it."

She smiled. "I won't."

He had to leave immediately, or he would never go. Rutherford left and started walking towards Duelers' Alley.

He wore his Saint Christopher's medallion and wondered if it could save him one last time. Rutherford knew word had gotten out about the duel. He just hoped Sally wouldn't find out until it was over.

He arrived to find a rather large crowd milling about in anticipation of seeing someone die. Charlestonians loved duels.

Mr. Restin was waiting for him.

Rutherford walked over to him and shook his hand. "Good morning. It sure is a nice day," Rutherford said as if they were on their way to a picnic.

Mr. Restin's face was ghostlike. He tried to force a smile, but his lips wouldn't cooperate. "Morning, John," he said rather weakly. "How do you feel?"

"Scared." Rutherford laughed nervously.

Mr. Restin shrugged his shoulders and looked around. "Johnstone isn't here yet."

"He will be."

Five minutes later, Johnstone and his second showed up.

They met each other in the middle of the red brick street. Johnstone's second introduced himself as Andrew Butler, and they shook hands.

Butler cleared his throat. "Before we continue," he said in a stilted British accent, "are the both of you sure this disagreement cannot be settled in a less dramatic fashion?"

Rutherford looked at Johnstone. "No, it is too late for that. We settle our differences here today."

Butler looked at Johnstone, who shook his head.

Rutherford noticed a bit of apprehension in his face that he had never seen before.

"Very well, then," Butler said.

Butler took a set of pistols out of a wooden box and handed them to Mr. Restin for inspection. He checked the barrel and trigger. Mr. Restin nodded to Butler.

Butler took the box over to Rutherford. "Your choice, sir."

Rutherford picked up one of the pistols and looked directly at Johnstone. Did he see fear in his eyes? He wondered if Johnstone could see the fear in his.

The remaining pistol was handed to Johnstone.

Butler announced in dramatic fashion, "The two gentlemen will pace a distance of ten steps. I will count one, two, three, and then give the command to fire. Both men will empty their chambers. If either is incapable of carrying on, then the match has concluded."

He asked the men, "Are these terms acceptable?"

Rutherford and Johnstone both nodded.

They stepped off the paces and turned to face each other. Butler and Mr. Restin stood off to the side. The crowd waited nervously, no one uttered a sound.

Butler looked at both men one last time, as if hoping one of them would change his mind. No one did.

"Gentlemen," he announced, "please raise your pistols."

They both slowly raised their pistols and took dead aim at each other.

"Please cock your pistols."

Rutherford could hear seagulls flying overhead. A gust of wind kicked up, and he could smell the sea.

They both knew what was coming next.

Butler's voice sounded softer, almost reluctant. "One."

Rutherford wondered what Sally was doing right now. Was she thinking of him?"

"Two."

He could see the whites of Johnstone's eyes. Rutherford's senses were heightened to a level he had never experienced before. It felt as if he was outside his body, far away in the distance, observing what was about to take place.

"Three."

The next word would mean the end to one of them forever.

"Fire."

Rutherford pulled the trigger.

A bullet takes exactly one tenth of one second to travel a hundred feet – less time than it requires to take a breath of air. Time no longer had any meaning; it had come to a standstill. The bullet left the end of his barrel, and a puff of dark gray smoke gently rose from the breech. It slowly rose in the air until the breeze dissipated any memory of it.

Rutherford's pistol recoiled slightly in his hand. The bullets passed by each other and continued moving closer toward their targets with only one objective: to kill.

Rutherford blinked and felt the bullet's wake as it passed between his shoulder and neck. Johnstone had missed.

Rutherford stared straight ahead, but Johnstone had disappeared from sight. Where had he gone? Time finally returned to normal, and then he saw him. Johnstone was lying on his back, in the middle of the red brick alley, with a pool of crimson blood underneath his head. Butler ran over and knelt down beside him.

Rutherford looked at his pistol and then lowered it to his side. He watched with horrid fascination as Butler checked Johnstone for any sign of life.

Butler stood up and announced solemnly. "He's dead."

There was a loud hush from the crowd, as if they were shocked someone had died in a duel. Butler shook his head and walked away. It wouldn't be long before the undertaker showed up to take Johnstone's body away. The crowd slowly started to leave, talking to one another in hushed tones.

No one said a word or came near Rutherford, except for Mr. Restin, who walked over to him. Rutherford hadn't moved an inch. He couldn't take his eyes off of Johnstone's lifeless body lying in the street. It could have been him.

"Are you all right?" Mr. Restin asked.

"I think so."

With great effort, Mr. Restin pulled the pistol from his hand.

"John," Mr. Restin began.

"Yes?" Rutherford asked, still staring at Johnstone's lifeless body.

"Don't ask me for any more favors."

Mr. Restin walked off, leaving Rutherford alone.

Rutherford reached inside his shirt, pulled out the Saint Christopher's medallion, and looked at it. Finally, it felt as if the weight of the world had been lifted from his shoulders.

Printed in the United States
27230LVS00005B/424-474